OFF COURSE

Brantley Walker:

Off the Books

By Nicole Edwards

The Walkers

Alluring Indulgence

Kaleb
Zane
Travis
Holidays with The Walker Brothers
Ethan
Braydon
Sawyer
Brendon

The Walkers of Coyote Ridge

Curtis
Jared
Hard to Hold
Hard to Handle
Beau
Rex
A Coyote Ridge Christmas
Mack
Kaden & Keegan
Alibi (a crossover novel)
Trey
Rafe

The Jamesons of Coyote Ridge

Hot Chocolate Wishes

Brantley Walker: Off the Books

All In
Without A Trace
Hide & Seek
Deadly Coincidence
Alibi
Secrets
Confessions
Bounty
Off Course

Austin Arrows
Rush
Kaufman

Club Destiny
Conviction
Temptation
Addicted
Seduction
Infatuation
Captivated
Devotion
Perception
Entrusted
Adored
Distraction
Forevermore

Dead Heat Ranch
Boots Optional
Betting on Grace
Overnight Love
Jared (a crossover novel)

Devil's Bend
Chasing Dreams
Vanishing Dreams

Misplaced Halos
Protected in Darkness
Salvation in Darkness
Bound in Darkness

Office Intrigue
Office Intrigue
Intrigued Out of The Office
Their Rebellious Submissive
Their Famous Dominant
Their Ruthless Sadist
Their Naughty Student
Their Fairy Princess
Owned

PIER 70
Reckless
Fearless
Speechless
Harmless
Clueless

PRIMAL INSTINCTS
Chase (Volume 1-3)
Capture (Volume 4-6)
Claim (Volume 7-9)

SNIPER 1 SECURITY
Wait for Morning
Never Say Never
Tomorrow's Too Late

SOUTHERN BOY MAFIA/DEVIL'S PLAYGROUND
Beautifully Brutal
Without Regret
Beautifully Loyal
Without Restraint

STANDALONE NOVELS
Unhinged Trilogy
A Million Tiny Pieces
Inked on Paper
Bad Reputation
Bad Business
Filthy Hot Billionaire
RULE

NAUGHTY HOLIDAY EDITIONS
2015
2016
2021

OFF COURSE

Brantley Walker: Off the Books, 9

NICOLE EDWARDS

NICOLE EDWARDS LIMITED
A dba of SL Independent Publishing, LLC
PO Box 1086
Pflugerville, Texas 78691

This is a self-published title.

OFF COURSE

Brantley Walker: Off the Books, 9

COVER DETAILS:

Image: © rotorania (203196640) | 123rf.com ***Design:*** © Nicole Edwards Limited

INTERIOR DETAILS:

Formatting: Nicole Edwards Limited

AUDIO DETAILS:

Image: © rotorania (203196640) | 123rf.com ***Narrators:*** Tor Thom & Fiona Clare

ISBN: (ebook) 9781644180860 | (paperback) 9781644180877 | (audio) 9781644180884

BISAC: FICTION / Mystery | FICTION / LGBTQ

To the fans of the Walker universe.

Something is coming. Enjoy the ride.

"You're tryin' to distract me. That, or you're stalling. Which is it?"

"Why would I do either?"

"You don't want to share your coffee."

He flashed a smile and picked up his mug. "You can't *have* coffee."

"Sure I can." She rushed toward the kitchen island, moving as fast as her pregnant belly would allow. "Just don't tell Baz."

Although JJ was the one to put herself on a caffeine diet, she'd enlisted Baz to hold her to it. And Brantley got the feeling JJ was just as worried about disappointing her baby's daddy as she was overdosing her unborn baby on caffeine. Love really did look good on her.

Brantley glanced out the door to ensure Baz wasn't standing there, ready to bust him. He knew if the man caught him supplying coffee to JJ and their unborn daughter, he would not be happy. It was bad enough that each week he had to hear at what stage their child was in—based on the book JJ was reading, at twenty-nine weeks, the baby was now over a foot long and close to two and a half pounds. He seriously doubted something that size needed the caffeine.

"Come on, B," JJ pleaded. "I promise, the peanut won't care."

Peanut was the nickname they'd given their unborn child back before they found out the sex of the baby. Now that they knew, he wasn't sure why they didn't refer to her as princess or baby doll or some other unnecessary nickname. It would've been simpler if they'd given her a name already. Then Brantley could start learning it, and he wouldn't risk forgetting by the time she arrived.

If she ever got here. No one told him that pregnancies—while being nine months long—felt like they lasted an eternity. He couldn't remember his sisters' pregnancies dragging on like this. He couldn't imagine how JJ felt.

The coast was clear, so Brantley set his mug on the counter and turned to the refrigerator.

"Oh, I love you, B." JJ pulled out a stool and dropped her laptop bag on the countertop. "More than you could ever know. Cream, please."

He grabbed the bottle off the top shelf, shut the door, and turned back to his best friend.

"I swear, I won't tell—"

He passed over the bottle.

JJ frowned. "What's this?"

"It's the only form of coffee I'm allowed to give you."

"This is juice, Brantley."

He flashed another grin and picked up his mug.

"I can't believe you'd betray me like this," she pouted.

"I can't believe you didn't steal my cup when you had the chance."

JJ glared at the mug in his hand. "I would have. If I'd … thought about it." The glare shifted to his face. "And if I'd known you were a Judas."

Brantley pointed toward the back door, which was now sliding open as Sebastian Buchanan, the father of the peanut and the manager of JJ's coffee intake, stepped inside. "Talk to him about it. I'm just doin' what I'm told."

"Yeah? You never do what you're told," she grumbled. "Why start now?" JJ turned a sweet smile on Baz. "If I break up with you, I'll get coffee."

"True," he said. "But then you won't get my—"

JJ slapped her hand over his mouth, cutting him off.

Baz slowly moved her hand from his mouth. "I was gonna say eggs Benedict. You won't get my eggs Benedict. What did you think I was gonna say?" Baz asked, feigning innocence.

JJ rolled her eyes and glanced at Brantley. "He does make really good eggs Benedict."

Brantley's upper lip curled. "If that's some kinda double entendre, I'm gonna throw up."

"Double entendre? For what?" JJ asked, eyes wide and sparkling with payback. "Did you think I was thinkin' about his—"

Baz saved the day this time, placing his hand over JJ's mouth so that the word was muffled.

Brantley watched her eyes, noticed the smile a second before Baz pulled his hand away and wiped his slobbery palm on his jeans.

"Penis!" she blurted.

"JJ," Baz scolded with amusement.

"Penis, penis, penis," she sang.

"What's that entail?" JJ asked, then formed air quotes with her fingers. "'They knew enough about the neighborhood.' I mean, did they know that Susie Homemaker put her kid on the bus every morning at eight? Or that Joe Schmoe's Doberman barks all night long? I don't get it. How do you trust someone online when you've never met them face to face? Don't they know you can learn far too many intimate details about a person and their habits just from what they post on social media?"

That was the question of the hour. And it was true. Some people didn't realize when they complained on Facebook or Twitter about missing their kids because they were spending a week at Aunt Susie's house that they'd given people a little too much information. Now the bad guys knew to check out Susie, their target's Facebook friend, to see where she lived. Or when they ranted about Fido waking the neighbors when he snuck out the dog door that they'd told everyone there was easy access to the house—through a dog door.

"No idea," Brantley admitted. "But they're takin' the lead on this one. I'm just in the loop."

"It's hard to believe it's been so quiet the last couple of weeks," JJ noted.

Brantley looked at Baz and sighed.

"What?" JJ's gaze bounced between them. "What's that look you just gave him?"

"We're gonna get a case."

"How?" She glanced at Baz. "When?"

Baz shrugged. "It's bound to happen now that you've jinxed us."

JJ's grin was slow and wide. "Jinxed? Seriously? You believe in superstitious bullshit?"

"Watch," Brantley told her. "I guarantee within a week, we'll have a case."

She rolled her eyes again and grabbed her juice. "That's not a bad thing, B. It's what we do. We work cases." JJ got to her feet. "Now come on. Let's see what trouble's brewing at the barn."

"DON'T BE MAD AT ME," REESE SAID.

He glanced in the rearview mirror, recognizing the pout.

"It had to be done. And deep down, you know it feels better." Reese flipped the signal to turn. "Seriously. I do it at least twice a day. You can handle havin' your teeth brushed once a week, easy."

Tesha's eyebrows twitched.

"Keep lookin' at me like that, and we'll do it daily."

Reese chuckled when she turned her attention out the window.

If it was weird that he talked to his dog, he didn't care. He did it all the time. These days, he didn't even care if anyone was around to hear him, either. He considered it fate that almost two years ago, he and Brantley had been called down to Houston to work a case that had turned out not to be a case at all. It had led Reese to the home of Tesha's former owners, the parents of the kid they thought was missing but had, in fact, been sneaking around with a girl from another school. Tesha had been neglected and tied up in the backyard without any shade and just out of reach of the food and water bowls that had both been empty. Without hesitation, Reese had revoked her former owner's rights to own a dog by carrying Tesha out of that backyard.

As far as Reese was concerned, aside from falling in love with Brantley Walker, it was the best thing he'd ever done. Never had he figured that, at thirty-three, he would be settling down, making a life with a man and a dog. Yet that was what he was doing.

"Almost home, girl. I bet JJ's there."

He watched Tesha in the rearview to see her reaction. The moment she heard JJ's name, her ears cocked, and she started looking around. It wasn't a secret that Tesha loved JJ. Strangely enough, Tesha had become more protective of her since JJ got pregnant. How the dog knew, he wasn't sure, but it was another of Tesha's many endearing qualities.

"When we get to the house, you can go to the barn and see her. Cool?"

Tesha leaned forward and rested her head on the corner of the seat back, her snout pressing on Reese's shoulder. He reached back and gave her head a scratch.

"I'm glad you forgive me."

A few minutes later, Reese pulled up to his house, parking behind Brantley's truck so he didn't block the exit from the parking area everyone else used. He climbed out and opened Tesha's door. She waited patiently until he unbuckled her leash from the seat belt clip.

"Go," he told her. "Have fun."

With a flurry of speed, Tesha launched out of the truck and took off at full speed for the barn, weaving around to the back where the dog door was.

Reese was still smiling when he walked into the house.

Brantley leaned out of the kitchen, watching him. "If brushing teeth makes you smile like that, you're welcome to do mine whenever you want."

Reese chuckled, joining Brantley.

"Although, if you're up for that task, I could think of *something else* I'd prefer you to put in my mouth," Brantley said, his voice husky.

Reese felt his face heat. It was a reaction he couldn't help. Didn't seem to matter how long he was with this man, Brantley still had the ability to make him blush.

"How'd it go? At the vet?"

"All good."

"Tesha mad at you?"

Reese laughed. "Not anymore. JJ's here. She's forgotten all about it." He jerked his chin toward the barn. "Anything happenin' that needs our attention?"

"Not yet. But beware. JJ jinxed us again."

"Yeah? We've got a week, then?" It seemed whenever JJ mentioned things were slow, they would get a case that would have them running around like chickens with their heads cut off. They'd spent the better part of the summer doing just that. Only this week had they slowed down long enough to catch their breaths.

"If we're lucky."

Brantley passed Reese a cup of coffee.

"Thanks."

With cup in hand, Reese followed Brantley upstairs to their offices. Back when they'd originally modified the house for their business, they had spent more time in the barn than behind their desks. Now that they had a full staff, unless there was an active case or one of their weekly debriefs, they spent most of their time here tackling paperwork or making calls to check on cold cases, or—the worst part of their job, as far as Reese was concerned—sitting on conference calls with the Sniper 1 Security team.

They had fully integrated into the day-to-day of one of the country's most successful private security agencies. With that came access to a variety of cases and assignments. Although they still worked missing persons cold cases, they were also on rotation for personal security assignments of high-profile clients and events. From what he could tell, the team was enjoying the shake-up.

"You workin' on somethin'?" Reese asked before they parted ways into their separate offices.

Brantley turned to look at him, a gleam in his eyes. "Can't say I am. Why? Did you wanna take me up on my oral offer?"

Reese was grateful he hadn't taken a drink. "I … that …uh…"

Brantley's grin intensified. "The offer stands. Always. Day. Night. Just say the word."

Shaking his head, Reese turned toward his office. He grinned so hard his cheeks hurt. That man never ceased to amaze him. Who else could turn a toothbrush into a euphemism?

Evan should've remembered that, considering he'd been relying on Darius as his research analyst since avoiding Becs had become commonplace for him. Good thing he had Holly to rely on as a backup when Darius wasn't available. Thanks to the two of them, he didn't have to put in too much time behind the desk, nor did he have to fumble through a conversation with Becs, both of which required him an intimacy with her he couldn't deal with anymore.

Perhaps intimacy wasn't the right word, but it was the only way he could explain it. Being around her … fuck. It made him want things he hadn't wanted in a long damn time.

"What about Holly?" Becs inquired as she took a seat at her desk, cutting off his view of her perfect ass.

"Upstairs with JJ," Luca muttered, still focused on his monitor.

Becs chewed her bottom lip but didn't ask anything more.

Evan could almost feel bad for Becs. He was sure she thought they were shutting her out when that wasn't the case at all. Luca was merely being Luca, doing his best to keep her at arm's length. The guy had been doing it ever since Becs made it clear she was interested in him as more than a co-worker or friend. Not that she'd said it outright—not that Evan knew, anyway—but Luca acted like she'd declared her love for him on a billboard for the world to see.

As for Evan, it hadn't been his intention to ignore her, nor did it have anything to do with her skills. Becs was brilliant, from what he could tell. But she was also a complication he did not need in his life. And since they'd become friends outside the office because their daughters were BFFs—a term his daughter said he *had* to use because *best friends* wasn't cool—Evan was spending far too much time in Becs's presence as it was.

"Anyone heard from Jay or Charlie?" Slade asked.

Luca grunted.

Slade laughed.

Evan realized Slade wasn't asking because he cared. He probably did, but Slade was running through the list of employees in an effort to frustrate Luca, who preferred quiet in the mornings.

Evan found it interesting that all these personalities somehow managed to gel. More than that, they worked well together. The Off the Books Task Force had earned a reputation with local law enforcement as a go-to for help when they needed it. And thanks to their affiliation with Sniper 1 Security, federal agencies were now occasionally looking to them for assistance.

Despite the recent changes in the team, they were as strong as ever. Perhaps more so now that Jay Hernandez had officially transitioned from an analyst to an investigator after Trey left the task force. Jay's position had been filled by Holly, who had initially been hired as JJ's assistant. Now Elana filled that role. As far as investigators went, the task force was back to having four teams of two now that Atticus James had come on board. And though they gave Atticus shit about it, there was no relation to JJ. The kid couldn't have come at a better time since Sniper 1 Security called Decker Bromwell to the home office back in June.

"Do you need me to help with anything today?" Becs offered.

"Whad'ya think, boss?" Slade asked, his question directed at Evan.

"We're good. Nothing pressing," Evan answered, sparing a glance at Becs so she wouldn't think he was avoiding her. Which he was.

He probably should've leaned on Becs more, but spending too much time with her was not a good thing as far as he was concerned. It was bad enough that he couldn't stop thinking about her. Day, night. It didn't matter. And when she wasn't plaguing his thoughts, she was often stopping by his house to pick up her daughter. Because of their chaotic schedule, Evan's mother was now filling in as a full-time babysitter for both girls, so it wasn't uncommon for Becs to be lingering in his living room talking to Kaye about her day.

Those social chats were the very reason Evan had started going to the gym. Not because he'd needed it, although he had, but because he preferred to be whipping his body into shape rather than risk asking Becs out on a date when he knew that would be the worst thing that could happen. Technically, he was merely trading one form of torture for another.

"Is Sophia excited about her birthday party?" Becs asked.

And if shit like that hadn't been obvious, Becs had figured it out on her own when she saw Luca with another woman after work one day. Rather than go straight home, Becs had headed to downtown Coyote Ridge to stop in at the bookstore. Turned out Luca'd had a similar idea, only she was sure he wasn't there searching for a book for an eight-year-old. If he had, she didn't know how he could've found one while playing tonsil hockey with a stunning brunette near the back door.

Not that seeing him had broken her heart or anything. Becs had thought he was an attractive, intelligent man when they first met, and she'd indulged in the fantasy that one day, she might date a cowboy.

But she'd gotten over him quickly. Not only because she realized they had absolutely nothing in common outside the office but also thanks to an infatuation she wasn't quite as capable of shrugging off. Seemed to be a trend she was starting. Finding herself attracted to men in the office. And in this case, one particular man she had no business whatsoever fantasizing about.

Evan Vaughn.

In all fairness, she had far more in common with Evan than anyone else on the task force, although she was sure he would say differently. On the personal side, they were both in their thirties. It didn't matter to her that there were seven years between them. Evan had turned thirty-nine back in June, and she'd turned thirty-two last Monday. He claimed he was now on the fast track to forty, but Becs had never been one to gauge age by a number.

Plus, they both had daughters who were the center of their worlds, respectively. Career-wise, they'd both started out pursuing legal careers before shifting into law enforcement. Evan had done two semesters of law school before dropping out and becoming a police officer in Tampa. Becs had been a paralegal prior to this job. On the past relationship front, Evan had lost his wife to violence, and Becs had divorced her husband because he inflicted it.

Okay, so the last point wasn't really a similarity. Becs did not relate her abusive marriage to the fact that Evan's wife had been brutally murdered by a serial killer. Aside from the fact that the experiences had shaped who they'd become, there was no correlation at all. And while she knew Evan hadn't fully recovered from the loss, Becs found herself wanting to help him move on even if it wasn't in her best interest.

But while they did have things in common, and she was certain they'd make a great couple, Becs didn't want Evan to know she had a crush on him. Over the past few months, they'd developed a rather wonderful friendship outside the office, and she had no desire to give that up. Not even if it would quench her long-running dry spell.

Becs cut her gaze to Evan, waiting to see if he was getting ready to leave. Based on his routine, he would get up from his desk in roughly three minutes. He would make a quick stop at the restroom, then he'd come back to his desk, grab his phone, his wallet, and his keys before heading out the door. The man was nothing if not a stickler for routines, and if he didn't get lunch at the appropriate time, his natural grumpiness level dialed up about ten notches come mid-afternoon.

Countdown begins in three … two…

Becs locked her gaze on her computer screen when Evan pushed his chair back from his desk. She skimmed her email while he stretched and waited another minute when he went to the back of the barn where the restroom was.

Once she was alone in the space, she began running through what she wanted to say to him.

Hey, Evan. Your mom and I thought it would be best if I stayed the night and helped with the birthday party.

Hmm. No, that sounded like it had been Kaye's idea. Since it hadn't, she figured it was best not to blame Evan's mother.

Hey, Evan. I talked to your mom the other day. I was thinking maybe I could spend the night and help with the birthday party.

No, that wouldn't work. Without a direct question, Evan would likely shrug her off.

Hey, Evan. What do you think about me staying the night to help with the birthday party?

Maybe that was too forward.

Shit.

No matter how she worded it, she could imagine the look on his face. It was almost a foregone conclusion that he was going to stroke out when he thought she was inviting herself to stay the night. Of course, she wasn't thinking she would spend the night in his bed. She figured the girls could build blanket forts in the upstairs game room, and Becs could sleep in Sophia's room.

Hey, Evan. Mind if I camp out in your daughter's bed this weekend? I'd like to help with the party.

God, she sounded like a moron.

Becs cleared her throat when she saw Evan coming toward his desk.

It was now or never.

"Hey, Evan."

Before he fully turned toward her, his cell phone rang. Because he was always worried that something had happened to Sophia, he went to his desk and squinted at the screen.

He held up one finger, signaling he needed a minute.

"Hey, Mom. What's up?"

Becs did her best not to eavesdrop. Or to look at him. Neither was easy for her. First of all, they were in the same room, so she couldn't very well tune out his conversation when no one else was around. Not without putting in her earbuds, but then she risked him leaving before she realized he was finished. And two, she really liked looking at Evan. Over the past couple of months, she'd noticed a few changes. When he first started working with the task force, he was one of those guys who seemed to blend with the background. With his light brown hair and dark brown eyes, he looked like a lot of guys one might see on a daily basis. At six feet tall, he'd been a little overweight, although he'd looked even bigger than he was because he wore suits that were too large for him.

She knew for a fact he'd started spending time at the gym. He'd lost twenty-two pounds, or so she had heard him telling his mother. And now that the weight was gone, so were the suits, which was a good thing. They would've swallowed him whole. She got the feeling Slade had worn off on him because Evan's wardrobe had shifted from cheap suits to jeans and casual shirts that were cut to accentuate his muscular physique.

The interesting thing was it hadn't been his physical changes that had drawn her to him. Becs had liked Evan just the way he was before he'd undergone the physical transformation. This version of him … well, he was hot. That's what he was.

"All right, Mom. I'll ask her, but I can't imagine she'd say yes." He paused for a moment before saying, "Yep. I'll be home by five. Tell Sophia to relax. Her birthday weekend'll start when it starts."

Evan disconnected the call and tucked his phone in his pocket before grabbing his wallet and keys.

"Was that Kaye?" Becs asked, aiming for casual.

"Yeah. She's got it in her head that I should ask you if you'd like to hang out this weekend to help with the party."

"Hang out?"

His gaze shifted to the floor. "Stay the night or whatever."

God, he was cute.

"I'm more than happy to help," she said.

"You've probably got plans."

"Nope," she blurted a little too quickly. "I mean, you know. There's the grocery store. But I can do that anytime."

Evan met her gaze again. He nodded. "It's up to you."

"Yeah. Sure. I'll hang out this weekend."

For a brief moment, they stared at each other, and Becs felt the heat building somewhere deep in her soul. She knew she needed to ignore it, but by God, she wasn't sure she was strong enough to do so.

CHAPTER THREE

Reese stood at the grill, in charge of the food for the night's festivities, while everyone else chatted and chilled. They'd been having these Friday night cookouts at the house for most of the summer. It hadn't been intentional, but Reese enjoyed how the team came together outside the office as much as in it. It allowed them to socialize and talk about something other than work. It had become routine at some point, something Reese looked forward to at the end of a busy week.

"You need any help?"

"I'm good for now," Reese told Baz as he rolled the line of sausage links on the grill. "I've got JJ's burger almost done."

"Has anyone else noticed how much we spoil her?"

Reese laughed, staring down at the grill as though noticing for the first time that there were sixteen sausage links and one hamburger patty.

Baz was right. They'd all been spoiling JJ for quite a while now. Sometimes, they were running out to get her something she was craving. Other times, they pitched in at her house when she wanted something moved or changed completely now that they'd moved in. Sure, Baz was doing most of the work, but everyone else did their best to help simply because they wanted to.

Reese wanted to say it was because of the pregnancy—which was partly true—but he knew it was more than that. Considering all JJ'd been through over the past year and a half, she deserved to be spoiled by all of them. First, she woke up to a grizzly scene in her house because her ex-boyfriend had staged his own kidnapping and used JJ to make it look real. Later that day, things had gone from bad to worse when her house blew up because that idiot ex-boyfriend had trusted the wrong people to help him. Thanks to Juliet Prince's psychotic need to punish Travis Walker, they'd all ended up with targets on their backs. Then there was the guilt JJ still felt because she hadn't been able to find Juliet before the unthinkable happened, and they lost a good friend.

As though that hadn't been enough karmic injustice, throughout all of it, JJ'd had to sit back and watch when Baz thought he was having a baby with a one-night stand.

So, yeah, JJ deserved for them to treat her like a princess. And because she was pregnant, they could disguise it as merely helping out because she needed to take it easy. There was no way JJ would've sat back and accepted their help any other way.

"Did you crumble the bleu cheese into it?" Baz asked, looking over Reese's shoulder.

Reese flipped the turkey burger once more. "Yeah. Just like she asked."

Baz lowered his voice, a slight hint of fear in his tone. "And the pickled okra? Was someone able to find that?"

Reese grinned. "Elana has it all taken care of."

"Thank God," Baz huffed.

It was safe to say Baz was a good man, and he was good for JJ.

"Grab a plate," Reese told him.

When Baz presented it, Reese set the turkey burger stuffed with bleu cheese on it.

"Lifesaver," Baz muttered. "That's what you are."

Reese wouldn't go that far, but he grinned. He grabbed his beer and took a sip while shifting the sausage links again. His gaze strayed to Brantley, who was in the yard, standing by Slade and Atticus, throwing the ball for Tesha while listening as Atticus told one of his animated stories.

Reese had stopped keeping a close eye on Atticus when he realized the kid only flirted with Brantley when he was around. No one else knew that he was aware of the ruse, and he maintained his defensive, jealous stance when the moment called for it, but not because he wanted to wring the kid's neck. He didn't. Not anymore.

No, Reese kept it up because he knew Brantley enjoyed it. The Navy SEAL who'd been hardened by life enjoyed that Reese was possessive. And he was. Brantley was his, and after all they'd been through, nothing and no one was going to come between them. Now that he knew Atticus was on the up and up, Reese liked him more.

"Dinner's ready," Reese announced, directing the statement at Luca, Elana, and Holly, who were inside, setting out everything they'd pitched in to buy for the meal.

"Feels kinda thin this week, huh?" Luca said, taking the plate of sausage links from Reese.

It was thin. Decker was off doing whatever assignment he'd been called up for. Charlie and Jay were still in Chicago finishing up so they could return home for a while. Darius was enjoying some family time at his sister's wedding. Evan and Becs were also doing the family thing at Evan's daughter's birthday party. That left only nine of them. But it was exactly enough.

When everyone slipped inside to get food, Reese grabbed another beer from the cooler and walked over to where Brantley threw the ball to Tesha.

"You gonna eat?"

Brantley turned to him and smiled. "I figured I'd let them get theirs."

Reese passed Brantley the beer.

He took it, but not before he leaned in and kissed Reese, lingering for longer than he normally did when people were around. Reese didn't mind anymore. It no longer mattered to him where he was or who was around. Provided he had the chance to kiss this man for the rest of his life, he didn't give a shit who witnessed it.

He'd come a long way in the past two years, and he wouldn't change a thing.

Except maybe for Atticus to shift his attention to someone else's man.

And fine, maybe it did still bother Reese.

Just a little.

"CARLY'S HERE!" SOPHIA YELLED. "CARLY'S HERE, DAD! She's here!"

Evan nodded at his daughter, doing his best to conceal his reaction. If Carly was there, then her mother was also there, which meant Evan's weekend with Becs was about to begin.

Not that it was a weekend *with* Becs. She would merely be there. In the house. With him.

Why the hell did he agree to this again?

Evan should've told his mother that they didn't need the help. Between him and Kaye, they could easily handle everything half a dozen eight- to nine-year-old girls could need. Seriously, how hard could it be to ensure they were fed and not running amok?

Oh, who was he kidding? He was outmaneuvered when there were only two. Multiply that by three, and he was in way over his head. At least with Becs there, they stood a chance.

As for whether he would survive the weekend … well, that was anyone's guess. If Becs mentioned Luca even once, he would likely hide in his study until Sunday afternoon when the kids' parents would return to get them.

A loud squeal sounded from the front of the house. It was followed by another loud squeal. That was how little girls communicated. Somehow, those squeals translated to "You're here!" and "Yep! I am!" and "Let's get this party started!"

"You'll survive," his mother said, patting him on the shoulder.

"They're barely four feet tall. Of course, I'll survive."

Kaye grinned. "Sure. Let's pretend you're worried about the *little* girls."

Evan frowned. "What?"

His mother chuckled. "I've seen the way you look at Becs."

"You've seen no such thing," he muttered, taking a sip from his coffee to keep from having to continue the conversation. It was six thirty in the evening. The last thing he needed was coffee, but he figured the girls would stay up until at least ten, and since his bedtime was nine at the latest, he needed the caffeine if he was expected to make it.

"Hey," Becs greeted when she walked into the kitchen. Her pretty blue eyes shifted between him and his mother. "Are we the first ones?"

"You are," Kaye answered. "Shelly's mom called a few minutes ago. She's on the way."

Evan focused on breathing while Kaye ran through the list of girls who were coming and the status of their arrival. He did his best not to look at Becs, but she made it damn near impossible. She was wearing a black tank top with white shorts, both of which showed off her silky alabaster skin. Her shoulders were sprinkled with freckles, as were her nose and cheeks. He'd never found freckles sexy until Becs.

"I've made finger foods for dinner," he heard Kaye say. "Little sandwiches. Bologna, turkey, ham. I figured they could have a selection. I've also got carrots and celery. Ranch dip and peanut butter if they want it. Would you like some tea? Or I made a pot of coffee for Evan if you'd prefer that."

"Tea would be great," Becs answered.

"Why don't the two of you take a breather before the other girls arrive," Kaye suggested. "Enjoy the calm before the storm."

Evan sipped his coffee, staring out the back window to avoid looking at Becs.

"Evan?"

Frowning, he looked at his mother. "What?"

"You. Becs. Find a quiet place for a little while."

"I don't need quiet," he said petulantly.

"Go. Now."

As he had growing up, Evan reluctantly did as his mother instructed.

"Is everything okay?" Becs asked, following as he led her toward his study.

No. No, it certainly was not.

He wouldn't tell her that, of course, so he grunted, hoping she would take that as a positive response. Why ruin her weekend, too?

He stopped at the door to his study. It was more of a man cave than an office. A place for him to escape when Sophia or Kaye (or both) took over the living room. It didn't matter that there was a game room upstairs with a television, Sophia preferred to be downstairs most of the time. And since their choice of television programs differed dramatically, he'd made a space for himself so he could watch sports while she binged the Disney channel.

Becs chuckled when she walked into the room. "I love the sign on the door."

No girls allowed, it read. Handmade by his daughter. Sophia had declared the space his, and so far, she'd abided by the rule.

Not that he cared whether she joined him. When Evan was home, spending time with his daughter was all he cared to do. With her around, he could keep his mind from wandering to other things.

Looked as though Becs's presence had the same effect because now that she was here, his full attention was in the present, not lingering in the past where it drifted often.

Evan gestured toward the black leather sofa that faced the television.

She paused in front of him. "Are you okay?"

He nodded, answering with another grunt.

Her voice softened. "I can go if it bothers you that I'm here."

When her gaze shifted to the wall, Evan looked over. She was checking out the eight-by-ten of him and Gayle. It had been taken when Gayle was pregnant with Sophia, the two of them smiling at one another. A happier time, for sure.

"It doesn't bother me," he told Becs.

It did, but not the way she was thinking. This house had no memories of his dead wife. Gayle had never left Florida. She was buried there, along with the happy life Evan had once had. Back before a serial killer shattered his very existence.

And while Evan had never imagined that he would find a woman who could capture his interest for more than a minute, it wasn't because he was still in love with Gayle. He loved her, sure. He always would. But if he'd learned anything in his job, it was that life was fleeting. And getting attached to something never ended well. The only exception to that rule was his daughter. Evan would move heaven and earth for Sophia, and that would never change.

Everything else … well, he ensured that was temporary.

Becs could tell her presence was bothering Evan. He claimed it didn't, but he was far too tense.

Perhaps she would've believed it was because he was about to have six little girls descending on his domain for the next forty hours or so, but if anyone could handle a slumber party, it was Sophia's dad. Becs was convinced he was born to be a father. It was in the way his eyes lit up whenever Sophia walked into a room, in the way his smile remained in place whenever she spoke.

She knew his discomfort had to do with her because Becs had noticed it before. Not only in the office but also here, in his home. If Becs were here picking up Carly when Evan came home, he would make a beeline in whatever direction would lead him away from her.

Figuring it might be good to clear the air, Becs took a seat on the sofa, attempting to get comfortable. Kaye came in to give her the glass of iced tea she made. On her exit, she closed the door, sealing her in the room with Evan.

"Would you please sit down?" she asked when Evan continued to pace near the small desk in the corner. The man wasn't known to pace. He was the sort who made as few physical movements as necessary, which was another clue that he was uncomfortable.

His eyes snapped to her face, and his feet stopped moving. She noticed the way his Adam's apple bobbed slowly. Knowing him, he was wondering what she would do if he ran from the room.

Nothing, probably. Becs wished she could say she would follow him and force him to talk to her, but that was bullshit. She didn't have an assertive bone in her body. Not when it came to men, anyway.

It took a minute, but Evan finally sat on the opposite end of the sofa. There was only a single cushion between them, but it felt like there was an ocean.

"Did I do something to offend you?" she prompted.

"Why in God's name would you think that?" he asked, his voice gruff with surprise.

"Because you're purposely ignoring me at work."

"I am not."

"Don't," she said firmly. "Don't do that, Evan. I'm not an idiot. I get that from Luca all the time. His purposeful attempts to keep me at a distance because he doesn't want to risk me liking him. Then he acts surprised when I mention it. I expect that from him, but I thought you were better than that."

His dark brown eyes skimmed her face, his thick eyebrows coming down over them.

"You don't have to worry," she said, keeping her tone gentle like she was talking to a wounded animal. "I'm not here to seduce you, I promise."

His expression softened, and a self-deprecating grin formed on his mouth. "Trust me. I never thought you were."

"What does *that* mean?"

Evan stared at her for so long she thought he'd forgotten the question. It wasn't until she was trying to come up with a way to get past this awkward situation that he finally spoke.

"It doesn't mean anything." He shook his head. "I know you're not interested in me. I'm not worr—"

"Oh, I'm interested," she blurted.

Oh, crap. What was *wrong* with her? After thirty-two years in this world, *assertive* decides to make an appearance now?

"You … um… You are?" His eyebrows lifted. "In me?"

"Don't forget we're goin' to Moonshiners tonight."

Reese grinned. "Didn't forget. Couldn't have even if I wanted to."

"Atticus?" Brantley chuckled. The kid had made it his mission to irritate the shit out of Reese. The most interesting were the times Atticus blatantly flirted with Brantley. If ever there were something that would make the strong, even-keeled Reese Tavoularis break, it would be Atticus's incessant flirting.

But Brantley knew the kid was harmless. The flirting never happened when Reese wasn't around, which was how Brantley had realized Atticus's intention was to get a rise out of Reese. No doubt, Atticus found it amusing. It kinda was. Plus, it didn't hurt to know the man Brantley loved was capable of jealousy.

"One hour," Brantley echoed Reese. "Then the store."

Reese shifted his ear protection down and walked away. Brantley took a moment to admire him before he picked up the SIG he'd brought and headed to his assigned lane.

Two hours later, as Brantley was driving home from the grocery store, he glanced over to see Reese looking at his phone.

"I thought we weren't working today."

Reese looked up, his expression confused. "What?"

Brantley lifted his eyebrows and nodded at Reese's phone. "Something's got your attention. What is it?"

Reese exhaled and put his phone down. "Nothin'. I was goin' through the checklist JJ sent."

The wedding checklist, or what JJ had dubbed the *Breese List*. Personally, he hated that. She'd also referred to it as her You-Do-It-Or-Die List.

He grinned. "What's on it for next week?"

"They sent the invitations out last week, so she's startin' to collect the RSVPs."

"Her job, not ours," Brantley noted.

"The rings are picked out," Reese said, "so that one's checked off."

"So we're ahead of the game."

Brantley was glad they were. Considering JJ, Cindy, and Iris were planning the wedding, they'd required far more input from Brantley than he'd thought he would have to give. Evidently, *planning* did not entail picking out what the invitations looked like or sampling the food that would be served in order to create the menu. Or getting a stomachache from all the damn cake they'd had to taste. Brantley wanted simple, but from what he could tell, they were designing a three-ring circus.

However, Reese didn't seem to mind the effort going into the wedding, so Brantley was dealing with it. If it made Reese happy to review the guest list and pick out venues, more power to him. Like Brantley kept telling people, as long as he and Reese were at the altar while Pastor Bob was doing his thing, he didn't give a shit.

Reese glanced his way. "Do you want to write our own vows?"

The tone of Reese's voice told him he was worried about Brantley's response. Logic told him he had a fifty-fifty chance of guessing the right way to answer. Unfortunately, his track record of trying to predict what Reese was thinking wasn't great, so he opted for the simple answer.

"What's *your* preference? Because honest to God, I don't care. As long as you promise to spend the rest of your life with me, we can recite Shel Silverstein poems for all I care."

"Shel Silverstein?"

Brantley glanced over. "Yeah. You know. *Where the Sidewalk Ends.*"

"Oh, I know who he is," Reese said. "I just didn't think you did."

"What? I read."

"You do, sure. But I've never seen you read poetry."

Reese was right. He didn't. When he had time, his preference leaned toward non-fiction. Mostly military-related.

Brantley shrugged. "When I was a kid, I did."

Reese was quiet for a moment. Brantley didn't attempt to fill the void. There was something on Reese's mind—something not related to Shel Silverstein—and with time, he would get it out.

They were pulling into the driveway when Reese cleared his throat. "When you were a kid, did you ever think about what your weddin' day would be like?"

Brantley chuckled. "You mean when I was reading *Where the Sidewalk Ends*?"

"No, I'm serious."

That sobered Brantley instantly. Never could he have imagined himself answering a question like that, but he figured Reese deserved the truth.

"No. Did you?"

"A fleeting thought from time to time, yeah." Reese sighed. "Maybe it's just me."

"It's not just you, I'm sure." He considered making a joke about how women tended to focus more on those things, but he didn't. One of the many things Brantley loved about Reese was his vulnerability and his wistful spirit. Reese did a good job of masking it for the world, but deep down, he was a romantic. Another of the many things Brantley loved about him.

He parked the truck near the house, and before Reese could get out, Brantley put a hand on his arm, stilling him.

He took a deep breath and shifted so he could look at Reese. "I've known I was gay since I was young. Probably twelve or so, I guess."

"Wow. That's … young."

"I didn't know what it meant at the time," Brantley clarified. "But that's when I noticed Jeremy for the first time. He was my best friend. I'd seen his face every day for years, but one day, I noticed he had green eyes. I knew they were green, of course, but I saw them differently. I found the color fascinating. And then I found the way he spoke fascinating. One little thing after another until I saw every part of him in a different way."

"You were in love with him," Reese stated.

"I guess so. My infatuation grew from there, but I kept it to myself. At first, I didn't want him to know. Then, I didn't want other people to know. I wasn't ashamed, but it wasn't something you flaunted. Trey was a year older than me, and I knew he was gay. We all did because we come from a supportive family, so it was okay to be ourselves.

"But we learned that it wasn't something you shared with everyone. When they knew, they looked at you differently because it wasn't socially acceptable to be out and proud in the nineties. Certainly not in a small town. Yeah, Coyote Ridge has come a long way, as has the nation as a whole, but it's still not acceptable to a lot of people. Younger generations have an easier time being open about it."

"They have more support than our generation did," Reese noted.

"True. And that's a good thing. I look forward to the day when our differences don't divide us. Race, sexual orientation, religion. It would be a better world."

Reese nodded, his brown eyes glittering like honey in the sun.

"With that said, when I was a teenager plotting the rest of my life, marriage wasn't an option for me."

"Shit," Reese muttered. "I'm sorry. I didn't think about that."

Brantley reached over and squeezed his hand. "But it's what I want now. To marry you. And if you want to recite our own vows, I'll put in the time and effort to write mine. If you want to recite whatever Pastor Bob has in store for us, I'll do that, too. I don't care. No, maybe I didn't imagine what it would be like to stand at the altar, but if you did, let's do it your way, Reese. Whatever that looks like." Brantley thought about that for a moment and tacked on, "Provided it does *not* involve me wearing a wedding gown. That shit won't fly."

Reese barked a laugh, and suddenly, the tension disappeared. "All right."

"Good." Brantley opened the door and got out.

They grabbed the groceries from the back seat and headed for the front door.

"So which is it gonna be?"

Reese smiled. "Lemme think about it for a bit. I'll let you know."

"Fine." He opened the front door. "But that doesn't mean you get a head start on writing vows. If that's the route we take, you get the same amount of time I do."

Reese chuckled. "Fair enough."

THEY SPENT THE REST OF THE AFTERNOON hanging out.

Reese tossed the ball to Tesha until she was too tired to move from the cool tile in the kitchen. He camped out on the couch with Brantley for a bit, flipping through channels. When Brantley stopped on the History channel, Reese knew it was time to put his plan in motion. Without saying a word, he got up and headed for their bedroom, taking his time. He knew it wouldn't take Brantley long to come searching for him, and he was right.

"I assume I've got time to shower before—"

Reese remained where he was when Brantley stopped, framed by the doorjamb of their bedroom.

"Fuck me," Brantley rasped softly, his blue-gray eyes heating instantly.

To say Reese was nervous and anxious would be an understatement, but he didn't stop stroking himself, willing Brantley to join him on their bed.

"My, my, Mr. Tavoularis. I do believe you've been a naughty boy."

Reese groaned. Leave it to Brantley to tease him.

"I have to say, I'd much rather do this than go to the bar for drinks."

Reese grinned. "We promised we'd go."

"Yeah, well. What awaits me on that bed is worth breaking every promise I've ever made."

The man knew exactly what to say to fortify his nerves. Reese was making it a point to step out of his comfort zone from time to time. He figured it was only fair since Brantley was doing the same. And since Brantley was usually the one coming up with the sexual innuendo or brazenly instigating their passionate moments, Reese thought he would contribute, too.

So here he was, naked on their bed, his cock in his hand. He fought the gasps that filled his chest as he stroked himself, eager for Brantley to come closer.

When he stepped into the room, Brantley paused to close the door, then proceeded to admire Reese from all angles, walking around the bed on all three sides, his gaze lingering on Reese's iron-hard dick. Oh, man. Those eyes. They saw so much more than Reese ever intended for Brantley to see. They were so expressive, relaying Brantley's emotions even when he probably didn't intend for them to.

"At this rate, I might come without you," he told Brantley, his voice a husky whisper thanks to the lust constricting his vocal cords.

"Trust me, I won't let that happen."

Brantley pushed the waistband of his shorts down and wrapped his fist around his cock, allowing only the swollen head to peek out. Reese's gaze locked in on the sight. It was a tease; one Brantley knew he thoroughly enjoyed because he'd busted Reese watching him in the shower once or twice as he jacked off.

"Did you get lube?" Brantley asked, pushing his shorts down a little more, giving Reese a view of his thick, veiny shaft.

Reese picked up the small bottle that was beside him on the bed. He dropped it back down. At the moment, he didn't have enough brain power to focus on anything other than the exquisite tug and pull on his cock and Brantley mirroring his movements.

"You want this?" Brantley offered, angling his dick toward Reese.

"Yes."

Brantley stepped forward, slowly approaching while Reese's heartbeat throbbed in his shaft.

Reese released his cock, intending to meet Brantley halfway, but Brantley stopped him with a subtle shake of his head.

"Keep strokin' it."

Reese gasped, gripping his dick again and tugging on it. He really would come if Brantley kept this up. He was so fucking hard, so turned on. Any second, his trigger was going to flip, and he would come.

Brantley grabbed Reese's ankles and pulled him to the end of the bed. Reese's cardiovascular system shot into hyperdrive. He didn't know why he found it so fucking hot when Brantley manhandled him, but fuck, he loved it.

"Keep strokin'," Brantley snapped.

Reese focused, continuing to jerk himself while Brantley leaned forward, pressing a kiss to his knee as he reached for the lube.

"Brantley…" he gasped.

"I won't make you wait. I promise."

Reese slowed himself down, caressing his cock versus tugging, trying to hold himself back. It wasn't easy when the man he loved was standing there, shirtless and so damn sexy it made Reese's mouth water.

Brantley pushed Reese's right knee back. "Hold it."

Using his left hand to stroke, Reese freed his right hand so he could curl his fingers behind his knee and hold his leg back, opening himself to Brantley.

"Fuck me. Fuck me now, Brantley," Reese pleaded.

Brantley smirked, flipping the top on the lube and pouring a generous amount in his hand. Reese swallowed hard, watching as Brantley transferred the lube to his cock, massaging himself. If that were all he did, Reese would've survived, but then Brantley slicked the greasy liquid on Reese's balls as his fingers dipped lower, caressing his taint before sliding inside his hole.

"Oh, fuck." Reese dropped his head back and closed his eyes as the exquisite sensation tore through him. Brantley knew exactly what to do to send him right to the peak.

"Give me one of those pillows," Brantley commanded.

Reese slapped the mattress over his head until he found one of the small throw pillows Brantley had made fun of him for adding to the bed. He tossed it to Brantley. A second later, Brantley had the pillow wedged at the small of Reese's back.

Bent the way he was, Reese couldn't see between his legs, so he turned to look in the mirror on the armoire Brantley had also teased him for getting. In this position, he could see Brantley guiding his cock to his hole.

"You sure you're ready for me?"

"Yes," Reese whispered when the blunt head pressed against him, stretching the tight ring of muscle as he pushed inside.

Brantley grunted. "Take me, Reese. Relax and let me in."

Relaxing took effort because he was so worked up, adrenaline flooding his veins. Reese took deep breaths, welcoming Brantley inside him. He loved this. He'd come to crave this intimacy. Being with Brantley had changed him in so many ways. No longer was he nervous about their encounters. He looked forward to them.

Once the head of his cock had breached the tight ring, Brantley grabbed Reese's ankle, holding him still as he began sliding in. An inch or two in. Back out. In. Out. Deeper each time.

Reese took deep breaths in, slowly exhaling as the pleasure pulsed through him. He watched Brantley in the mirror, admiring every beautiful plane and angle of the man's big body as he fucked him. The man could go for hours just like this, his stamina incredible. However, Reese wasn't quite as disciplined. He longed for Brantley to fuck him hard and deep until he was lost in the sensations.

Reese looked up at Brantley's face, saw the sheen of sweat forming on his brow. Brantley made it look easy, but he knew resisting was as difficult for Brantley as it was for him. He tormented them both with his restraint, watching as his cock disappeared inside Reese one inch at a time.

"Fuck, you feel good." Brantley's hold on Reese's ankle tightened. "I wanna bend you in half and ram my dick inside you."

"Do it," Reese pleaded. At this point, he didn't fucking care. He was hovering on an edge made of razor wire. Any second, he was going to split apart.

"Oh, God, yes. You're so fuckin' tight." Brantley shivered as he pulled out, then drove in again, more forcefully this time.

Reese pressed his elbows into the mattress and held his legs, trying to keep himself in place, needing Brantley to fuck him.

"More, Brantley."

Brantley met his gaze. "I'll give you more. But don't you come until I tell you to," Brantley warned, pumping his hips faster as he leaned against Reese's legs.

"Not makin' any promises," he grunted, using the muscles in his legs to support Brantley's weight.

Brantley planted one knee on the bed, angling his cock down, driving in deep and hard. Reese was a goner. He could barely hold on as the pleasure singed every fiber of his being, drawing every muscle in his body taut as he let it consume him.

When Brantley put his other knee on the bed, Reese was bent like a pretzel, but he didn't fucking care. Brantley was untethered and watching him was all Reese needed. Their eyes met and locked as Brantley impaled him, driving them both to that space where time split between reality and ecstasy. Reese was there, lingering as Brantley's hips slammed against his legs. The discomfort only intensified the sensation until pain morphed with pleasure, and Reese was soaring on the high that preceded orgasm.

More of Brantley's weight pressed against him when Brantley reached for Reese's cock, stroking it in time with his thrusts.

At that point, the unraveling began, the intensity igniting the electrical current that sparked at the base of his spine and radiated outward.

"Fuck … Reese … Fuck, baby, I'm gonna come," Brantley growled roughly. "Come with me, Reese. Oh, fuck … come with me."

Reese gritted his teeth and let go while Brantley's cock swelled and pulsed inside him. A thunderous roar echoed through the room. Might've been Brantley. Could've been Reese. He didn't know because, as was the case whenever they came together, Reese splintered into shards.

It would take long minutes before he would pull himself back together.

CHAPTER FIVE

THE FIRST TIME SLADE MENTIONED MOONSHINERS, ATTICUS thought the guy was joking. Being that he was from Dallas, Atticus didn't think small-town bars like this existed. Even the small towns outside Dallas were big or expanding, drowning out anything that might've once resembled Coyote Ridge.

Moonshiners was proof that there was life in a small town.

It didn't matter which day of the week he came in here, it was always the same. A handful of people at the bar, a group congregating near the pool table, a few more scattered in chairs at the dozen or so round tables or the booths along the back wall. Everyone knew everyone. The only difference between Wednesday and Saturday was that there were more people. Not many, but more. And yes, they all knew each other, it seemed.

For Atticus, the increase in volume was a plus. He'd been in here enough times to know that the pickings around these parts were slim, so his chances of finding someone who might scratch the itch for a night increased immensely with more people. Unfortunately, most who came in for a drink were happily settled down with a significant other and a handful of kids. On the off chance they were single, they tended to be of the female persuasion, and Atticus didn't swing that way.

He was hoping that would change tonight. Not the direction of his swing, of course. That was set in stone at this point in his life. No, he was hoping to find a handsome stranger he could create some sparks with.

So far, no dice.

As he sipped his beer, he listened to the conversations taking place around him.

"Anyone know the new guy stayin' at the B and B?"

"I heard he's some big-shot writer."

"Why's he here?"

"I saw him talkin' to Rafe the other night."

"He was with Bailey at the concert in the park last night."

Atticus could hardly keep track of the people he encountered. He damn sure couldn't be expected to keep tabs on those who were keeping the gossip mill running. But that was what these people did. If they weren't talking about their kids or their jobs or the fact that the general store started selling boxed wine a few weeks ago, they were chatting about what people were doing.

He figured he had been the topic of many conversations recently, but these people were too nice to say whatever they were thinking when there was a chance that person might hear it. And since Atticus had become a regular of Moonshiners, he was comfortable knowing they wouldn't be debating where he was staying, who he was doing, or where he came from. At least not in his presence.

As for the second one, the answer was a big fat no one. At the moment, Atticus's sex life was on the fritz. Not for lack of trying on his part, mind you. Of course, he hadn't put any real effort into it. Certainly not when Slade or Evan were around, and it seemed he was rarely anywhere without one or both of them.

Tonight, he didn't have to endure those confused glances from Evan since he was at home having a birthday party for his daughter. But Slade was keeping an eye on him. Every so often, Atticus would feel his gaze burning holes in his flesh, but he had no idea what the guy was expecting him to do. He'd been on his best behavior lately.

Unfortunately, good behavior makes Atticus a dull boy.

It seemed the only thing he had time for these days was work. For the past couple of months, Atticus had been trying to find his footing with the task force. The people were great. Becs, Holly, and Elana welcomed him with open arms, offering to help him to get acclimated. Luca wasn't quite as friendly, but he wasn't hostile. Not the way he seemed to be with Becs. Atticus hadn't spent much time with Charlie or Jay because they'd been focused on a particular case that had taken them out of town quite a bit. Brantley and Reese were cool, and they were helping him to get his footing. He appreciated the assistance since this was new for him. And then there was Darius. They called him NostraDarius for a reason. The guy was stupid-smart, and he kept his nose to the grindstone, not welcoming too much personal interaction because he was always learning everything he could learn about everything. Atticus no longer attempted small talk with the man.

That left Baz and JJ. As a team, they were pretty unstoppable. Separately … well, Atticus liked Baz. He seemed like a stand-up guy. The only one he was hesitant about was JJ. She scared him. But he liked her. As long as she was smiling, he didn't fear she was going to beat him over the head with the closest blunt object.

Then again, most people reacted to Atticus with the desire to club him in the head. He'd been told he had that effect on people, but whatever. He happened to like who he was, and he made no excuses for it. When people couldn't handle him, they generally told him so. At that point, he went on his merry little way. He'd been on his own since he was seventeen, and he'd done all right for himself without relying on anyone else, so why on earth would he start giving a shit now?

For the next few minutes, Atticus sat silently by and listened while Slade and one of his many cousins shot the shit. By the time his ears were on the verge of bleeding, he'd gotten the lowdown on everything going on in Happy Married Man's world. He'd been so bored he'd honestly forgotten the guy's name.

As soon as he noticed two more hot married men coming their way, Atticus knew it was time for him to make his escape. So, while Beau and Ethan Walker took seats at the table, Atticus hopped up.

"I'll be back," he told Slade, although he didn't know whether it was true. He was hoping to find something interesting to distract him from the sameness of this place.

Luckily for Atticus, there were enough people at this small town watering hole that he could find plenty of trouble to get into.

As he was heading to the bar to get another beer, the front door opened. Several people shouted a greeting, making the guy flash a grin that had Atticus doing a double take.

Now *that* was some serious man candy. Dark brown hair, whiskey-brown eyes, and a body built for sin. Exactly what Atticus was on the hunt for. Now he just needed to answer the pressing question: which way did he swing?

"Hey, Rafe. Can I get a beer?" the handsome stranger drawled.

"Sure." Rafe looked at Atticus, popped an eyebrow.

"Yeah," he said. "I'll take another."

Rafe nodded and turned away.

"You come here often?" Atticus asked Tall Dark and Do Me, purposely using the cheesy line. After all, he wasn't looking to hitch himself a husband. One night was about all he was good for.

"You use that line a lot?"

"Whenever I can." Atticus gestured toward everyone else in the bar. "But don't feel special. I've asked everyone here. It's a survey. I'm compiling the responses for a book."

That earned him a laugh, and his dick got with the program.

He held out his hand to the stranger. "I'm Atticus James."

"Spencer Elliott," the guy responded, shaking his hand.

"Elliott, huh?" Atticus glanced Slade's way. "Any relation to that one?"

Spencer followed his gaze and grinned. "My brother."

Oh, now this was getting interesting. He'd known Slade for two months, and not once had he heard the man mention his brother.

"You know him?" Spencer inquired, leaning on the bar and giving Atticus his full attention.

"You could say we work together."

"That task force thing?"

"Yeah. You have any more brothers?"

Spencer turned his attention back to the bar, still grinning. "I'm the youngest of six."

"Only brothers?"

"Seems to run in the family."

Holy fuck. Atticus wasn't sure what was in the water in this town, but whatever it was, he made a vow not to drink it because, yes, even the gay ones had kids. Every damn person he met seemed to have half a dozen siblings and almost as many offspring. And to think he'd been surprised when he'd learned that Brantley had three brothers and three sisters.

Atticus waited until Spencer looked his way. "Any of 'em gay?"

That was always a risky question, but Atticus usually learned the answer before words were ever spoken. Like now, as Spencer's gaze trailed over him from head to toe. That wasn't revulsion in those golden eyes.

"And single?" he tacked on because seriously. Atticus had no problem bending the rules, but he wasn't a damn home wrecker.

Spencer's attention shifted to the bar when Rafe set two bottles in front of them.

"Put his on my tab," Spencer told the bartender.

Nope. Definitely not revulsion.

"And how're the kids?" Slade asked Ethan and Beau.

Both men beamed at the mere mention of Aiden, John Michael (a.k.a. Jack), and Kiera—their three-year-old triplets.

"They're fantastic," Beau said with a grin.

Slade noticed the man never used simple words like "good" or "fine" when he referred to his children. They were always "fantastic" or "awesome". For whatever reason, Slade liked that.

"And Kiera? Is she still insistin' on wearin' their clothes?"

Ethan chuckled. "She's a tomboy through and through."

The first time they'd mentioned their daughter wanting to wear boy's clothes, Slade had asked if they were worried. He quickly learned the error of a question of that nature when Beau and Ethan informed him she was her own person and could dress however she wanted. Slade had asked if they'd feel the same if Jack or Aiden wore girl's clothes. Beau's answer had been simple: "They're kids. Let 'em wear what they want. If that's the least of our worries, I'll be a happy dad."

Slade found he liked the simplicity.

"What's goin' on with the task force?" Ethan prompted.

The question had Slade glancing around to find Atticus, realizing the man hadn't returned from the bar. The moment he saw him, his jaw tensed, and his back straightened.

"Problem?" Beau asked, clearly picking up on Slade's sudden mood shift.

"Oh, hell no," Slade bellowed, shoving his chair back from the table when he saw Spencer talking to Atticus.

He felt Ethan's and Beau's eyes on him as he stormed across the crowded bar toward the two men who were standing too fucking close for Slade's liking.

"What the fuck is this?" Slade asked, glaring at his brother.

"What's it look like?" Spencer's countenance was as sweet and innocent as ever. "Just two guys gettin' to know each other. You have a problem with that?"

Slade didn't miss the slight edge to his brother's tone when he asked the question.

"Fuckin' right, I do," he countered hotly.

Spencer grinned. "Is this a new development, big brother? Last I knew, you were straight as an arrow."

"Fuck you. This ain't about me, and you fuckin' know it."

"I think I'll give you two a minute." Atticus's green eyes shifted between them.

"No," Spencer said firmly, his eyes narrowed. "We don't need a minute." Spencer looked at Atticus and smirked. "I was thinkin' maybe we could get outta here. It just got a little too crowded for my taste."

Slade never looked away from Spencer when he said, "He's gonna fuck you over, Atticus. It's what he does. Just ask my ex-wife."

Spencer's lip curled. "He's a grown man. He don't need you to fight his battles."

"Perhaps you should tell him your interests shift based on who's available. For the record, Jennifer *wasn't* when you fucked her."

A vicious laugh escaped his brother. "Man, I was just tryin' to prove a point."

"What? That you could fuck her? Or that you could fuck me over? 'Cause you did both, *little brother*."

A careless shrug preceded Spencer's, "It wasn't intentional. She was hittin' on me."

"So it was innocent. You just took what was bein' offered?"

"Damn right, I did. I needed to know just how far she would go to fuck my brother over. Look on the bright side. It all worked out. She left you for an old man anyway."

Yeah, Jennifer had left him for a guy nearly twice Slade's age, but that didn't change the fact that his own brother had fucked her while Slade had been married to her. He hadn't learned about it until Jennifer decided she was leaving. At that point, she had no problem cutting Slade off at the knees. Telling him all about the night she spent with Spencer had done the trick.

Truth was, Slade had expected Jennifer was cheating more than once during the three years they were married. He'd even suspected she'd done so when they were dating. But Slade had let it slide because he'd loved her. Or at least he thought he had. He was starting to think it was nothing more than an obsession since he seemed prone to those.

No, what shocked the shit out of him was that his own brother could do that to him. Slade would forgive Jennifer long before he would ever forgive Spencer. And it would be a cold day in hell before he accepted an apology from Jennifer.

"You really do need to get over yourself, Slade. That was nearly ten fuckin' years ago."

Yeah, but the blade from that betrayal was still lodged to the hilt in Slade's back.

"Now, where were—" Spencer looked around.

It was then Slade realized Atticus had disappeared.

He couldn't help it. He laughed. Served Spencer right.

CHAPTER SIX

"SOMETHIN' TELLS ME THAT MIGHT NOT END well."

"What's that?" Reese followed Brantley's gaze toward the bar. He saw Slade and his brother Spencer standing toe to toe, Slade's finger stabbed into the younger man's chest.

"I'm surprised Grady's not here tryin' to play referee."

Reese only knew what he'd heard via the grapevine about the rift between the youngest Elliott brothers. And he'd only heard that much because Grady, the third oldest of the brothers, had been bitching about it one night at the diner after a nasty argument between Spencer and Slade in which Grady had ended up taking a fist to the jaw.

"I'm sure Grady's fed up with their bullshit by now," Reese told Brantley. "You know what started it?"

"You mean tonight?"

Reese nodded. He knew the major rift had to do with Spencer having an affair with Slade's wife nearly a decade ago. To be fair, Reese wasn't sure he would ever get over that either. Reese wasn't usually one to take sides, but he was fully in Slade's corner on this one. Family didn't screw family over the way Spencer had. And sleeping with Slade's wife had been the ultimate betrayal.

"If I had to guess, it has somethin' to do with *him*."

Reese followed Brantley's finger to where he was pointing to the bar. Atticus was standing there watching the pair of them, shaking his head in disbelief.

"What the fuck did he do now?" Reese grumbled.

"You say that like you've already determined him guilty."

"Yeah, well. When the shoe fits."

Brantley chuckled. "The fact that Spencer'll screw anything that walks upright on two legs isn't a secret in this town." He tipped his beer bottle to his lips. "Knowin' Atticus, he tapped into that and thought he'd hook him one for the night."

"Why would Slade give a shit?" Reese wondered aloud.

"He hates his brother. Probably a knee-jerk response."

Reese relaxed when Slade backed up a few steps. His lips were moving, but they couldn't hear a word being spoken. Whatever it was earned Slade a middle finger when Spencer shoved his hand in his face.

"Son of a bitch," Brantley growled when Slade shoved Spencer.

Reese was out of his chair a second behind Brantley. The brothers got in a couple of punches before they managed to pull them off each other, shoving them in opposite directions.

"You wanna do that, you take that shit outside," Brantley snarled. "You don't disrespect Mack's place like that."

Spencer wiped his bloody lip with the back of his hand and glared at Slade. "You need to get over yourself, asshole. It's time for you to move the fuck on."

Brantley didn't allow Slade to say a word, planting a finger in his chest. "Not here."

Slade nodded, his gaze following Spencer as he walked toward the door. The man paused to say something to Atticus. The room seemed to hold its breath as Atticus glanced at Slade and then back to Spencer. A second later, he was following the man out of the bar.

"He's gonna fuck him over," Slade snarled.

"Atticus is a big boy," Brantley told Slade. "He can take care of himself."

Reese figured no truer words had ever been said. He didn't know much about Atticus other than the bits and pieces they'd learned while working to find Tobias Land and what little he'd picked up on the past couple of months, but he knew Atticus wasn't the laid-back, happy-go-lucky guy he wanted everyone to think he was. He was hiding something. Pain, anger, Reese wasn't sure. But it was damn sure something.

ATTICUS KNEW HE WAS MAKING A MISTAKE leaving with Spencer. He knew it, and he did it anyway.

Or, at the very least, he was considering it with his final decision weighing heavily on the getting laid side. For that to happen, he had to go with Spencer.

So why the hell was he even second-guessing himself?

Because going will be a silent "fuck you" to Slade.

Goddamn. Why the fuck did he go and grow a conscience now?

Did he really give a shit about Slade?

The answer to that was not really, but even so, Atticus had no business getting in between Slade and his family drama. Which meant decorum dictated that he cut his losses and either go home alone or go back inside the bar and get shit-faced.

Shit-faced or laid?

Shit-faced or laid?

Which is it gonna be?

Atticus squared his shoulders. Decorum could go fuck itself because tonight he was thinking solely with his dick.

"Follow me back to my place. That's me right there," Spencer said, pointing toward a candy-apple red Camaro.

"Where do you live?"

"Not far."

With one last chance to do the right thing, Atticus looked at the bar. He recalled the look on Slade's face when Spencer rubbed it in that he'd fucked his wife. It was a dick move; that was for damn sure. Worst part was Spencer wasn't the least bit apologetic. In fact, there might've been a glimmer of victory in Spencer's eyes. Atticus was all for bucking the system, but did he want to go down that road? Where he no longer gave a shit about other people's feelings?

"You comin' or not?" Spencer called out as he opened his car door.

Could he do that to Slade? Could he put a rift between them so early in their relationship? They were only co-workers, but it wasn't like they worked in an office building and would only see each other on occasion. Atticus would have to see the man every damn day. And hell, there was a good chance that one day, he might have to rely on Slade to have his back.

Atticus found himself shaking his head. "Actually, no. I'm not comin'."

In more ways than one, he thought as he started toward the bar.

"Your loss," Spencer shouted after him.

Yeah. It probably was, but Atticus's dick had gotten him into trouble more than once. Only once when it had mattered, though. A couple of years ago. Turned out the guy he'd gone home with had been helping a friend evade arrest. Atticus ended up losing a large bounty thanks to thinking with the wrong brain.

Sure, sex was a great way to take the edge off, but it wasn't a requirement. He didn't *need* to get fucked. He simply wanted to.

With a sigh of regret that he'd missed an opportunity, Atticus opened the door and stepped inside. A round of greetings echoed, and like usual, no one looked up. Had they, they might've said, "Welcome back."

He scanned the room, looking for Slade or Brantley. He found Slade standing near the hallway that led to the bathrooms. He had a beer in his hand and a scowl on his face.

Atticus made a beeline for him. With each step, his frustration grew until he found himself up in Slade's face. He ignored the fact that he had to go up on his toes since Slade was several inches taller.

"The next time you wanna protect my fuckin' virtue, don't."

Slade stared at him, his brown eyes glittering. "Virtue? Among other things, that's one thing you're lackin'."

Great. And now Slade was going to take his anger out on him.

Atticus rolled his eyes. "And to think, I gave up gettin' fucked for you."

Slade's expression changed, and for a moment, Atticus thought he saw a hint of remorse. If he had, Slade had no intention of apologizing because he walked away, heading back to the table where Ethan and Beau were once again watching them.

With a sigh, Atticus returned to the bar. He flagged Rafe down and ordered another beer. When he got it, he found an empty seat near the pool table and took a load off. He figured he'd finish his beer and head back to the cheap, rent-by-the-week motel he was staying in until he could find a place of his own. He'd been hoping to find an apartment close to work, but so far, there weren't any available rentals. None that he could afford, anyway. He'd been calling those in his price range every week, hoping someone had turned in their notice. So far, no luck.

"You chose wisely."

The gruff rasp came from his left. Atticus looked up to see a dark-haired cowboy holding what looked to be some fruity drink. He was dressed like nearly every other redneck in this bar, wearing scuffed boots, ball-crushing Wranglers, a faded, seen-one-too-many-washes graphic T-shirt, and a Stetson made of straw—a summer staple, or so Slade had told him—resting on his head.

In a word, he looked fucking delicious. The rugged cowboy look definitely did it for him.

The guy nodded to the empty seat beside Atticus. "You mind?"

"No."

He took a seat on Atticus's left, leaning back with a casualness so many of these cowboys exuded. As though he didn't have a care in the world. That or he needed to recline to take some pressure off his balls since those damn jeans looked molded to his mile-long legs.

"What was the wise choice I made?" Atticus prompted, not wanting to think about the guy's balls or his legs and risk getting a hard-on.

The guy nodded his chin toward the door. "Not gettin' in between those two. Slade and Spencer've been fightin' since they were kids. Got worse when Spencer screwed Slade's girl."

"Yeah, well." Atticus huffed. "In between wasn't where I was hopin' I'd end up tonight. You related to them or what?"

"Not directly, no."

"What does that mean?"

"Means my cousins are their cousins."

Atticus didn't have the brain power to make sense of that, so he said, "Then who *are* you related to?"

"Well…" The guy looked around the room and started pointing. "That one. And him. And that one over there. Her. Her. And yeah, that one, too."

Atticus noticed he'd pointed at Brantley first, then to Ethan, and then some others Atticus didn't know.

"Cousins," the guy said, twisting so he could offer a hand. "Name's Carson. And you are?"

"Let me guess, your last name's Walker."

"Nope. Briggs." Carson flashed a grin. "My mama's maiden name is Walker, though. And you are?"

"Atticus." He shook the man's hand, and as soon as their palms touched, Atticus knew his night was looking a little brighter.

"Nice to meet ya."

"I'd say the same," Atticus told him, "but I'll refrain until I see if one of your kin is gonna come over here and warn me off you."

Carson laughed. "Ask anyone. I've got no skeletons in my closet."

"With or without, are you still locked up tight in that closet?"

A sexy curve pulled at the corner of Carson's lips until he was doing that whole half-smirk thing. Carson raised his pink drink. "What do you think?"

Oh yeah. His night was definitely looking up.

CHAPTER SEVEN

"I HAVE TO SAY, THIS HAS BEEN easier than I expected," Becs said when Evan joined her in the kitchen.

It had been a long day. Freakishly long since somehow they'd managed to get the girls to go to bed early last night. That backfired when they woke up at the ass-crack of dawn this morning ready to party.

On the flip side, they'd been so busy keeping up with the kids they hadn't had a chance to finish the conversation they'd started last night.

"Which part?" he replied. "Dinner or getting them to agree to go to sleep?"

She smiled. "Both."

Damn, she had a beautiful smile.

"Be careful what you wish for. The night's still young."

Her smile widened. "True. Last night, we got lucky."

Yes, they had.

"You want something to drink?"

Becs glanced around the empty kitchen. "I should probably turn in. If, by chance, we get lucky again, I'm sure they'll be up early in the morning."

"Yeah. Probably." Evan knew he should go to bed, too.

If he were tired, that wouldn't have been a problem. He should've been. Chasing six kids around all day took it out of you. He could blame it on the coffee, but it would've been a lie. The woman standing two feet away was the reason for his insomnia. More accurately, her admission last night. Not a minute had gone by since then that he hadn't thought about it. It had taken every ounce of self-control he possessed not to broach the subject last night. Since she hadn't either, Evan was starting to think he'd dreamed it all.

"Did you wanna keep talking about … you know … what I said last night?" Becs asked. "I mean, we were interrupted, so we didn't get to finish the conversation."

Their quiet time had certainly come to an end faster than he'd anticipated. The moment the third girl showed up, Sophia decided they should get in the swimming pool, which meant Evan was needed to keep an eye on things. The party was in full force from that point on. Right up until they had tucked the girls into their fancy blanket forts that Becs had helped them make in the game room. At that point, Becs had been invited to hang out with them, leaving him to ponder the conversation alone.

"We don't have to talk about it if you don't want to," Becs said, her voice softer than before. More hesitant.

If he didn't know better, Evan would've said she was as nervous as he was. But he wasn't sure that was even possible.

Becs was the first woman Evan had been interested in since his wife. At least for more than an intimate encounter. And since Gayle had been his high school sweetheart and the first woman he had slept with, Evan didn't have a long, sordid track record with women. He hadn't actually been on a date in more than a decade. Not since before Gayle died. The women he'd been with over the years had been ones he picked up in bars, ones he ensured understood he wasn't looking for anything more than sex, so there'd been no subsequent dinners or movies or any of that social shit required to maintain a healthy relationship. Evan didn't do relationships, so as far as he was concerned, it wasn't necessary.

And while he wanted to take this woman to bed—God, he wanted that more than his next fucking breath—Evan wanted more from their relationship than that. Even if it was only friendship, he wanted more. The problem was sex muddied the waters. Intimacy increased affection in many cases. Evan wasn't ready for something complicated. Was he?

"Sorry I brought it back up," Becs said with a sad smile. "Would you mind if I slept in Sophia's bed? If and when I get them to sleep, I mean."

Evan heard her words, but he wasn't listening. He was stuck on her apology and the fact she thought he was bothered by the topic. Sure, it made him uncomfortable, but he admired her boldness. The fact that she'd brought it up had surprised him. Hell, everything about Becs surprised him.

She took a deep breath and nodded. "I guess that means the decision's mine to make."

Decision? What decision?

Becs stepped around him. "Good night, Evan. I'll see you in the morning."

Before she could pass him, Evan reached for her. He cupped her face, pivoting to face her as he did. Without thinking about the repercussions—there would certainly be time to do that later—he kissed her.

The moment her soft lips met his, his senses were overwhelmed. Her sweet smell, her smooth skin, the barely audible whimper that escaped her as she leaned into him, her cool hands curling on the sides of his neck. And when her lips parted, allowing him entry, he knew he was in over his head.

She was sweet. Her taste, her touch. Their tongues met, a hesitant, languid mating. Evan wasn't sure he'd ever been as turned on by a simple, innocent kiss as he was now. It was intense despite the lack of urgency. He savored her for long minutes, unable to release her even when his brain told him it was the only option.

When their lips finally separated, Evan didn't pull away, nor did she. Her hands remained on his neck, his cradling the back of her head. Evan rested his forehead against hers and let his heart rate return to normal.

"I've wanted you to do that for a long time," she whispered.

"Not as long as I've wanted to do it," he assured her.

Footsteps sounded on the stairs, and the moment was broken. Evan stepped back just as Carly and Sophia appeared in the doorway, grinning from ear to ear.

"Aren't you two supposed to be in bed?" Becs asked, her eyes glittering with both remembered passion and renewed amusement.

"We want popcorn," Carly said.

"Popcorn?" Becs put her hands on her knees and bent to their level. "I think popcorn sounds like the greatest birthday sleepover snack ever."

"Yay!" Sophia shouted, hopping up and down.

"You two go on up. I'll bring it up as soon as it's ready."

There was more bouncing, followed by Sophia's exuberant, "Goodnight, Daddy!"

"Night, baby," he called after her.

"I think it might be wise if I sleep in the game room with them again," Becs said when she turned around to face him. "I'm not sure sleep's gonna come quickly tonight."

"No, it won't," he agreed, but he wasn't only referring to the girls.

"How about a deal?" Becs said. "I stay up with them tonight, and you get up early with them tomorrow?"

"I can handle that deal."

She moved closer. "About that kiss…"

Evan swallowed and waited for her to finish that sentence.

Her voice was soft when she said, "I hope we get to do it again sometime."

"Me, too."

"I won't lie. This isn't somethin' I normally do."

"What's that?" Atticus asked, glancing over at Carson.

They'd been sitting at the back of the bar for the past two hours, simply talking. Mostly about mundane shit like the weather, but there were a couple of instances when Atticus had gotten a glimpse into who Carson was.

"Come to this bar and not spend the entire time shootin' the shit with my cousins and catchin' up on what's goin' on in their lives."

Atticus motioned toward the tables where a handful of people still lingered. "Well, don't let me keep you."

Carson tilted his head and regarded Atticus from underneath thick, dark lashes. "I didn't say I'd *rather* be doin' that."

Atticus wouldn't admit it, but he was glad. He was enjoying Carson's company.

He'd learned quite a bit about the sexy Carson Briggs over the course of the time they'd spent together. At thirty-one, he was the youngest of six. His mother, Maryanne, was Brantley's father's youngest sister. Carson had two brothers, Jaxson and Wyatt, and three sisters, Piper, Renee, and Cara. Jaxson, the oldest, had his own handyman business in Coyote Ridge, and he helped out at Walker Demo whenever Autumn, who happened to be dating Charlotte Miller, one of Atticus's co-workers, needed assistance. Carson's oldest sister, Piper, was a psychiatrist who'd recently started a practice in town after moving back with her son when she divorced her cheatin' bastard of a husband—Carson's words. Renee was married to a lawyer, and they had four kids. They lived in San Antonio. Cara, the youngest sister, was an internet influencer—whatever that was—and made more money doing it than most of his siblings combined. Oh, and in Cara's spare time, she was a volunteer fireman for the Coyote Ridge Fire Department. And Carson was an electrician.

There was no doubt Atticus wouldn't remember most of those names come morning, but he'd enjoyed hearing the stories. What he found interesting was that Carson liked to talk about himself the least. He could go on and on about his family, but when Atticus tried to get too personal, he somehow managed to steer the conversation elsewhere.

"Excuse me for a minute," Atticus told Carson when he felt his eyes on him. "I'm gonna hit the head."

Carson nodded, then tipped back the rest of his pink drink. Atticus hadn't asked what it was, but he knew one thing for sure, there was alcohol in the damn thing. If he had to guess, Carson was past the point of wasted, which was why his ass had remained glued to the chair. He doubted seriously that the guy was interested in what little bit Atticus had to say throughout the night. Guys like Carson never did. They entertained the notion for a little while but usually came to their senses before the night ended.

No, there was no way a guy as nice and stable as Carson had any interest in Atticus. It didn't work out that way for him. The guys he generally went home with were the ones who were out of work for one reason or another. At twenty-five, Atticus had never had a serious relationship, much less a stable one. Then again, he wasn't serious or stable, either, so it wasn't surprising that was the type of guy he attracted.

He shoved open the bathroom door, moving to the side to keep from getting plowed over by a tall cowboy on his way out.

After taking a piss and washing his hands, Atticus used the rough paper towels to dry them while he stared at himself in the flaked and peeling mirror. He'd spent most of the last hour debating whether he should invite Carson back to his motel room. If he did, they'd likely have a fantastic night, but no doubt he wouldn't see Carson after that. Maybe if their paths crossed in town.

As for why Atticus wasn't keen on that idea, he didn't know. He liked Carson. And that usually meant he needed to steer clear of him. As far as sex went, anyway. Otherwise, it would get weird later on down the road.

No, what Atticus needed to do was go back to his motel room. Alone. He'd stopped drinking an hour ago, and he'd only had three beers all night. He was fine to drive, and there was no better time than the present to make his exit. He would tell Carson he enjoyed meeting him and hoped they could hang out again sometime.

Simple.

Tossing the paper towel in the trash, Atticus opened the door and found Carson standing in the hallway, one booted foot resting on the wall.

Damn, the man was fine. With his blue-gray eyes and the dark stubble that lined his jaw, not to mention a body honed from physical labor, Carson was the sort of man you looked at twice to see if your eyes were playing tricks on you. His weren't.

"You got a phobia of bathrooms?" Atticus asked, gesturing toward the door behind him. "No one's in there, in case you're wondering."

"Not wonderin'," he said simply.

"Then why're you standing there?"

"Just 'cause."

His words were slurred, the twang even thicker than it had been earlier.

"I wasn't gone *that* long, was I?" Sure, he'd gotten lost in his head for a minute or two, but not long enough to warrant a search party.

"Anyone ever tell you you talk too much?"

Atticus grinned. "Daily."

Carson's eyes glittered with amusement, but his expression was full of heat.

"I think I'm gonna call it a night," Atticus told him when it was clear Carson didn't have anything more to say.

"Good idea."

Well, that was easy.

Not sure what to do or say, Atticus tipped his chin. "I guess I'll see you around then."

Before he could take a step, Carson had him up against the wall. His hands were hard, almost rough, as they moved along his sides, but his lips were soft, his tongue sliding into Atticus's mouth, making it impossible for him to resist.

Not that he would. Fuck no. A man like Atticus did not resist a man like Carson. It didn't happen. Tomorrow, Carson would no doubt kick Atticus to the curb, but for one night, they could enjoy the hell out of each other.

"Dayummm," Carson groaned, his breath fanning Atticus's mouth. "I've wanted you since the first time I saw you."

"Two hours ago?" Atticus laughed, holding Carson's hip to keep from dry humping the guy in the hallway.

Carson's thumbs pressed against Atticus's ribs as though the man was fighting to keep them still. "Try two months."

"Two—huh? Where?"

"Here."

Atticus shook his head. "No way. I would've certainly remembered seeing you before."

Carson's grin was wickedly sexy. "I come in here maybe once every three months to see what's goin' on. Since I saw you back in June, I've been in here every fuckin' weekend." He nodded toward the bar. "Ask Rafe or Mack. They'll tell you."

"Why didn't you say somethin'?"

He chuckled. "I did."

"Before now."

"'Cause I wanted to know if you were for real."

Atticus managed to lean back enough to meet Carson's gaze. "How fucking drunk are you?"

Carson chuckled. "A little. But not so much I can't think straight."

That was debatable.

"Did I pass your test? Your *is he for real* test?"

Carson leaned into him, their hips pressing together. Atticus sucked in a sharp breath when he felt the hard ridge of Carson's cock pressed against him. His entire body reacted to the proximity, his muscles tensing, his cock throbbing.

"I don't usually do this."

"I think we've already established that," Atticus retorted with a laugh.

"I'm talkin' about comin' on to someone I just met."

"Well, if it's any consolation, you're pretty fucking good at it."

He felt Carson's smile against his lips. "I wanna take you home."

"Let's go th—"

"But if I do, I'm gonna fuck this up. I always do." Carson pulled back, met his stare. All amusement was gone. "I don't wanna fuck this up."

Atticus honestly didn't know what to say to that.

"Tell me I can see you again if I don't take you home tonight."

Atticus swallowed.

"If I can't, I'll gladly take you back to my house and fuck you until the sun comes up."

Atticus shivered. "You realize it's pretty damn difficult to resist a proposition like that, right?"

"If I *can*, I'm gonna get your number, walk outta here, call an Uber, and go home to sleep it off."

Shit.

Why the fuck did he have to meet the one guy who could proposition him with no sex and make it sound so damn appealing?

Carson stood up straight and pressed his hands down the front of his shirt to smooth it. "Which is it gonna be, Atticus?"

"Why don't I drive you home, and I'll decide on the way?"

Carson's gaze bounced over his face. When he finally nodded, Atticus knew this man was going to be nearly impossible to resist.

Twenty minutes later, Atticus was trying to figure out if this was a test. If so, he knew he was going to fail.

He'd never been good at tests. Not in school or in life. He tended to let people down at every turn. Since Carson was hoping Atticus would make a decision that would result in them seeing each other again, Atticus figured he was going to let him down, too.

"You good over there?" Atticus asked, glancing at Carson, who was leaning against the window.

"Peachy," he muttered.

Or maybe fate would intervene, and Atticus wouldn't have to decide. There was a good chance Carson was going to pass out before Atticus pulled up to the guy's house.

"Take a left."

Atticus followed Carson's direction into a neighborhood. It was one of many in Coyote Ridge, lined with older homes designed with brick fronts and wood siding on the sides. Some had driveways made of solid concrete slabs, some were designed with narrow strips meant as a path for tires, and the rest were dirt. There weren't any of the new, two-story cookie-cutter houses in this area. Not like in the next town over, where they'd sprouted up in recent years based on the age of the trees. Or the lack thereof. Here in Carson's neighborhood, the tree trunks were enormous, meaning they'd been there for a while.

"Up here. White house on the right."

Atticus pulled into the single slab driveway of a little white house with black shutters and black iron railing around the front porch. The yard looked as though it had been mowed recently, the shrubs that lined the base of the structure had been trimmed. And the porch light glowed yellow by the front door.

There was a single-car detached garage set back farther than the house. A floodlight came on when Atticus stopped near the sidewalk leading up to the porch.

"Which is it gonna be?" Carson asked, tipping his hat up. "Your phone number? Or are you comin' in?"

Atticus put the truck in park. "I haven't decided yet. You live here by yourself?"

"Yeah."

Atticus stared at the house. "Stable. Good job. Nice house."

Carson looked at him. "What's that?"

"Nothin'," he grumbled. "I was just outlining all the reasons I should leave and never look back."

Carson leaned forward and squinted out the windshield. "It ain't *that* nice."

Atticus chuckled.

"You can sit out here and think on it," Carson told him, reaching for the door handle. "I'm gonna go in and get some water."

When Carson got out of the truck, Atticus had no choice but to follow.

Well, technically, he had a choice, but something told him not to let this guy get too far away. This was a first for Atticus, and while he was still confused about which path to take, he wasn't ready to let Carson go completely.

He reached the front porch before Carson had made it into the house. He was listing to the left while trying to get the key to line up with the deadbolt. Atticus helped him along, unlocking the door and pushing it open.

"Thanks." Carson stepped inside and flipped on a switch by the door. "I don't usually drink this much."

Atticus looked around. The house Carson claimed wasn't *that* nice was even nicer on the inside. The furniture matched, the painted walls were clean, and the hardwood floors gleamed. Maybe it wasn't expensive shit, but it was definitely cared for.

"I knew I'd need some liquid courage to talk to you," Carson continued as he ambled toward the kitchen.

Atticus followed.

Carson fumbled around but managed to get a glass and fill it with water. He held tight to the counter as though he might fall over if he let go.

"Is the room spinnin'? Carson drawled. "Or is it just me?"

Atticus smiled. "You need to sleep it off."

Carson set the half-empty glass of water on the counter. "Don't have to tell me twice."

Atticus stood in the doorway between the living room and the kitchen, watching as Carson headed toward a hallway that led to the back of the house.

"If you go, just flip the lock on your way out."

Atticus debated, remaining firmly rooted to the floor. It wasn't until he heard a loud thud that he followed the route Carson had taken. He found the man in his bedroom, a bedside lamp on, his Stetson sitting on top of the lampshade, and Carson draped across the bed, his long legs hanging halfway off, the toes of his boots on the floor.

At what point in his life had he become the caretaker, Atticus wondered as he helped Carson out, turning him so he was on the bed the right way, his head on a pillow.

"I want you to stay," Carson whispered, his hand sliding under the edge of Atticus's T-shirt.

Atticus knew he was fucked at that point.

Never in his life had anyone ever asked him to stay. Not ever.

Before he could tell Carson his plan, the man's eyes closed, and his arm fell listlessly to the side. A soft snore sounded a moment later.

Atticus grinned, then proceeded to pull Carson's boots off. He wasn't sure how those jeans could possibly be comfortable to sleep in, but Atticus wasn't about to help out with those. He was a lot of things, but Atticus had never taken advantage of a drunk man, and he didn't intend to start now.

Leaving would've been the smart thing to do, but he couldn't. For whatever reason, Atticus wanted to take Carson up on the offer of seeing him again, so he did the only thing he could think to do. He wandered back to the living room, dropped on the cushy leather sofa, and drifted off. If come morning, Carson still wanted to see him again, Atticus would give him his phone number, and they'd go from there.

If not, then no harm, no foul. At least this way, Atticus could walk away without leaving a piece of himself behind. Something told him Carson Briggs was the man who was going to slip under the protective walls he'd built around his heart, and he wasn't sure he was ready for that.

At the same time, he didn't think he was strong enough to resist.

CHAPTER EIGHT

Sunday, August 7, 2022

BRANTLEY STIRRED FROM THE SOUND OF HIS cell phone ringing on the bedside table. Out of habit, he reached over and touched Reese's leg, ensuring himself he was there. With a sigh, he rolled onto his back, glanced at the clock.

0416—this couldn't be good.

He grabbed his phone. "Walker."

"I hate to wake you this early," Zachariah Tavoularis said, "but I'm gonna need your team on an assignment."

"Local?"

"No."

Reese moved beside him, relaxing when Brantley put his hand on his leg and patted, a signal that it wasn't a dire emergency.

"How long do I have to get the team in?"

"An hour. Hour and a half tops."

"All right. How many do you need?"

"Your best and brightest, at the minimum."

"Lemme call 'em in. I'll call you back."

Brantley disconnected and set the phone on the nightstand.

"Z?" Reese's voice was thick with sleep.

"Yup."

"Local job?"

"Nope."

"Figures."

Brantley grinned at Reese's grumble. Since they'd officially shifted under the umbrella of Sniper 1 Security, their jobs were taking them out of town more often. Brantley didn't mind, and he knew Reese didn't either, but due to the diverse situations of their team members, it often required a bit of juggling.

"I'll call JJ," Brantley told Reese, still lying on his back, eyes closed. "You text Slade and Evan—"

"Evan's got his daughter's birthday party this weekend."

"Right." Brantley sighed, rearranging the puzzle pieces in his head. "Text Slade, Atticus, and Becs. Let 'em know we'll need 'em to be ready when we give the signal."

When Reese didn't say anything, Brantley rolled toward his nightstand. Before he could reach for his phone, Reese was spooning up against him.

"How long did Z give us?" Reese asked, his lips trailing along Brantley's shoulder.

"Hour and a half tops."

"I only need a small percentage of that."

"Oh, the sexy things you say, Tavoularis," Brantley teased. His chuckle turned to a groan when Reese reached over his hip and gripped Brantley's cock.

"I'd say you're on board."

"Baby, when it comes to you, I'm always ready and willin'."

Reese pressed closer, the warmth of his chest against Brantley's back, his cock hard and eager against his ass. The silence morphed into a steady hum of grunts and moans as Reese teased him with his hands and lips sliding across his back. Brantley took the liberty of getting the lube, then slicking Reese's cock by reaching behind him. He knew Reese liked this position, and Brantley had no desire to move from where he was.

When Reese finally pushed inside him, Brantley closed his eyes and moaned softly, savoring the stretch as the man he loved drove him to the brink, never giving him what he needed to go over until they were both ready.

"Come with me, Brantley," Reese whispered in his ear.

Brantley took over stroking his cock, timing it with the increasing pace of Reese's thrusts.

"You close?"

A grunt was all Brantley could manage. He was holding on by a thread.

"Fuck, you feel so good." Reese grabbed Brantley's leg, lifting it as he began thrusting in deeper, harder. A few seconds later, Brantley felt the exquisite pulse of Reese's cock, and he let himself go.

Evan came awake slowly, alerted by a sound in his bedroom. He didn't open his eyes, didn't move a muscle. If it was Sophia, she usually planted both hands on his chest and shook him.

No one shook him.

"Evan?"

Yep, that was what had woken him—Becs's sweet, lyrical voice calling his name.

Her soft, cool fingers trailed over his arm. "Evan."

"Hmm?"

"I hate to wake you, but Reese texted me. They're gonna need me for a case."

He opened his eyes. The room was dark. The clock on his bedside table read 4:47 A.M.

"What's the case?"

She continued to whisper, answering with, "He said he didn't know yet. Only that it's not local."

Evan forced himself to sit up, reaching for the lamp as he dropped his feet to the floor.

He didn't think about the fact that he was wearing only a pair of shorts and nothing else. He was certainly covered where it was necessary, but it wasn't exactly appropriate for his co-worker to see him like this.

Becs stepped back, her pretty blue eyes lingering on his chest. Evan didn't want to admit how much he liked the way she was looking at him. It had been a long damn time since a woman had eyed him like she wanted to devour him.

"When do you have to leave?"

Her gaze jerked to his face. "Reese said he'd text with the time. Do you think Kaye will have a problem watching Carly?"

Evan shook his head. Kaye adored Carly. So did Evan. She was always welcome at their house.

"Of course not."

"She's a lifesaver."

"You want some coffee for the road?"

"I didn't mean to get you out of bed," she said quickly. "I just didn't want to leave without telling you. The girls were up until a little after one, so I'm sure they'll sleep for a while. You should—"

"I'm up," he said, pushing to his feet.

Becs's eyes raked down his entire body, from his neck to his toes.

"Honey," he said smoothly, "if I'm expected to be a gentleman, you'll have to stop looking at me like that."

Her lips parted with a gasp, her eyes shifting to his face. "I'm so sorry."

He chuckled softly. "Don't apologize. I'm not complaining. But…" He gestured toward the door.

She nodded curtly. "Right. Coffee. I'll get it started."

With that, she darted out of his bedroom.

Evan stared after her for several seconds before his feet got with the program. He ignored his eager cock, hoping the damn thing hadn't started tenting his shorts until after she left.

An hour after Z had woken him up, after Brantley called JJ, unwilling to risk her not seeing a text message, and after a shower with Reese that lasted as long as the hot water did, Brantley was in the kitchen waiting for the coffee to finish brewing.

Reese was pulling eggs and bacon from the refrigerator, getting to work as he always did on Sunday morning. It didn't matter that they had a case or would likely be on the road in a matter of hours; this was Reese's way of creating some semblance of stability in their routine. Although Brantley had been driven by routine early in his military career, that had shifted when he joined the Teams. For the last several years of his career in the Navy, it had been lacking in his life. He figured that was the reason he'd begun to appreciate the sense of normalcy it provided.

While Reese worked at the stove, Brantley prepared Tesha's food, delivering the bowl to her. While she chowed down, he rinsed and filled her water bowl. She was so focused on eating that Brantley heard the sound of footsteps outside before she did.

Clearly sensing there was no threat, Tesha let out a soft bark, sparing only a few seconds on the back door before it finally opened.

Baz was there, stepping out of the way so JJ could come inside.

"Are you wearin' pajamas?" Brantley asked, staring at her long cotton pants, which had clouds all over them.

"Shut it," she groused. "They're comfortable."

Brantley's gaze snapped to Baz. He shrugged, a silent confirmation that, yes, he'd noticed that JJ wasn't her usual chipper self this morning, too.

"I'm makin' breakfast," Reese said. "You two want some?"

"I'll never turn down bacon," JJ told him, pulling out a stool at the island. "Especially not when you're cookin' it."

Baz nodded in agreement, and Reese went to work doubling the amount.

"Since you dragged me outta bed on a Sunday, this better be a damn good case," JJ said, accepting the juice Brantley passed over to her.

"Might I remind you, this is your fault," he quipped.

"Mine?" She frowned, glancing between the three of them. "How's that?"

"You jinxed us," Reese said without looking up from the skillet.

"He's right," Baz chimed in.

"Y'all are idiots," she muttered. "What's the case?"

Brantley shrugged. "Z said to get the team together. All I know is it's not local."

JJ sighed. "Don't tell me he's gonna have us playin' bounty hunters again."

Brantley grinned.

"The last time your brother"—JJ pointed a finger at Reese—"wanted us to help, he had us chasin' a man up and down the I-35 corridor between here and Dallas."

She wasn't wrong. They'd been in pursuit of Tobias Land, affectionately known as Uncle Toby to Reese and his brother Z. For a guy who was a bit off his rocker, Toby had given them a run for their money. And that was before he'd kidnapped Reese's mother.

"Well, if he plans to put us to work, he better remember you've got your tux fittings on the fifteenth. I pushed it out as far as I could. Whatever this is, better not take more than a week."

Brantley practically had the day burned into his brain since JJ had been reminding them of it for the past month. As had been the case with everything JJ had needed them to address, it was a big deal and would require the presence of their mothers. Brantley had no idea why, but he'd stopped asking questions. His intention was to show up at the wedding and marry the love of his life. If his mother insisted on picking out his tie, he didn't care.

"I figure there's only one way to find out," Reese said, pointing his spatula toward Brantley's phone.

He was right.

Brantley dialed Z's number and put the phone on speaker.

"About damn time."

"You said an hour and a half. It's been—" Brantley looked at the clock.

"Seventy-seven minutes," Z chimed in.

"Still less than ninety," Brantley countered. "I've got JJ, Baz, and Reese here. Tell us what's goin' on."

"Mornin'," Z said with that slow drawl that was eerily similar to his brothers. "One of our agents and the client he's assigned to have gone missin'."

Brantley stood tall, all teasing falling away as he waited for Z to continue. If the guy had mentioned that earlier, they could've been on the road by now.

"At the family's request, we assigned an agent to keep an eye on a New York socialite. I've received daily updates for the past three weeks without a missed check-in. Four days ago, that stopped. I gave it a day before I got worried. On the second day, I sent one of the local agents to look for him. No luck. That's where y'all come in. The jet's on its way to you, and I need at least four of you on it when it gets there."

Brantley hadn't worked for Sniper 1 Security for long, but he knew the agents were kept to a strict check-in policy. The rule was every twelve hours, and if they hadn't heard from him in four days, he'd missed eight check-ins.

"You know for a fact they're in New York?" Brantley asked, glancing between the faces watching him closely.

"At last check-in, they were."

"Four days ago? With that amount of time, they could be anywhere, Z."

"Are you opposed to gettin' on the damn plane, Walker?"

Brantley rarely heard Z get angry or frustrated, and it was apparent he was both. "Who's the agent?"

Z sighed. "It's Deck, Brantley."

Frowning, Brantley looked at Reese for confirmation. Decker Bromwell had worked for the task force since the end of last year, but Sniper 1 had recently requested him to return temporarily. Brantley hadn't been given any details about his assignment, nor had he asked.

Reese's shrug told him it was news to him, too.

"This isn't the first time Deck's done this," Reese said, his tone hard. "The guy's not exactly known for followin' the rules."

Brantley was surprised by Reese's vehemence. Although RT and Z had been the ones to suggest they bring Deck onto the task force, Brantley hadn't seen any signs that the guy was anything but dedicated. Sure, he was more of a boots-on-the-ground kind of guy, but when they needed him to step in, he did.

"This time's different, Reese."

Reese looked up for the first time and met Brantley's gaze as he spoke to his brother. "What aren't you tellin' us, Z? Who's the client?"

"I take it they're not the ordinary socialite?" Brantley stated.

Z sighed heavily. "No. She's very high profile."

Brantley noticed the curiosity on JJ's face. She stirred her hand in his direction, urging him to ask.

"Who?"

"Saoirse Kavanagh."

"Holy shit," JJ muttered, clearly not meaning to speak loud enough for Z to hear her.

He did.

"I echo that sentiment, JJ. If you haven't heard of her, you've been livin' under a rock."

Brantley didn't bother admitting his residences tended to be under rocks. He had no idea who she was or why she was famous.

JJ noticed his confusion because she attempted to fill in the blanks. "Saoirse Kavanagh is the youngest of the Kavanagh siblings. The very same siblings who hold the reins to Kavanagh Holdings Group. They're a titan in the investment and insurance world, with headquarters in Dublin, Ireland, as well as New York. The Kavanagh siblings are the only family members who reside in the US."

"Why'd they ask for protective detail specifically?" Brantley inquired. "If they're *titans*, as JJ said, shouldn't they have around-the-clock security?"

"They do," Z answered.

"So why this specific request?"

There was a beat of silence, and Brantley knew he wasn't going to like the response.

"Deck made the request after Ronan Kavanagh contacted him directly."

"Ronan's the oldest of the four," JJ supplied.

"I take it they've got history?" Brantley asked, looking at Reese again. He wasn't sure why his partner was so quiet.

"Friendship," Z said. "And no, I don't know the specifics on who, why, or how. At this point, it doesn't matter. What does is that we find Saoirse and Deck."

Brantley knew he could argue until he was blue in the face, but Z was right. They needed to find Decker and the woman he was responsible for looking after. To do that, they'd need a hell of a lot more information than Z could provide, so continuing to ask questions was moot. It would be a better use of their time to get JJ and Luca digging up dirt. They were damn good at it.

"Fine," Brantley said. "We'll go to New York."

"Just you and Reese?" Z asked.

"No. I'm gonna bring along more of my team. You're footin' the bill for this, Z. Don't forget that."

This time, the chuckle was a little lighter. "Understood. There's somethin' else you should know."

Brantley didn't like the tone, but he refrained from reacting.

"The Kavanaghs have ties to the Irish mob."

"No shit?" JJ grinned. "That's cool."

It wasn't cool, but Brantley glanced over at Reese.

"Hold up a minute," Reese said, dropping the spatula with a clatter. "Tell me this isn't the agent you sent in to be the eyes and ears."

Z didn't answer, which likely meant Reese had hit the nail on the head.

"Eyes and ears of what?" Brantley asked Reese.

A heavy exhale preceded Reese's response. "A coupla months ago, Z mentioned he was sendin' an agent to be the eyes and ears inside an organization." Reese glared at the phone. "He wouldn't tell me which organization, but now it all makes sense."

Then it clicked for Brantley. "Let me guess, Max is lookin' for some dirt."

"He's actually lookin' for a person," Z clarified.

"Jesus fucking Christ, Z," Reese bellowed. "You couldn't've put someone else on this?"

"No." Z's tone hardened. "I've got a missing agent. I want the best I've got. That's you. I know you've got a beef with Max, but I need you to set it aside. Find Deck and proceed with your hatred of the man, but until then—"

"Brantley, I had no idea this—"

Before Reese could apologize for something far out of his control, Brantley stepped up to him. "We're gonna find Deck and the woman. That's our case. Nothing else matters."

Reese nodded, but Brantley could see the uncertainty in his eyes.

When Z spoke, it was apparent he was frustrated. "You'll be wheels up in forty-five, Walker. Can you make it?"

"We'll be there."

"Keep me in the loop," Z said.

"Yep."

"Who's goin' with you?" JJ prompted when the call disconnected. "And remember, Evan's got his daughter's party this weekend."

"And you've got Charlie and Jay in Chicago," Baz noted.

"We've already given Slade and Atticus a heads up," Brantley informed them.

"And Becs," Reese noted.

"I want you runnin' it from this end," Brantley told Baz directly, then looked at JJ. "I want you and Luca to give me everything about the Kavanaghs. Get every available person on this. I wanna know where they've been, who they've talked to. Hell, I wanna know what the fuck they ate for dinner before they went missing. I wanna know what we're dealin' with. And I want to know who the *fuck* Max Adorite is tryin' to find and how it's related to them."

Baz nodded while JJ said, "Sure thing, boss."

ATTICUS ROLLED OVER AND GROANED WHEN HIS phone vibrated in his pocket. He'd fallen asleep on the damn thing.

"I think it's safe to say someone's lookin' for you."

Forcing his eyes open, he lifted his head, searching for the owner of the voice. He found Carson sitting in the upholstered armchair, a cup of coffee in his hand.

"What time is it?"

"A little after five. That's not the first time your phone went off."

Shit.

He grumbled as he sat up, shoving his hair back from his face as he dug his phone out of his pocket. He squinted at the screen, attempting to read the latest text message from Reese.

We'll be wheels up in forty-five. Expect you at the airstrip on time.

"Dammit," he muttered, pushing to his feet. "Mind if I use the head?"

Carson gestured toward the hallway.

Atticus used the bathroom, then took a minute to splash water on his face. He glanced at the toothbrush in the holder and considered borrowing it. Instead, he used toothpaste on his finger to get the foul taste out of his mouth. He could change on the plane or when they got to wherever they were going. The last thing he wanted was to risk being late. He'd been toeing the line with the team until he could figure out the rules. Something told him that being late for a flight would likely get him booted from the case, and Atticus happened to like working on the task force—more specifically, a steady paycheck—so he wouldn't be doing that.

When he returned to the living room, Carson was still sitting in the chair.

"Did I wake you? Was I snoring or something?"

"I'm an early riser."

Well, that was good to know.

"But you do snore."

Atticus grinned. "So do you."

"Only when I drink," Carson defended.

"I'll have to take your word for it." Atticus looked toward the front door. "I hate to run out, but we've got a case, and there's a plane waiting for me."

Carson set his coffee mug on the small table beside him, then pushed to his feet. "Thanks for drivin' me home last night."

Atticus nodded. He didn't want this to be weird, so he started toward the door.

"And for givin' me your phone number."

Atticus stopped and turned. "I didn't."

Carson's smirk was slow and wicked. "Not yet."

Atticus pulled his phone out of his pocket. "What's your number? I'll text you so you have mine."

Carson rattled off the number, and Atticus entered it into a text message. He sent an emoji, then tucked the phone back in his pocket.

"I guess I'll see you when I see you."

His hand was on the doorknob when Carson grabbed his arm. Atticus pivoted slowly, then found himself up against the door, Carson's lips sealed to his. Relief was sharp and potent, surprising him. He hadn't realized how much he hoped last night was real. That Carson had been serious about seeing him again.

"Text me when you get a chance," Carson told him, nipping his lower lip. "And I'll see you when you get back to town."

Atticus nodded, smiled, then opened the door and slipped out. He smiled all the way to the airstrip.

CHAPTER NINE

WHILE BRANTLEY ROUNDED UP THEIR WEAPONS, REESE packed the rest of their things.

He grabbed enough to get them through four days, figuring that would be plenty. If not, they'd figure out what to do at that point. Reese knew Brantley preferred to pack light, and now wasn't the time for Reese to worry about the piddly shit. From the instant his brother had informed him that Decker Bromwell was officially MIA, a switch had been flipped on. And while he wanted to explain away Deck's absence as a result of his lack of maturity, he couldn't brush it off. He recalled all too well what it was like to be captured and held prisoner, wondering if anyone was even looking for him. No way would he leave Deck to wonder, regardless of where he was or what he was doing.

Brantley appeared in the bedroom doorway, phone to his ear. "You want to bring Tesha or leave her with JJ?"

"Bring her."

"We're gonna take her with us, JJ," Brantley said, turning away.

Reese made a mental note to grab Tesha's fresh food from the refrigerator, along with her go-bag, which he kept stocked and ready with everything she might need. Although he didn't mind leaving Tesha with JJ from time to time, he preferred she go with them, and now that she was undergoing advanced training, it benefited her to get some field action.

Forty minutes after the call ended with his brother, they pulled into the private airport with Tesha riding in the backseat. Sniper 1's private jet was waiting for them. Reese wouldn't pretend this wasn't his preferred method of travel. It allowed them to bypass the rigorous security as well as giving them the ability to take their weapons along with them. He figured the only thing that might've been better would be if he were the one in the cockpit. There were times he missed navigating the sky.

"There's Slade and Becs," Brantley announced as they parked the truck inside the private hangar. "Let's hope Atticus—"

Reese pointed toward the plane's nose, where Atticus was talking to one of the maintenance workers. If he had to guess, Atticus was unabashedly flirting because that was what the guy did. The only upside was that it kept the kid from flirting with Brantley. Which he *also* did unabashedly. And yes, it appeared he wasn't as cool with it as he was pretending to be.

"You ready, girl?" Brantley asked Tesha as he opened the driver's door.

Reese got out and went to the rear of the truck while Brantley got Tesha out of the backseat. He opened the tailgate and grabbed their bags from the bed, shouldering his and Brantley's, then passing over Tesha's when Brantley came around for it.

The three of them made their way to the plane, with Slade and Becs falling into step with them when they neared.

"Any word?" Slade asked, glancing between them.

Reese answered with a shake of his head. JJ and Luca were already working on it, and he figured they would have plenty of information once they were in the air. At least enough to give them a foundation to build on.

"Wow," Atticus gasped when he stepped into the plane. "Y'all aren't playing around, huh?"

"The only way to fly," Slade told him.

"No, shit." Atticus looked around. "Do I sit somewhere specific?"

"As long as there's a seat belt, you can sit there," Brantley told him as he moved deeper into the plane.

Reese got Tesha settled in and buckled. He'd learned she actually preferred to be secure when they traveled, and it made him feel a hell of a lot better. Because she'd spent so much of her life chained up, Reese always ensured she could reach him or Brantley and that she had her blanket and a bully stick. She'd gotten so used to traveling that she would even nap from time to time.

Reese looked up as Atticus was glancing at the seat beside Brantley.

"Sit there, and I'll cut your dick off," he told him, keeping his tone even.

Atticus laughed. "Got it, boss."

Brantley snorted a laugh, his gaze meeting Reese's.

Reese winked.

Fifteen minutes later, they were airborne, everyone settling in for the four-hour flight.

"I didn't realize Decker was on another assignment," Slade said casually, pulling his laptop out of his bag.

"Where'd you think he was?" Brantley asked, amusement in his voice.

"Hell if I know. The guy's not exactly an open book."

"He's been gone for two months," Becs relayed. "You didn't think to question whether he quit?"

Slade shrugged. "Not my business."

In all fairness, they had been busy the past couple of months, ever since they'd staged Uncle Toby's death after he got himself mixed up in a mafia turf war. It was a never-ending cycle when it came to cases. As soon as they finished one, another would pop up. And now that they were doing personal security assignments, their time was becoming increasingly limited.

They rarely had time to work on the cold ones anymore. Since June, they'd assisted on two active cases with local police departments and were making some headway in the social media case they'd been working on. With new members on the team there to assist, Decker's absence hadn't been as glaringly obvious as it would've been if they were short-handed.

"I've got JJ gettin' us the details on the Kavanaghs," Brantley noted, skimming his phone.

"We know nothing about her?" Atticus asked, reclining back like this was a vacation, not a job.

"If you watch television, you should know enough," Becs said, crossing her legs. "I'm just confused because the last I heard, the Kavanaghs were gearing up for the wedding of the century. Or maybe that's why they needed extra security."

Reese stared at Becs, waiting for her to elaborate.

She frowned and glanced around. "I'm seriously the only one who knows?"

Slade shrugged. Atticus smirked. Brantley's eyebrows rose.

"Saoirse Kavanagh is the youngest of the four. They moved to New York from Ireland a couple of years ago when they opened a new headquarters. I don't know much about the business, but I can tell you anything you want to know about the billionaire playboys and their sister."

"Don't leave anything out," Atticus urged. "Any of them single? And gay?"

Becs giggled. "I don't know about their sexual preferences, but I do know they're all single. At least now, they are. Saoirse's the baby and the only girl, so they treat her with kid gloves. She turned twenty-nine this year, and according to the gossip blogs, to celebrate, she had a soiree to rival even the ball dropping in Times Square a few days before. It was there she met Lawson Nova."

"*Casa*nova?" Slade asked.

Reese recalled the name, but he remained quiet.

Atticus smirked. "I thought they called him *Super*nova."

"They did," Slade said. "Back when he was in his prime. But his shitty career took a backseat to his playboy ways. His stats have taken a downward trend for the past five years. Rumor was he was tryin' to get traded."

Reese could feel Brantley's eyes on him, so he did his best to explain. "Starting quarterback for the New York Surge."

"Football," Brantley nodded. "Got it."

"Yep," Becs continued. "And they say it's been a storybook romance between him and Saoirse. They dated for three weeks before he popped the question. They're supposed to be getting married in ten days."

"I heard he was a hothead with a superiority complex," Atticus added.

"I don't think you're off on that," Becs said. "There's been plenty of media coverage about their fights."

"Thought you said it was a storybook romance?" Reese asked Becs.

"Is there really any such thing?" she countered with a shrug. "Honestly, I don't know. When I hear Kavanagh, she's not the first one I think of."

"Well, I think yours is a storybook romance, boss," Slade drawled.

"If the storybook's a crime novel, maybe," Atticus added.

Brantley flipped them off even as his other hand brushed Reese's knee.

Reese couldn't help but grin.

"HOW GOES IT?"

JJ looked up from her computer screen and pursed her lips at Baz. "It goes."

"Feeling better?"

She nodded. She'd been grumpy when she woke up this morning, having been jarred awake by the ringing of her cell phone. For the most part, she was a morning person, so it didn't surprise her that Baz had noticed. She probably could've apologized for it, but there was a good chance it would happen again in a day or two. The last thing she wanted was to make him think she could change her mood on a whim. It wasn't happening, so why bother?

"You get the info Brantley asked for?"

"And then some." She exhaled heavily and leaned back in her chair, drumming her fingers on the desktop. "To say the Kavanaghs are high profile would be an understatement. I kicked off a program to pull some images from the internet, using one I found on the company website. I think it blew up my program. There are probably more pictures of this girl than … than I have no idea."

"As my dad likes to say, a shit-ton, huh?"

"Exactly." JJ grinned, recalling the last conversation she'd had with Wesley Buchanan.

They'd gone to dinner with Baz's parents the weekend before last, and when JJ got to the restaurant, she hadn't been surprised to see not only Aretha, Baz's stepmother, but also Baz's mother, Julie. Since Julie and Wes learned she was pregnant, they always seemed to be together. How Aretha could stand it was anyone's guess. She was Wes's sixth wife, and JJ hated to say it, but she was starting to believe there was only one woman Wes would ever truly love, and that was Jules. Not that their relationship was any of her business, but she wouldn't deny that she was expecting them to get back together at some point.

As for the conversation, Wes's use of shit-ton had been in reference to the amount of diapers they were going to go through when the peanut was born.

Baz moved closer, so JJ clicked the mouse to bring up the picture of Saoirse Kavanagh.

"She's gorgeous," JJ noted, staring at the black-haired woman with light green eyes. Her face was absolute perfection, not a blemish or wrinkle in sight. And it was that way in every photo, so she knew it wasn't photoshopped.

"*That's* how you spell her name?" Baz leaned closer. "Holy shit."

JJ laughed. "*That's* what you got from that picture?"

He pointed at the name as though that explained everything. And in a way, it did. JJ had thought the same thing when she saw the name for the first time. She never would've gotten the phonetics correct if Z hadn't said it first. To get ser-shuh from a word with that many vowels was beyond her abilities.

"She's got three older brothers," JJ informed him, flipping through the other photos she had open. "I was wrong earlier when I said Ronan was the oldest. Callum is. He's thirty-three. He's got the most responsibility at the company, and from what I can tell, all work and no play makes Callum a dull boy." She flipped to the next photo. "And then there's Ronan, he's thirty-one. Recently divorced, he's back on the dating scene, and the New York nightlife is his playground." She tapped the mouse. "And last but not least is Liam. He turned thirty earlier this year, and while he's dedicated to learning the ropes at Kavanagh Holdings, he's trying to break a record for dating as many supermodels as humanly possible. Sometimes more than one at a time."

Baz's eyebrows inched upward.

"Yep. He's been known to date them in pairs."

The man she loved was smart. He had nothing to say to that.

"Why would the brothers want someone looking after their sister?"

JJ turned to the keyboard and typed. "If I had to guess, they want to keep an eye on this guy."

"Lawson Nova?"

She peered up at him. "You know him?"

Baz chuckled. "Well, no. But he's a football player, so I know *of* him."

"He's also Saoirse's fiancé as of a few months ago. They're supposed to get married in ten days."

"Anything to say their relationship's not solid?" the sexy detective asked as he perched on the edge of her desk.

"You mean, aside from the fact they just met and got engaged?"

Baz's eyebrows rose. "There's no time limit on love. When you know, you know."

Right. He might believe that, but JJ wasn't of the same mind. And when it came to rich people, she was pretty sure they should have a time limit. A required one. Something that forced them to get to know each other versus hyping things up for the cameras and riding the wave of pheromones and lust right to the altar. It rarely seemed to end well.

"Fine," she conceded. "And to answer, yes, I turned up a few things that raised red flags for me."

"Like?"

"For starters, there are very few factual details of their relationship. Most of what's on the internet are fan pics. Even a few videos." She figured letting him see for himself made more sense, so she pulled up one and clicked play.

"You crazy bitch!" Lawson shouted, his hand raised as he stood over Saoirse.

JJ hit the pause button.

"Looks like they're at a club," she told Baz.

"Tell me he doesn't hit her," Baz seethed.

"No. He doesn't, but the rest of the video is much of the same. Him hollerin' at her. You can't make out anything *she* says, but from her expression, she's as pissed as he is. By the end, they're sucking face like they've been apart for a year. Besides those videos and a few photos taken shortly after they announced the engagement, there aren't many of them together. Considering how much they're photographed individually, that feels off to me."

"Off?" Baz crossed his arms over his chest. "How so?"

"They're both glory hounds, from what I can tell. The news of their engagement broke, and for the two weeks after that, they were everywhere. Then suddenly, they're out of the limelight as a couple? I'm not buyin' it."

"Maybe they broke up," Baz mused.

"I don't think so. That video was taken last Friday."

"Was Deck in the video?"

JJ shook her head. "Not that I could tell. And I haven't seen a glimpse of him in any photos I've come across. If he's keepin' an eye on her, he's doin' it from a distance."

She turned back to the screen and stared at the frozen image of Saoirse. The way she was looking up at Lawson … it felt off to her.

"It's something in her eyes," she mumbled.

"Meaning?"

She shrugged. "It could be my imagination, Baz. Seriously. I don't trust my instincts right now, so I can't be sure."

Baz frowned, canting his head to the side as he studied her.

JJ felt the scrutiny in his gaze and was compelled to explain. "I'm hung up on that woman from Ava's case. I still can't find her, and I've done everything short of takin' out an ad."

Although Harrison Rivers was dead and Ava March was no longer in danger from the crazy bastard who attempted to kill her, JJ was still trying to find a woman she suspected was Harrison's first victim. Admittedly, JJ wasn't spending as much time on it as she had been, but she knew she wouldn't rest until she found the woman. Dead or alive.

She sighed. "I know I should move on, but I can't."

Baz's smile was slow and sinful. "One of many things I love about you."

JJ's chest squeezed, just as it did every time he said that. She figured she should be used to it by now, but she wasn't. In fact, every time Baz said those three little words, she felt as though it was the first time. Except for Baz, she honestly couldn't say when the last time someone told her they loved her. Not her mother, not her father, and since she had no one else…

"JJ?"

She focused on the present. "Hmm?"

"Where'd you go just then?"

Forcing a smile that quickly turned genuine, she pushed to her feet. "Nowhere. I'm good."

Baz's arms lowered, widening to allow her to step in close. The moment she did, he put his hand on the baby bump that was getting bigger by the day.

"How's the peanut?" Baz asked softly, pressing his nose to her cheek.

She was twenty-nine weeks pregnant, and while the first few months had been uneventful except for the wicked bouts of morning sickness, she was seeing drastic changes in her body, most notably, the protrusion of her belly and the size of her boobs. But more than the outward differences, she was hyper-focused on every single move the baby made. Whenever the peanut wasn't moving, JJ would begin to worry. She would kick as though she knew her mom was starting to panic. Sometimes just once, but it was enough.

"The peanut's good," she said, sighing with contentment.

"Can I get you anything?"

She had to think about that one for a minute. Pregnancy had brought on a whole new slew of cravings and, each day, a unique combination. Yesterday, she'd convinced Baz to go to the store and buy her sweet gherkins, saltines, and Colby Jack cheese. Last week had been easier when she'd wanted chocolate-covered Ritz crackers and Nutella.

"I could really use some coffee," she decided.

One of his dark eyebrows rose slowly. "I take it you're not referring to *regular* coffee."

Her grin exploded. "A caramel Frappuccino with mocha drizzle."

"Decaf?"

"Definitely."

"So basically, you want a caramel milkshake with mocha drizzle?"

"Even better."

Baz smirked as he stood tall, then leaned down and pressed a kiss to her forehead. "Coming right up, hot mama."

JJ's eyes narrowed. "Eww. No. Not that."

Baz laughed. "Yeah. I heard it as soon as it came out of my mouth."

He walked away, still laughing, making JJ's heart expand with even more love for him. She wasn't sure she would ever get used to loving someone as much as she loved him, but she was enjoying the hell out of the journey.

CHAPTER TEN

"HOW DO YOU WANT TO HANDLE THIS?" Brantley asked Reese when they arrived at the hotel after picking up the SUV Z had rented for them.

Luckily, they'd arrived during a lull in activity, so checking in only took a few minutes. A little longer for them since Reese had informed the concierge they required a refrigerator. Not because he was a diva but because they had to have a place to store Tesha's food.

Since the hotel was booked, they'd had to settle for having a refrigerator delivered to their room. She assured them it would be there by the time they went up. Brantley was skeptical, but stranger things had happened.

"Put our stuff in the room," Reese said, talking to him as well as Becs, Atticus, and Slade. "Let's meet in the business center in, say, thirty?"

"Forty-five," Brantley corrected.

"Forty-five," Reese amended, his eyes narrowed.

"You think maybe we could get some food when we meet?" Slade prompted as he hitched his bag higher on his shoulder. "I skipped breakfast."

"Order it," Brantley told him.

Slade pointed toward a sandwich shop across the street. "That work?"

"Yep. Put it on the company card."

"Actually," Reese said, fishing his wallet out of his pocket. "Put it on mine. I'm not fightin' Z on this. He wants us here, he's payin' for all of it."

Brantley knew Z liked to pick apart their expense reports from time to time. Probably had to do with the fact the task force was the only team Z oversaw. Everyone else reported to RT, Z's husband. To prove he was good at managing people, Z often nit-picked the little things. That or he simply liked to get a rise out of Brantley. It could go either way. It was safer to force Z to take it up with Reese than to leave Slade fending for himself.

Slade plucked the card from Reese's hand. "Sure thing, boss."

With that, Brantley nudged Reese toward the elevators, Tesha trotting along between them. Thankfully, there weren't many people coming or going on a Sunday afternoon. However, they hadn't been so lucky in the selection of rooms. The hotel was booked, which meant they'd only had three rooms available. To give Becs her own room, Slade and Atticus had to share. Based on what Brantley had witnessed at Moonshiners last night, he wasn't certain that was a good idea, but for now, they were going with it.

Once they piled on the elevator, everyone was quiet on their way to the floors. Slade was the first to exit, his room on the third floor. Atticus followed him out. Becs was on the sixth, and finally, they reached the seventh, where they were staying.

"You think we should worry about Slade and Atticus?" Reese asked as they walked down the hall.

Probably, but Brantley wasn't going to. "They're big boys. They'll figure it out."

"This is us, girl," Reese told Tesha after he swiped the key card across the reader, causing the lock to disengage.

Tesha waited for a proper command, which Reese gave before she trotted inside to check out their accommodations.

"I don't see a refrigerator," Reese said as he walked in first.

Brantley didn't let him get two feet into the room before he grabbed his arm and spun him, shoving him against the wall.

"They'll get it. I promise."

When he was about to argue, Brantley crushed his mouth to Reese's and all but inhaled the man.

"That's for putting pleasure before business this morning and starting the day right," Brantley told him as he let his bag slide down his arm to the floor. He was still thinking about how Reese slid up behind him and fucked him. He loved waking up like that.

"For a man who got laid not too long ago, you don't seem all that satisfied," Reese mumbled against his mouth.

Oh, he was satisfied. He simply hadn't gotten his fill yet. He never would. With every breath he took, he wanted Reese more.

"I know how to resolve that." Brantley flipped the button on his jeans from the loop, then lowered his zipper.

"And what makes you think you deserve it?" Reese countered, his eyes heating as he peered down at Brantley's rigid dick. The damn thing had been straining against his zipper for the better part of the flight, and now that they were alone, he wasn't wasting another second.

"This is for denying me on the plane. I want your mouth on me, Reese."

He stroked himself once, twice, then took Reese's hand so he could take over.

Reese grunted. "It is tempting."

God, he loved this man.

"Come on," Brantley urged. "We don't have time to waste."

"Mmm." Reese moaned as he lowered to his knees. "This is why you requested fifteen extra minutes."

"And you're wastin' time," he told the sexy man.

Brantley would be the first to admit he wasn't exactly fond of them stepping out of their newly formed routine. On the flip side, it did allow for moments like this.

"Reese…"

"I love it when you beg." Reese stroked his cock firmly in his fist. "You want my mouth on you?"

"Yes." He gasped and groaned. "Fuck, yes."

Normally, Reese would've teased Brantley for long minutes, but they were pressed for time. As it was, they could get a knock on the door any second with that refrigerator being delivered. Brantley had tacked on fifteen additional minutes for good measure, but he could get lost fucking Reese's sinful mouth, so he figured they should get on with it.

Sliding his hand into Reese's hair, Brantley guided his head forward. "You better suck me good … first chance I get, I'm gonna fuck you so hard…"

"Like this?" Reese took Brantley's cock to the root.

Brantley grunted, using the wall behind him to keep him upright. The heat of his mouth enveloped him, that wicked tongue tormenting him.

Oh, yeah, Brantley loved the way Reese gave himself fully to the moment. It didn't matter what they were doing, Reese was in it for pleasure, the same as Brantley. The fact that Reese was always willing and ready turned him on so fucking much.

"Fuck. That mouth," Brantley mumbled. "Suck me."

Brantley was in heaven, Reese's lips sliding over his shaft, taking him as deep as he could. He pulled back, did it again. At that point, Brantley gripped Reese by the ears and shoved his cock deep into his throat. Reese submitted, letting Brantley own him. And he did. They owned each other—heart, body, and soul.

"Gonna come," he warned, letting the intensity build until he couldn't contain it any longer.

Reese hummed.

Brantley came.

Less than a minute later, there was a knock on the door.

Talk about perfect fucking timing.

Forty-three minutes after they'd agreed on a time, Brantley walked into the business center behind Reese and Tesha. Becs and Slade were already there, sitting at a large conference table. Becs had her laptop in front of her, her fingers tapping the keys.

"Where's Atticus?"

"I placed the order online," Becs said. "He went to pick it up."

"We ordered sandwiches," Slade explained. "Got enough for all of us."

"And a few extras," Atticus said as he walked into the room carrying a large paper bag.

"Thanks," Brantley told him. He was starving, but as usual, his mind was already on the case, and since he had too little room in his head to think about food and sex, he always opted for sex. He was glad someone was looking out for him.

As he took a seat, Brantley dialed JJ's number, putting the phone on speaker.

"Hey. You got the team with you?" she asked when she answered.

"Yep."

Atticus stood at the end of the table, passing out sub sandwiches to each person.

"Good. I only want to detail this once."

Brantley glanced at Reese, wondering if he noticed the frustration in her tone.

Reese's eyebrow lifted slightly, but he didn't say anything.

They listened while JJ walked them through the information she had. It wasn't much. Not nearly what Brantley had hoped to have at this point. The fact that Saoirse Kavanagh fought with her boyfriend in public didn't give him much to go on.

"I did manage to get in touch with Ronan," JJ explained. "He's willin' to meet you in his office whenever you can get there."

"On a Sunday?" Slade asked, looking around at them.

"No rest for the wicked," JJ noted.

"All right, JJ. Spill. What's bothering you?" Brantley demanded, staring at the phone.

"Nothing."

"Then put Baz on the phone. He can tell me."

JJ huffed. "It's … it's nothing, really. I just…"

It wasn't like her to be so tongue-tied.

And then it hit him. "Let me guess. It has something to do with Max Adorite."

Silence filled the room like a toxic gas. No one spoke, no one moved. Hell, Brantley wasn't sure anyone was breathing. He found it amusing that they walked on eggshells whenever the man's name came up. Oddly, it happened more often than Brantley cared for. The night Reese got shot, the bastard had ordered his lackey to rescue Max's sister but had left Reese to die. Brantley would never forgive him for that. And it seemed no matter how hard he tried, they were never going to put that man behind them.

Finally, JJ spilled. "Fine. I don't like this. I don't like that Max inserted someone into other people's business. And now that someone is missin'. And Max doesn't give a shit."

Brantley glanced at Reese as he said, "Please tell me you didn't call him."

"Well…"

"What did he say?" Reese asked.

"Basically, he told me to mind my own business. In no uncertain terms."

"Did you expect anything less?" Brantley couldn't hide his frustration.

"No. But we helped him out at one point. I thought he'd help us out."

"This isn't tit for tat. He's a mob boss, JJ. He's only interested in what'll benefit him."

"Yeah, well…" she grumbled.

"Any chance you were able to track their last movements?" Slade asked. "Do you know where they went during the hours before they disappeared?"

"Not yet. Luca and Holly are lookin' into it, though. I asked Z to get me Decker's credit card charges to see if they'll tell us anything. He said he'd get right on it. In the meantime, I suggest you talk to Ronan. If anyone knows what she's been up to, it's him. But, like Max, he's not willin' to talk to the help."

Brantley laughed. "JJ, you're not the help."

"Tell that to the mob. They seem to think I'm your freakin' secretary."

Well, that explained her frustration.

Since talking her off the ledge wasn't something he could do from nearly two thousand miles away, Brantley decided to let Baz soothe her ruffled feathers.

"We'll head to his office in a few minutes," Brantley told JJ. "Send me directions."

His phone chimed.

"Done."

No, she certainly wasn't anyone's secretary. If he were being honest, he would have to say that JJ was pretty much the heart of this operation. Without her, they'd be lost.

"SHOULD I GO BACK TO MY ROOM and wait?" Becs asked after they'd finished their sandwiches, and Brantley and Reese were getting ready to go to the Kavanagh Holdings building.

Although she hadn't directed the question at anyone specifically, Reese looked at Brantley. They did that a lot, she noticed. Becs figured that was what made them great partners, both at work and in love. They looked to each other for advice and direction, which made them stronger as a team. At least from her viewpoint.

"No," Brantley said, looking at her. "You'll stay with us. It'll be good for you to get a firsthand account."

She fought the urge to smile. Becs had hoped he would say that. Although her job as an analyst required her to be glued to her computer, spending most of her time researching, she was fascinated by the fieldwork.

Not that she was hoping to become an investigator. That was too far outside her comfort zone, but it didn't hurt to occasionally get in on the action. More importantly, it allowed her to get outside and enjoy at least a small part of the Big Apple.

While Atticus and Slade cleaned up the trash from lunch, Becs stowed her laptop in her backpack and slid her arms under the straps before following Brantley and Reese out the door.

"We can leave the SUV as long as you're up for a walk," Becs informed them when Brantley pulled out his phone. "Or we could take a cab. It's probably faster to walk, though."

"You realize it's ninety degrees, right?" he countered.

"You realize the traffic's at a standstill," Slade retorted.

All eyes shifted to the street. Yep. Even on a Sunday afternoon, the street was crammed with vehicles.

"Plus," Becs said, "it's New York. Temperature means nothing."

Brantley gestured for her to lead the way.

Becs didn't hesitate.

Their hotel was on 7th Avenue between 55th and 56th, so they headed northeast toward Central Park. They walked against traffic, and Becs didn't hide her interest in the city. She'd never been to New York, but she'd always wanted to. She always imagined one day bringing Carly here so they could walk the trails in Central Park and go to the zoo. She also wanted to visit the 9/11 Memorial and Museum, as well as the Statue of Liberty and Grand Central Terminal. She figured they would check out the American History Museum, see the city from the 86th floor of the Empire State Building, and go to Rockefeller Center.

Today, she would settle for walking alongside Central Park as they headed toward Columbus Circle. She smiled, wondering if Evan would be interested in a vacation here. One day. They could bring both girls and spend a week checking out the sights. Getting caught up in a fantasy like that was silly, but Becs couldn't help herself. No, she wasn't getting her hopes up because a happily ever after didn't seem to be in her future, but it never hurt to dream.

The walk took less time than she expected because she'd been so caught up in the sights and smells of the city. She nearly passed the Kavanagh Holdings building, which was sad because she'd actually been looking for it. She probably would've kept going if Reese hadn't called out her name.

"Right." She grinned sheepishly. "Sorry."

"You've never been here?" Reese asked.

"To New York?" Becs shook her head. "Always wanted to."

"Maybe you'll get a chance to see the sights," Brantley noted.

Her eyebrows rose, and she hoped he would elaborate, but he didn't. She loved the idea, although going alone wasn't something she was willing to do. Too bad Evan hadn't come along on the trip.

They moved as a group up the stairs toward the towering glass building. The front was lined with a dozen glass doors, allowing multiple people to come and go at once. Reese reached them first, opening one and stepping back, allowing them to go inside before him.

Becs did her best not to express her awe when she saw the lobby. If she didn't know better, she would've thought it was an art museum. The marble-lined walls were decorated with a variety of large canvas paintings, and a few sleek statues stood throughout, looming proudly over the elegant marble floor. High above them were chandeliers that dangled, the lights glittering like diamonds.

The space had no benches or desks, only a discreetly placed reception stand that blended in with the marble walls. Three uniformed people stood, two watching computer monitors and one woman tracking them closely.

"How may I assist you?" she asked as they approached, stepping out from behind the stand as though gearing up to tackle them before they reached the elevator.

Becs noticed she spoke with a distinct Irish accent.

"We're here to see Ronan Kavanagh," Brantley informed her.

"And your name?"

"Brantley Walker."

She glanced back at her counterparts. One of them nodded.

"I'll need to see some ID."

Brantley and Reese both pulled out their IDs along with their Sniper 1 Security credentials.

"I'll need ID for everyone."

Becs shrugged out of her backpack and pulled out her wallet.

She took each of the IDs and slid them under a digital scanner. Each one appeared on the monitors the other two were watching.

"I'll need to scan your bags," the woman informed Becs and Reese.

Interesting. She hadn't realized they were going to encounter the TSA.

Becs glanced at Slade and Atticus. Both gave single-shoulder shrugs, looking as bewildered as she felt.

Since she had nothing to hide, Becs passed over her backpack so the woman could slide it under what appeared to be an X-ray machine. After she finished, she passed it back, then did the same with the bag Reese carried. Becs knew it contained water, food, and treats for Tesha, as well as waste bags.

"Now I'll need you to check your weapons," she told the group as she returned Reese's bag.

"No," Brantley stated firmly.

Becs glanced around; it was the first time she realized they were all carrying weapons. Everyone but her. She found it strange that she'd gotten so used to them being armed that she no longer noticed it.

"Excuse me?" the woman said, glaring at Brantley.

"You heard me. We're licensed security agents. We won't relinquish our weapons. Call Ronan Kavanagh and tell him we're here. Either he'll meet with us, or he won't."

The woman glanced back at her counterparts. One of them picked up a phone receiver and made a call. Becs couldn't hear what he was saying, but when he disconnected, he glanced at the woman and nodded. Evidently, they'd been cleared.

The woman walked in front of them. "Right this way."

Becs wondered if it was customary to get an armed escort when coming for a meeting. And if so, what did regular people think of it? The ones who were coming here to do business. It seemed like overkill, but this woman was definitely armed. Not only with a gun but also what looked like a billy club and pepper spray, all mounted neatly on the utility belt around her waist.

The woman led the way to a bank of elevators and pressed the call button. A moment later, the doors opened, and she stepped inside. Looked like they were getting the royal treatment today.

Becs filed in along with Brantley, Reese, Tesha, Slade, and Atticus. The woman shielded the keypad mounted on the wall and pressed several buttons. A moment later, the numbered buttons lit up, allowing her to select a floor.

A lot of security for an investment firm, she thought as they rode the elevator up to the thirty-seventh floor.

Expecting the woman to return to her post in the lobby, Becs was surprised when she stood in the hallway in a parade rest stance, her feet spread apart, her hands behind her back, and her eyes facing forward. Becs knew that position only because she'd asked Brantley one day when she noticed him doing the same thing. Apparently, it was something he had learned in the military. He said at some point, it had become second nature, and he did it without thinking.

Hmm. Was this woman military-trained?

She didn't get a chance to ponder the question because they were on the move once again. Brantley led the way through a set of glass doors and into a reception area. No one was sitting at the large desk, which wasn't surprising. It was Sunday, and Becs figured they weren't expecting many visitors.

They stood there for a few seconds, all of them looking around. Was there a bell or something? Were they supposed to call someone?

She received the answer a moment later when a man strolled out from one of the offices.

Becs was glad she was at the back of the pack because her breath caught in her chest, and she prayed she was the only one who heard the gasp that escaped her lips.

She recognized Ronan Kavanagh from the photos she'd seen of him online, but there wasn't a photograph in the world that could do this man justice. He was breathtaking.

He strolled toward them, his expression pinched, his light green eyes practically glowing. His black hair was artfully tousled, styled to look as though he had just gotten out of bed, she was sure. She figured the scruff on his jaw and the well-manicured mustache and goatee took far more effort to maintain than appeared.

There was a reason he'd been slated as one of the sexiest men alive by more than one media outlet.

Recalling what she'd read, she knew Ronan was six feet tall, but he seemed larger than that. Even next to Brantley and Reese, who had four or five inches on him. He wore a white dress shirt and black slacks, his muscular frame discreetly masked by the conservative wardrobe. He wasn't as big as Brantley, but he was big enough.

Not that Becs was checking him out from a perspective of interest. More like intrigue because he was a celebrity. She hadn't met a celebrity before.

Ronan held out his hand to Brantley. "Ronan Kavanagh."

Brantley shook his hand and then introduced him to the rest of them. Becs didn't shake his hand, but she nodded when he said, "It's nice to meet you all."

She did her best not to swoon at the sexy Irish lilt.

"Follow me," Ronan stated before turning and going back the way he'd come.

Thankfully, she was at the back of the group, so she didn't get a chance to look at his ass. The last thing she wanted was to drool on her first field assignment.

CHAPTER ELEVEN

Ronan Kavanagh looked exactly like his photographs.

His class and sophistication weren't faked. The way he carried himself spoke of entitlement and wealth. As for whether he'd grown up in the lap of luxury or he was a street rat who'd clawed his way to the top, Brantley didn't know. The family history was steeped in secrets and mystery. Or so JJ had told him via text after another attempt to trace their origins.

The one thing he did know was that the family was as much a titan as the company they'd created.

Granted, Brantley had expected to see a laid-back version of the man on a Sunday afternoon, but he wasn't entirely surprised. Something told him that nothing about the Kavanaghs was typical. Or laid-back. Considering they had armed escorts for their visitors, this family appeared to have something worth defending. Could've been people, possessions, or even secrets. Perhaps all of the above. Whatever it was, they weren't messing around.

"Have a seat," Ronan stated, gesturing toward a dozen empty seats around a large conference table. "Can I get you anything?"

"No." Brantley wasn't here to have tea on a Sunday afternoon.

Ronan's gaze shifted to the rest of the team, one eyebrow cocked to extend the offer to them as well.

Everyone declined as Brantley pulled out one of the chairs and eased into it while he scoped the space around him.

Aside from the door they'd come through, it appeared there was a hidden exit at the back of the space. It blended relatively well with the glossy wood walls, but Brantley had been trained to seek out things like that. There were also two additional hidden compartments in the walls, both roughly waist high and long enough to hold anything from office equipment to a sizable cache of weapons. Brantley suspected it was the latter, considering the family was rumored to have mob ties. He figured they were loaded for bear and ready to take anyone on when the situation arose.

"Your secretary told me you're here looking for Decker Bromwell," Ronan said, glancing between all five of them as he pulled out a chair and sat.

"She's not his secretary," Atticus said at the same time Slade said, "Don't let JJ hear you say that."

Brantley cut his gaze to them and silenced them with a look. Slade mouthed *I'm sorry* before squaring his shoulders.

"Yes," Reese confirmed. "We are."

"Are you friends of his?"

"Are *you*?" Atticus retorted.

Brantley glared at him and got an impish smile in response.

Maybe he should've left them all at the hotel.

"Co-workers," Reese admitted.

"How well do you know him?" Brantley asked, wanting to maintain control of this conversation.

Ronan's eyebrow lifted, his all-seeing gaze shifting over each of their faces. "About as well as I know anyone. I met Deck a few years ago while he was on assignment for a family friend. We made our introductions over a glass of whiskey at the bar."

"You liked him enough to keep in touch?"

Ronan's eyes narrowed. "I hadn't seen or talked to Deck since then. At least not until he contacted me a couple of months ago."

According to Z, Ronan was the one who'd contacted Deck. Which was it? Who was lying? And why?

Opting not to point out that he'd already detected a lie, Brantley asked, "So you're not friends?"

"Friends?" Ronan shook his head. "No. Acquaintances? Perhaps. He's been around a bit more these past couple of months. I've had a chance to get to know him better."

"Is that something you usually do with people you hire?"

Ronan frowned. "I've come to trust Deck. To a degree."

Brantley wondered if that was something that came easily. Ronan's trust. Based on the fact he looked as though he was expecting one of them to draw a weapon on him at any moment, he seriously doubted it.

"More than the armed entourage in the lobby?" Slade questioned.

Ronan's black eyebrows rose as he glanced at Slade.

"We're trying to figure out why you hired Deck to keep an eye on your sister when you've got personal protection," Brantley clarified.

He had to give the man credit. Ronan managed to mask his expression. If he were surprised that they were here or that they were digging into his life, he didn't show it. However, it was obvious to Brantley that Ronan wasn't one to engage in conversation with people he didn't know well.

"Look, Mr. Kavanagh, we—"

"Ronan," he said sternly. "Mr. Kavanagh is my father."

There was a hint of hostility in his tone that had Brantley's hackles rising.

"Ronan," he drawled slowly. "To find Deck, we need to—"

Ronan sat up straight. "Find him? What makes you think he's missing?"

Brantley looked at Reese and frowned. What the fuck was going on here?

"That's why we're here," Reese explained. "Deck hasn't checked in for four days, and Sniper 1 Security has deemed him missing. We assumed he was with your sister."

The man pursed his lips and shook his head, his mask of indifference falling back in place. "Not to my knowledge."

"Where's Saoirse?" Brantley asked.

His answer came easily. "My best guess is that she's at home."

There was a casualness to his tone that told Brantley he was lying. He was trying to appear bored by the conversation, but the tense shoulders and constant eye movement were a dead giveaway.

"And home would be?"

Ronan's eerie green gaze slid over them. "I'm confused."

"That makes six of us," Atticus mumbled from the end of the table.

"You're here looking for Decker, and you think he's with my sister?"

"You hired him to protect Saoirse," Brantley stated.

Ronan's expression morphed into something that resembled amusement. "I did no such thing. As you said, I've got armed protection. And I don't mean only those you encountered in the lobby. Why would I need to hire him? And why on earth would I hire him to watch my sister?"

"That's what we're tryin' to find out," Reese said. "According to our information, you called Deck back in June and hired him to provide your sister with twenty-four-hour protection. He brought that information to his superiors and asked for the assignment specifically. Until four days ago, he'd been checking in regularly, every twelve hours."

"I'm sorry to hear that."

The man was talking them in circles, and Brantley got the impression that was how he got out of difficult discussions. By pretending not to have the answers.

"Where's your sister now?" Brantley asked, dropping all pretenses.

"As I said, she's probably at home, but honestly, I don't know. She's been spending a lot of time with that fiancé of hers."

Brantley didn't imagine the slight snarl that accompanied the word *fiancé*.

"We need to talk to her."

"You should call her."

"We've tried that," Brantley said, his patience dissolving.

Ronan didn't respond.

Brantley glanced down the table at Becs, Slade, and Atticus. "Would you give us a minute?"

Becs immediately stood. "Sure."

"Would you mind takin' Tesha?" Reese asked her.

Becs came around the table and took Tesha's leash, whispering to the dog as she led her out of the room.

"Go," Brantley told Slade and Atticus more forcefully.

He could tell they didn't want to, but they got to their feet and walked out behind Becs, closing the door.

"When was the last time you saw your sister?" Brantley asked when it was only the three of them in the room.

Ronan glanced at the door.

Brantley waited until he met his gaze. "Look. We're here looking for a colleague, and we're not leaving until we find him. With or without your help. If you help us, there's a good chance whatever it is you're attempting to hide will remain secret. But if you don't, we're gonna rifle through every inch of your life until we find what we're lookin' for. Your choice, *Ronan.*"

REESE WAS GLAD BRANTLEY WAS STEERING THIS conversation. Within the first minute, he'd realized Ronan wasn't going to give them any information. About anything.

The guy was as tight-lipped as someone else Reese knew. However, mentioning that there was a similarity between Ronan Kavanagh and Max Adorite didn't seem like the best way to approach this. God knows what would happen if he did. If the Kavanaghs had ties with the Irish mob—there was nothing directly linking them that he'd found so far aside from rumors and gossip—he figured that would put Ronan on edge. They weren't here to rile the man or taunt him with accusations. Reese wanted to find Decker. That was his only objective.

Clearly, this wasn't going to be an easy case. Ronan was hiding something. Reese had known it from the moment they stepped into the building. If he had to guess, those rumors were indeed fact, and the Kavanaghs were hiding their shady business dealings beneath this conglomerate. Since JJ hadn't yet unearthed anything concrete, they were doing a damn good job of it.

That didn't mean Reese wanted to find himself in the middle of some sort of mob war. And he prayed that Decker wasn't already there. If Decker was working for Max and had embedded himself in the Kavanagh's organization, there was a damn good chance the guy was dead in an alley somewhere. Or tied up in someone's basement, being beaten for information.

Reese was doing his best not to form the worst-case scenario, but it wasn't easy. Decker Bromwell wasn't the easiest man to work with, nor was he the most sociable in other settings, but that didn't mean Reese wished him any ill will.

With that said, Reese also didn't want to get taken advantage of, and based on Ronan's responses so far, Z hadn't been forthcoming about everything he knew. Reese intended to take it up with his brother as soon as he walked out the door.

"Where's Saoirse, Ronan?" Brantley asked, his tone rife with frustration. The longer Ronan was silent, the more intense it became.

Finally, there was a stirring of emotion in Ronan's olive-green eyes. He sat up straight, clasped his fingers together tightly, and rested his hands on the table.

"I do not know, but I don't think she's missing."

Finally, an inkling of truth. And now they were getting somewhere.

"When's the last time you saw her?"

"Four days ago. She came to the house with that twit of a fiancé. They got in a fight, and she left."

"Was Deck with her?"

"No."

"But he's been around?"

"Yes."

"Have you seen Deck since then?"

"No."

"What about Lawson?" Reese asked. "Have you seen him since their argument?"

Ronan shook his head. "He's a fucking cunt."

His Irish was thicker now. Rather than 'uh,' the u's took on a longer 'ooo' sound. *A fooking coont.*

Brantley relaxed some. "Isn't she getting married in a few days?"

Ronan shook his head. "That shit was never real. They did it for the publicity. My guess is she's hiding out until it dies down."

"So you do know where she is?" Reese prompted, growing tired of the runaround.

"I know she's not in danger. I'm kept apprised of her whereabouts, and last I heard, she was at home."

"Do you think Lawson's behind Deck's disappearance?" Reese asked.

"No. The little fucker doesn't know his ass from a horseshoe."

Reese had never heard that one before, but okay.

"We need somethin' to go on," Brantley told him. "Saoirse was the last person who was in contact with Deck. We'd like to talk to her."

Ronan swung a hand up. "If I were you, I'd start at that bloody club she's so fond of."

Finally. Something they could go on.

"Which one is that?" Brantley asked, beating Reese to the question.

"Obsession."

"I take it it's here in Manhattan."

Ronan nodded. "The owner's a close family friend."

"Do you have a name?"

"Kieran O'Rourke."

Reese made a mental note while the conversation volleyed between Brantley and Ronan.

"Have you spoken to him since you last saw Saoirse?"

"No, but not for lack of trying. Like most of us, Kieran's a busy man."

Too busy to help a friend? Reese had to wonder.

"We'll start there," Brantley informed him, getting to his feet. "We'd appreciate it if you kept us in the loop."

Ronan swallowed and stood. "I'll tell you what I can, but it won't be much. My family … we don't converse with outsiders about personal shit."

Yeah, Reese had already figured that one out.

They left the building the same way they entered, with their armed escort walking them to the main doors.

"What did he say?" Slade asked as they descended the steps to the sidewalk.

"Could we detour through the park?" Becs asked, still holding Tesha's leash.

Reese nodded, figuring it would give Tesha a chance to use the bathroom if she needed to.

"He basically told us we're on our own," Brantley answered Slade as they walked across the street to the park entrance.

Reese listened while Brantley relayed the high-level details of what little they'd learned from Ronan. The man hadn't been a fount of information, that was for damn sure. However, he didn't appear concerned about his sister's whereabouts.

"Does he know where his sister is?"

"He's not worried about his sister," Brantley said.

Reese joined the conversation. "Which tells us he knows exactly where she is, and she's safe."

Ronan didn't strike him as the sort to be left in the dark. As for whether the man was concerned about Decker, that was another thing entirely. There was a good chance the Kavanaghs had a hand in Decker's disappearance, and that was the reason they were putting up walls.

"And Deck?" Atticus asked. "What's that mean for him?"

"Either he's with her, or he's dead," Brantley said bluntly.

Becs stopped walking, her eyes wide as she stared at them. "Dead?"

"Probably not," Reese noted, although he wasn't sure he believed it. If the Kavanaghs were linked to the Irish mob, and they found out Deck was a spy, then all bets were off.

"Hopefully, JJ's got more information for us," Brantley said, clearly realizing he needed to refrain from harsh assumptions while Becs was around. "I'll call her."

"Have her look into the club," Reese instructed. "And Kieran O'Rourke."

While Brantley called JJ, Reese followed Becs and Tesha across the grass, watching as his dog checked out all the new smells. There were joggers on the path and people playing with their dogs, everyone oblivious to the fact that a man was missing. And while Reese wanted to believe Decker had pulled one of his stunts and went off the grid on his own, he couldn't help wondering whether he was in a cage somewhere, hoping someone was out there looking for him.

"Your friends … they do not be looking for you," the man said in heavily accented English, staring down at Reese through the bars above him.

Reese didn't bother responding.

"Two months. They should be here by now."

Reese's gaze slid to the concrete wall where he'd been tallying up the arrival of darkness. He wasn't sure exactly how many days he'd been here, but his marks matched up with the man's statement relatively well. Fifty-seven days and counting since Reese had been captured and thrown into this concrete hole.

"We'd like to meet them," the man said, his smile hidden behind his dark beard. "We hope they arrive soon."

"Reese? You okay, man?"

He dragged himself out of the memory and looked at Slade. "Yeah."

"You think Ronan's hidin' somethin'? Like perhaps Decker's dead body?"

Reese took a deep breath. "I think he's hidin' something, but I don't think he knows where Deck is."

"If he didn't hire Deck, how'd their paths cross?"

That was the question of the hour because what Ronan told them directly conflicted with the information Z had. One of them was lying. Or, at the very least, one of them was leaving out some pertinent details.

"I think we need to find Saoirse and talk to her."

"And the club Brantley mentioned? Think we'll find any leads there?"

Reese didn't think so, but he said, "Won't know unless we try."

Regardless of what they did or didn't find, he wasn't going to give up looking for Decker. Not until every fucking trail had gone cold.

He only hoped it didn't come to that.

CHAPTER TWELVE

"DIDN'T BRANTLEY SAY RONAN MET DECKER IN a bar?" JJ asked, her voice carrying from the living room.

From his spot at the kitchen sink, Baz grinned and called out his answer. "That's what he said."

He turned off the water and waited to see if she would ask another question. When she didn't, he flipped it on and finished the dishes.

Now that they were in their house, it was taking Baz some time to get used to the layout of the space. He'd gotten so used to his apartment he'd known where everything was without thinking about it. And though JJ had given him control of the kitchen, letting him put everything where he wanted it, he was still familiarizing himself with it.

Baz had to admit, he loved the house. It was even better than he'd anticipated, and the walk from his truck to the front door alone made house living so much better than apartment living. Plus, they had more space, which allowed their lives to mesh fully. Granted, they were still working on filling it up. Since JJ had lost most of her things in the explosion that leveled her house, she didn't have any furniture. They'd gone through and selected which of his things they wanted to take and the rest they'd sold. They were slowly but surely adding pieces here and there so that, hopefully, they would be completely settled by the time the peanut was born.

Of course, the peanut's room was completely ready. JJ had made sure of that within a week of them officially moving in.

Baz tucked the last dish in the dishwasher and added the soap pod before closing the door. He turned off the water, dried his hands, and hit the button to start the dishwasher before joining JJ in the living room.

"Whatcha working on?"

JJ looked up from her computer, her eyebrows angled in that way that told him she was attempting to unravel a mystery. He knew she couldn't focus during dinner, so he'd sent her off after they finished eating, assuring her he would clean up the kitchen.

"No matter how hard I try, I can't tie the Kavanaghs to the Irish mob."

"I didn't realize we were trying to," he said, perching on the edge of the cushion near her feet. JJ was leaning against the arm of the couch, her knees slightly raised and her laptop sitting on her thighs. He reached for her foot and lightly massaged it.

"We're not," she said with a sigh. "But if what Z said was true and Max is usin' Deck as a spy, you'd think I could find somethin'."

"Based on what Brantley told us this afternoon, I think it's safe to say Z doesn't have all the information."

"No, he doesn't." JJ closed her laptop and leaned her head back. "What's the real story, then? Did the Kavanaghs call Deck and Ronan lied? Or did Deck lie to Z? Or did Z send them on a wild good chase? If so, why? What's his endgame? Or Deck's? Is he really protecting Saoirse? Or usin' her to dig for information?"

Those were all really good questions. Questions the entire team was looking to unearth.

"Do you think this is personal?" JJ asked. "Maybe Deck is in a relationship with Saoirse."

Before Baz could answer, JJ continued.

"But how did they meet? He's older than her. By like nine years. Hell, he's older than her brothers. I don't understand where they connected. I know Brantley said they met when Ronan ran into Decker at a bar when he was on an assignment for a family friend, but is that true? Where? New York? Did they keep in touch?"

Baz smiled, leaning back and continuing to rub JJ's feet. Both now because he knew how much she enjoyed it.

"I get that Deck's been on assignment all over, but he happened to have a chance encounter with Ronan Kavanagh, and suddenly he's got an in with the family? What're the odds of that happening?"

God, he loved this woman. He loved the way her brain worked. He loved to watch as she untwisted her confusion until it made sense. It sometimes took her a while, but she always got there.

"I'm just tryin' to understand how Decker landed in the Kavanagh's world," she said, moaning when he rubbed her instep.

"And you think the mob affiliation is the key?" he prompted when she was quiet for a minute.

"It's what I was goin' on originally, but now…" She shook her head. "I'm startin' to think they really are rumors."

"What about their business dealings?"

"Oh, geez." She set her laptop on the coffee table. "Where do I start? This family … they're loaded. I mean, seriously, *seriously* loaded. Kavanagh Holdings started in Ireland, and it wasn't until a couple of years ago that they ventured to the US. Everything looks legit. It would take a forensic accountant to find something. If there's anything to find."

JJ canted her head to the side. "That's what I don't understand. If Max is involved, I can't imagine it's for legit reasons. Unlike the Kavanaghs, Max doesn't have a legit corporation to hide behind. His world is precariously built on drugs, guns, and protection money."

"I thought he started legitimizing his businesses when he married Courtney Kogan."

"Yeah. That was the rumor. And maybe he intended to, but that's not the case anymore. I was able to find some links between the Adorites and the actual Sicilian mob. Recent connections. Enough that makes me believe their family ties run deep."

"I thought the Southern Boy Mafia originated here. In Texas."

"I think that's what Samuel Adorite wanted the world to think. That his organization was homegrown. Maybe it was, but Max has created a stronger hold on his territory than Samuel ever had when he was alive. He's been fortifying his ranks since he started this turf war with Sabrina Moroso."

Baz knew some of what had transpired between the Adorites and the Morosos. The oldest of the three, Marco, had put a hit out on Max's sister, Ashlynn. He'd blown up her house. In retaliation, Max killed him. Then Dennis was released from prison and set out to kill Max. But he was unhinged, and when he started fucking shit up, Sabrina took him out, leaving his dead body behind Max's club. And then there was Sabrina. Based on what Baz had read, she was the real brains behind the operation and always had been. Now she was out for Max's blood.

The Southern Boy Mafia was known by every law enforcement agency in the country, but no one could pin anything on them. The FBI had run sting after sting to take them down to no avail. Baz wasn't sure whether Max had a guardian angel or merely had the right people in his pocket, but he was always one step ahead.

JJ sighed again and rubbed her temples. "It's givin' me a headache to think about. I just want to find the single line that connects Decker Bromwell to Saoirse Kavanagh, and I want it to tell me where he is. I'm not gettin' there. The only thing I'm almost positive about is that the connection has nothing to do with Maximillian Adorite."

"It's a start," Baz told her. "Hopefully, Brantley and them will get more information at that club they're checking out."

"They better," she said, her eyes widening. "Because if I have to enlist Luca's help on this…"

Baz laughed. He knew JJ admired Luca's talent, but his skills made him her nemesis. Together they were unstoppable, but it was their competitive nature that they had to get past before they teamed up.

Baz figured another day of these endless questions, and JJ would be ready to admit she needed his help.

"When was the last time you came to a club like this?" Reese asked Brantley as they stood inside the doorway of Obsession, one of the hottest nightclubs in Manhattan. Also one of the most difficult to get into.

"Try never," Brantley answered.

"I almost didn't think they were gonna let the kid in," Slade said, nodding toward Atticus.

"Not a kid," Atticus responded. It was the same thing he said every time Slade referred to him as such. "And I hate to break it to you, redneck, but I'm dressed nicer than you are."

Reese would admit Atticus had a point. His dark blue button-up shirt and dark blue jeans did have more flair than Slade's maroon Henley and ready-worn Levi's. Not that either would've gotten them in the door without a woman like Becs on their arm.

"Y'all owe Becs one. If she wasn't dressed like that"—Brantley nodded in her direction—"none of us would've gotten in."

Exactly what Reese was thinking. Although they'd all managed to scrounge up nightclub-appropriate attire, it had required shopping beforehand. Even then, they'd kept it casual. Everyone except Becs. Reese wasn't sure the dress she had on could actually be considered a dress. There wasn't enough material.

Then again, she looked good. With her hair styled and makeup on her face, she looked like she belonged in a place like this. In all the time he'd worked with her, Reese couldn't recall her ever dressing up. Not like this. She was more conventional with her attire, even when she was casual. He liked to see her getting out of her comfort zone for once.

Not that he would ever tell her that. She could dress however she wanted. He appreciated that she'd gone all out tonight because he was sure they would've been turned away at the door otherwise.

"Mind if we get a drink, boss?" Slade asked.

Reese glanced at Brantley, waiting to hear how he wanted to play this. Coming to this club didn't guarantee they'd find out anything that would help them locate Decker. The least they could do was enjoy themselves. They'd locked their weapons in their respective rooms to avoid hassle, so there was no risk there.

"A couple of beers," Brantley said. "No more than that. And while you're enjoyin' yourself, check with the employees and see if anyone recalls seein' Deck here in the past week or two."

"Will do, boss," Slade said.

To Reese's surprise, Atticus gestured for Becs to take his arm so he could escort her down the curved steps that led to the main bar. He hadn't thought the kid had a single gentlemanly bone in his entire body. Apparently, he'd been wrong.

"Let's see if we can get into the VIP area," Brantley said before heading for the stairs leading up to the second level.

Reese followed, checking out the space. He would admit it was impressive. Sleek and modern, with an over-the-top vibe to it. He figured that was due to the black velvet squares that covered the walls, crisscrossed by stainless steel. The geometric designs were the accent that drew the eye up to the two levels above the lowest level. There were at least two bars from what Reese could tell. One on the bottom floor and another on what looked to be the main level. The bottom floor was dedicated to congregating around two-top tables, although the music pumping through the speakers made it nearly impossible to think, much less talk. High above, lights flashed purple, pink, and blue, reflecting off a mirrored octagon dangling from the ceiling.

The second floor seemed to be where all the action was. There was an enormous dance floor, and above it, on what looked to be a third level, were stacked rows of seating, some with tables, others merely curved booths, that provided a birds-eye view of the dancers. Either he was stoned from the distinct aroma of weed he'd detected outside, or the seating area was moving in a circular motion around the dance floor. It was slow but noticeable.

"Any chance Mr. O'Rourke's here tonight?" Brantley asked one of the waitresses as she squeezed past.

She stopped and glanced up at the third level. "I believe he is."

"Would you mind lettin' him know I'd like to speak with him?"

"And your name?"

"He won't recognize it, so it won't matter. Let him know it's in reference to the Kavanaghs."

She nodded and slipped away.

"You think he'll talk to you?" Reese asked as they found an empty booth on the third level.

"Hopefully, I've intrigued him enough."

Yeah. Hopefully.

Two hours later, they learned they had, in fact, intrigued the mysterious Kieran O'Rourke. He emerged from what appeared to be an office on the third floor and made his way toward them, stopping to greet others along the way.

He approached each person as though he'd known them his entire life. He was quick to smile, his chiseled face lighting up with pleasant interest. He reminded Reese a lot of Ronan Kavanagh, only taller and with a roguish air. He wore charcoal gray slacks and a black button-down shirt with the top button unhooked, and his sleeves rolled up. His dark brown hair was styled with more product than Reese probably owned.

"You summoned," he said with a smile as he approached their table. "Kieran O'Rourke. Nice to meet you."

His accent was as thick as Ronan's when Ronan had allowed himself a moment to breathe. It looked as though Kieran embraced who he was a bit more than Ronan Kavanagh.

Reese was on his feet when Brantley was, holding out his hand to shake Kieran's.

"Brantley Walker and my partner Reese Tavoularis. We work for Sniper 1 Security. We're here lookin' for a friend of ours."

Kieran gestured for them to sit, and he did the same. "I received a call from Ronan this afternoon."

That didn't surprise Reese. Birds of a feather and all that shit. Ronan had mentioned that Kieran was a good friend of the family. Made sense that he would warn him.

"We're lookin' for Decker Bromwell," Brantley explained. "He's a private security consultant. We were under the impression he was here on assignment."

"Here as in New York? Or here as in…" Kieran gestured to the room around them.

"New York," Brantley clarified."

"But you no longer think that is true?"

Reese honestly didn't know what to think at this point, but he didn't intend to share that with Kieran. Or anyone else, for that matter.

"Do you recognize him?" Reese prompted, showing him a photo of Decker on his phone screen.

Kieran surprised him when he took the phone and gave it more than a cursory glance.

"He does look familiar," Kieran said, returning the phone. "I've seen him in here once or twice."

"With Saoirse?"

"Yes. Part of her entourage, I guess you could say."

Brantley leaned forward. "Can you tell me whether she had other security in place when he was here?"

Kieran glanced between them, and it was obvious he was crafting his response carefully. "Why would that matter?"

"We've yet to determine whether Decker was actually working for the Kavanaghs or if he was here for personal interests."

Kieran's navy-blue eyes shifted between them before he finally said, "Yes. She had other security in place. Her brothers wouldn't allow her to leave the house otherwise."

Which meant Decker's story didn't hold up. Either Z had been misinformed, or he'd purposely misled them. Reese wasn't sure why he would do the latter, but he wouldn't put anything past Z. If Decker were working a case that Z preferred not to disclose, there was a good chance he would create a story that sounded good enough to believe upon initial inspection. But why? What would it gain him to send them chasing their own asses?

Problem was Reese wasn't interested in doing his brother's dirty work. He wasn't interested in being left in the dark.

"Can you recall the last time you saw Deck?" Brantley asked Kieran.

"I want to say it was last week." Kieran sat for a moment, clearly thinking. "Tuesday night, perhaps." He glanced at the dance floor. "Saoirse was here with Mr. Nova. They stayed for a couple of hours, but I don't think your friend stayed that long."

"Did he talk to anyone else while he was here?"

"I truly can't say. I interacted with Saoirse a bit, then had to take care of other matters."

Reese asked, "Do you know if he left with them?"

"He did not. He left before them."

"With someone?"

Kieran shook his head. "Not that I saw."

Reese relaxed and exhaled heavily. That information didn't get them any closer to finding Decker, but it did clarify a few things. Decker hadn't been working as Saoirse's bodyguard, and Ronan hadn't hired him. So why the hell was he here, and what the hell was he up to?

CHAPTER THIRTEEN

BECS HAD BEEN TEXTING EVAN THROUGHOUT THE day to check in. According to him, the slumber party had gone well. All the other girls had gone home around noon, but Sophia and Carly had continued to celebrate. They were camping out in their blanket forts again tonight, but thanks to an exciting day, they'd passed out early.

Although she was enjoying this trip to New York and the opportunity for a field assignment, Becs wished she were at Evan's with him and the girls. She knew it was silly to form an attachment to him because he wasn't going to give her what she needed, but she couldn't help herself. It had been so long since she'd even dated a man. Even more, since she'd been with a *good* man. One who wasn't in the relationship while waiting for something better to come along. That was how she could describe her marriage and a couple of her relationships prior to that.

To say Becs didn't have a good track record with men would've been an understatement. She was horrible at selecting them and even worse at making the relationship work. It was her fault, she'd been told. She was too selfish or too petty or too *whatever* would make the man she was with feel better. And while she could argue she wasn't any of those things, Becs wouldn't deny that she had a bad habit of acting as a doormat. Letting people walk all over her. She tended to find herself attracted to unreliable men. Since she was a teenager, she'd had a thing for bad boys. The problem with bad boys was that they weren't capable of giving a girl like her the emotional stability she needed to be happy.

She'd promised herself she wouldn't even consider a relationship with anyone until she found one who would treat her with respect, someone who would love her and her daughter. Someone who would make them happy.

Not that Evan was that man. But her imaginary version of him was.

Despite his emotional distance, Evan Vaughn was everything Becs had ever wanted in a life partner. And she'd spent plenty of years dreaming up the perfect man, the perfect relationship. She wasn't an idiot. She knew neither was attainable, but a happily ever after certainly was.

Ten years ago, Becs would've turned her nose up at a guy like Evan. Her mother said she was a glutton for punishment. She wasn't wrong. Becs had self-deprecating tendencies, never believing she was worth something more, something better. Hence spending years with an emotionally and sometimes physically abusive man.

As the cab pulled up to the hotel, Becs texted Evan to tell him she would be going to bed soon and that she was checking in one last time for the night.

His response came as she was in the elevator.

Call me when you get a minute. I need to tell you something.

She read the text message several times while walking the long, brightly lit hallway to her room.

She grinned at her reflection as she got ready for bed, washing her makeup off and brushing her teeth.

Evan sighed. "You're right. It was amazing, and up until about ten seconds ago, I was feeling the same. However, I don't think now is the right time for…"

He left the sentence hanging, and her brain filled it in with a dozen different things. Fortunately, she kept them all to herself.

"I get it," she said.

Becs was familiar with rejection. Too familiar, really.

The silence lingered long enough to stifle the air around her.

Finally, Evan said, "I'll let you go. Carly's doing fine."

"Wait," Becs said before he could hang up.

"What?"

"What … um … what did you need to tell me?"

"Oh. Right." Evan exhaled heavily. "I'll be there tomorrow. In New York. Brantley called me tonight and told me he needs me there. Kaye's fine watching the girls."

Becs's heart slowed, and she was sure she had forgotten to breathe. Evan was coming to New York. He would be there with her.

And she'd just screwed it all up by being her normal, pessimistic self.

Lovely.

As Atticus walked into the hotel room, he was ready to land face-down in his bed.

The night had been a bust. He'd managed to talk to every employee at the club—at least everyone he'd seen—and no one had recognized Decker's photo. The same couldn't be said for Saoirse. They all recognized her, but the problem with flashing pictures of famous people was that no one recalled where they'd seen her. More than likely, it had been on their Instagram or TikTok feed rather than serving her drinks personally.

But Atticus had done his due diligence because that was his job. And while he traipsed through the club on the hunt for employees, Slade had spent the majority of his evening drooling over Becs while Becs did her best to blend in with the crowd. It had become apparent about ten minutes in that she wasn't comfortable in the place, but she was a relatively good actress. Probably would've been better if Slade's eyes hadn't been burning holes through her the entire night.

Like he said, the entire night was a bust.

Not even the limited information Brantley and Reese had collected would make up for it. They had nothing more to go on than when they went in. Only more questions.

Fortunately, it was time to crash, and it was still early enough Atticus could catch a decent nap before the day started again. *Un*fortunately, the hotel room wasn't the kind that had two queen beds in a single room. This one had a separate bedroom space, and the couch folded out into a bed. Atticus had offered to take the couch when they first arrived. It had been his attempt to apologize to Slade for what went down at Moonshiners last night. Slade's response had been a grunt, which Atticus took as confirmation.

"You need in the bathroom?" Slade asked.

Yeah, this room wasn't meant to be occupied by co-workers. The bathroom was in the bedroom, which meant Atticus would have to go into Slade's room if he needed to use it.

"Nah," he said, figuring he would go down to the bathroom in the lobby if he needed to go before Slade was up.

"We need to be up by six," Slade informed him before closing the door to the bedroom.

Atticus glanced at the clock on his phone screen. Thankfully, it wasn't quite midnight, which meant if he closed his eyes now, he'd be fully functional come morning.

He tossed the couch pillows onto the floor and shoved the coffee table toward the wall so he could drag the ancient sofa bed out from its hiding space. The mattress unfolded with a bounce. Atticus glared at the paper-thin excuse for a sleeping surface. No way that thing was meant for comfort.

As he was pulling off his shirt, the bedroom door opened. Slade walked out, coming to an abrupt halt when he saw Atticus. His gaze skimmed over his chest before darting back to his face. Slade tossed a pillow and a blanket in his direction, then disappeared back inside the room.

Was it his imagination, or had Slade *run* back into the room?

"Thanks," Atticus muttered before stripping off the rest of his clothes, opting to sleep in his boxer shorts.

At least the blanket wasn't scratchy.

Atticus clicked off the floor lamp in the corner, then flopped onto the bed. He grunted when a bar hit the middle of his back.

One day, he would have a real bed to sleep in again. One that hadn't been slept in by God only knew how many other people. As it was, sleeping in a motel room each night was beginning to wear on him. At least here, he felt like he was on assignment. Back in Texas, he felt as though his existence was only temporary.

He grabbed his phone so he could set the alarm for five forty-five and noticed he had a text message from Carson.

Call me. I don't care what time it is.

Atticus grinned, then pressed the icon to dial the number. A moment later, Carson's gruff voice sounded in his ear.

"Where're you sleepin' tonight?" Carson asked.

"Hello to you, too," Atticus replied, grinning from ear to fucking ear.

"Hey," Carson said with a soft laugh. "Sorry. In my head, I've been talkin' to you for a while now."

"Really?" Atticus liked that Carson was thinking about him.

"I hope the bed you're in tonight is more comfortable than my couch."

"Not a bed," Atticus corrected. "It's a couch, but it folds out into what they think passes as a bed. Yours is more comfortable than this one," Atticus admitted, trying to fluff the pillow under his head.

"You could always try my bed on for size."

That simple invitation had Atticus's dick swelling. It seemed to do that whenever he thought about Carson, which had been a problem for most of the day. He couldn't stop thinking about the man. The only time he'd managed to maintain focus had been when he was talking to employees at the club. Before and after, he'd been plagued by thoughts of the sexy cowboy he'd met at the bar last night.

"Or not," Carson added, sounding disappointed.

"It's a very tempting offer," Atticus said, keeping his voice down so he didn't bother Slade.

"Why're you whisperin'?"

"Slade's sleepin' in the next room."

"Sharin' a hotel room with another man. Should I be worried?"

Atticus chuckled. "I don't know. You think Slade swings that way?"

Carson didn't answer right away, but before Atticus could laugh it off, Carson said, "Rumor is he might've dipped his wick a time or two when he was with the missus."

Atticus looked at the door to Slade's bedroom, trying to imagine him with a man.

"Kinky sex games or some shit," Carson added. "His wife was all about mixin' it up."

Hmm. That didn't track for Atticus. He didn't see Slade as the sharing type. Then again, from what he'd heard, that had been a long time ago, so who knows?

"I'd prefer not to talk about my co-worker or his kinky sex games, thank you very much."

"What *would* you prefer to talk about?"

"You."

"Didn't you get enough of me last night?"

"Not even close," Atticus muttered.

He swore he heard a smile in Carson's voice when he said, "Is that so?"

"Maybe next time we hang out, we can do it while sober."

"I think I can make that happen. When do you think that'll be?"

Atticus stared up at the dark ceiling, grinning like an idiot. He honestly couldn't remember the last time he'd had a phone conversation with a man. A man he'd been interested in, at least. Even if he had, he was fairly certain it would've been done via text, not speech. That was the way of the world nowadays.

"I don't know," Atticus answered. "We're in New York right now."

"New York? Seriously?"

"Yep." Atticus sighed.

"You travel often?"

"The task force does. And since I'm now part of it, I've become a wanderer."

Carson was quiet for a moment, and Atticus didn't feel the need to talk. He was comfortable listening to the man breathe on the other end of the phone. If he closed his eyes, he could almost imagine Carson beside him. Only if they were in the same room, he would bet money they would be doing something that required more effort than this.

"I can't stop thinkin' about you," Carson whispered.

The words swam through Atticus's bloodstream, thickening his cock and making his skin prickle with heat.

"I seem to be having the same problem," he admitted.

"Yeah?" There was a rustling sound followed by, "What exactly do you think about?"

Jesus. When was the last time a man made him blush? Atticus could feel his cheeks heating, and the tips of his ears were warm.

"I'll tell you what *I* think about," Carson continued, his voice low and sexy. "I think about what would've happened if you'd been in my bed when I woke up this mornin'."

"What would've happened?" Atticus's voice cracked.

"You would've been nekkid. It's my bed. My rules." Carson chuckled. "I would've watched you sleep for a few minutes. When I started pullin' the sheet down, you would've stirred, coming awake slowly. But when I licked your nipple, your entire body would've jumped to attention."

Atticus hummed softly, his fingertip brushing his nipple.

"Are you touchin' yourself, Atticus?"

"Not yet," he lied, his voice sturdier than he expected it to be. "But keep talkin' like that, and I will be."

"I want you to," Carson rasped. "I wanna make you come like this. I wanna hear your voice in my ear when you do."

This was surreal. He'd met the man last night, and for the first time in his life, Atticus had resisted temptation. Was this his reward for it? If so, he was going to begin a life on the straight and narrow.

"Is the room dark?" Carson asked.

"Yeah."

"Are you covered up?"

"Mmm-hmm."

"I want you to pull the sheet slowly—"

"Blanket," Atticus corrected, although as soon as the word was out, he wasn't sure why it mattered.

Carson chuckled. "Slowly pull the blanket down. Let it scrape against your nipple."

Atticus glanced at the closed door to Slade's room, praying the man didn't come out because once he started this, he wasn't sure he'd be able to stop. The last thing he wanted was to make things weird with Slade.

He pulled the blanket down his torso, leaving his lower half covered.

"Now lick the tip of your finger and drag it over your nipple. Imagine that's my tongue."

Atticus did as Carson instructed, moaning as he imagined the man's mouth on him.

"I won't stop there," Carson continued. "Imagine my lips trailin' down your stomach while I pull the blanket back to reveal your beautiful cock."

Beautiful? Atticus wasn't sure his dick qualified as beautiful. Granted, it wasn't gross or ugly either, so yeah, he'd go with it.

Atticus's cock flexed and twitched, tenting the blanket. His hand followed the imaginary movement, pushing the blanket aside and shoving his boxers down until he was fisting his erection.

"I'm gonna take you in my mouth, Atticus. I'm gonna suck and lick until you're beggin' for mercy. Is that what you want?"

"Yes," he whispered. "God, yes."

"Is your cock hard?"

"So fuckin' hard."

"Mine, too. I'm strokin' it, Atticus. I've jacked off three times today thinkin' about you. It's drivin' me crazy. I've wanted you since the first time I saw you."

Two months ago, according to Carson's admission last night. Whether that was true, Atticus didn't know, but he couldn't fathom why Carson would lie.

"Wrap your fist tightly around yourself and stroke your dick for me, Atticus."

He groaned softly, tugging and rubbing while Carson's smooth, raspy voice sounded in his ear.

"Fuck, I wish you were here," Carson said, the tension in his voice growing. "I want you beneath me. I want to slide my dick inside you. I want to feel that tight ring squeeze me while I push deeper. I wanna look you in the eye while I do so I can see the pleasure on your face."

Atticus was going to come. He'd never done this before. Never had a man tell him what he wanted to do to him. Most of his encounters were cut and dry. Fucking for the sake of fucking. Limited pleasure. Nothing like this. The anticipation was building, and Atticus knew even if he came right now, it wouldn't matter. He would be hard for Carson come morning. He would be thinking about this moment for days.

"I want you to come for me, Atticus. I want you to come when I do."

He grunted again. "I'm so fucking close, Carson. Oh, God."

"I wish you were here," Carson said. "I want you in my bed. Fuck. I need to touch you, to taste you. I wanna *feel* you."

He listened to Carson ramble, loving the sound of his voice, the desperation in his tone. Atticus felt it. The tension was building, drawing his body tighter and tighter until he thought he would snap.

"I'm gonna come," Carson groaned. "Fuck. Atticus…"

That was it. The sound of his name on Carson's lips snapped his restraint. Atticus managed to cover his dick with his other hand seconds before he came, warm spurts shooting into his palm.

"Jesus, Atticus. I hope like hell you're comin' back soon."

He grinned into the darkness. For the first time in his life, he felt as though he had someone worth going home to.

CHAPTER FOURTEEN

Monday, August 8, 2022

"Any updates?"

JJ glanced over her shoulder to see Baz standing in the doorway.

They'd opted to work from home for the first part of the day since they had a doctor's appointment at ten. At her last appointment two weeks ago, Dr. Tinder informed her she would start coming in every two weeks versus every month. At least until thirty-six weeks, when she began coming in weekly. JJ didn't mind the visits, and she knew that Baz enjoyed hearing the heartbeat each time, so they'd been going to them together whenever possible.

"Not yet," she admitted glumly. "I gave up on tryin' to tie them to the mob. I asked Darius to start searchin' for hotels or motels where Deck might've checked in."

She figured it was a nearly impossible feat considering the size of New York City. With five boroughs, they couldn't restrict their search to only Manhattan. It was easy to think of it as only Manhattan, but the city was so much bigger than that. It would take significant manpower to search everywhere. JJ was starting to think they were in need of some serious luck, or they were going to keep coming up empty.

"Did you ask Z if they had his itinerary?"

JJ nodded. "I called him earlier. He had no idea. I get the sense this was truly an off-the-books op. I'm not even sure Z let the team know his concern yet."

And that was raising another red flag for her. JJ didn't understand why it wouldn't be all hands on deck for a missing agent. Why had Z selected the task force to look for Deck? Was he hiding something from everyone else?

"Maybe he doesn't want to worry them yet."

Yeah, maybe. She couldn't imagine the agents Decker had worked with for years wouldn't want to join in the hunt for their missing colleague. That or there was something else going on here that Z didn't want them to know about. Whatever it was, Z was being tight-lipped about details even though he wasn't hiding his concern for Deck's well-being.

"Luca's workin' to hack the security cameras at Saoirse's apartment." JJ raised a hand to cut Baz off before he could tell her that was a no-no. "It's not ideal, but we have to trace his steps before he disappeared, or we've got nothin', Baz."

"I get it. But why don't you have Brantley and Reese swing by her place?"

"They will. Eventually. He said Ronan didn't appear concerned for his sister. And since Ronan gave Kieran a heads up that they were askin' questions, he's probably alerted his sister as well."

"So what are their plans this mornin'?"

"I sent them the info I pulled up on Kieran O'Rourke. According to Ronan, he's the one who owns that club, but turns out the owner is Knox Montgomery."

"Why does that name sound familiar?"

"Probably because he's a filthy hot billionaire," she said with a grin, laughing when Baz's eyebrows rose. "I'm serious. He's got his own hashtag and everything."

Baz frowned.

"Knox Montgomery is the son of Jeremiah Montgomery, the man who developed Montage Markets."

"Oh, shit. That super chain store, right?"

"Yep. Like Walmart, only not. Anyway. I'm graspin' for anything that might give us a lead. Kieran told us he'd seen him, but that was before Deck fell off the map. I doubt Knox Montgomery could give anything more, but I figure it's somethin'. And since Brantley's got the entire team with him, they can hit the streets to search for Decker."

Again, considering the size of New York City, it would be impossible for them to even make a dent, but they were there, and it was all they could do at the moment.

Baz continued to watch her. "Did Evan get there yet?"

JJ glanced at the clock. "No. His flight left at seven. He'll be there by noon, their time."

"Speaking of time." Baz turned to walk out of the room. "We need to leave in thirty so we're not late."

"I'll be ready. I promise."

When he left the room, she turned back to her computer and finished the email to Elana. She'd detailed a list of things the team needed to start researching while she was out of pocket. That way, when she got to the office and Brantley called to find out what she knew, they wouldn't look like they'd spent the morning with their thumbs up their asses.

Just once, she would like the universe to send them a case that made sense from the start. This was getting ridiculous.

EVAN HATED AIRPORTS.

More specifically, he hated New York.

Where so many people saw a city rich in history and culture, Evan saw too many people and too much concrete. He would take Miami over New York City any day of the week. They both had diverse cultures and an electric atmosphere, but Miami had better weather and fewer people.

It was the people, he decided. The sheer number of people.

He hadn't checked any luggage, so he didn't have to wait before heading out into the smoggy morning. He hailed a cab, then held on for dear life while the man navigated toward the city. Evan stared out the window, his gut churning the closer they got to their destination.

He hadn't slept for shit last night. He blamed that on the phone call with Becs. All day, he'd looked forward to hearing her voice, only to talk to her and find out her thoughts had taken a dark turn somewhere since their kiss on Saturday night. He probably shouldn't have reacted so badly, but Evan couldn't help it. What was the point in attempting to see where this went if she already doubted him?

The cabbie dumped him at the hotel and gave him almost enough time to get out before he was on his way to pick up someone else.

Shouldering his bag, Evan headed inside.

"Good morning," the woman behind the check-in counter said with a pleasant, Monday-morning smile.

"Morning."

"What's the name on your reservation?"

"I don't have one. I just need a single room for a day or two."

As soon as the words were out of his mouth, Evan saw the woman's expression falter.

"I'm sorry, sir. We don't have any available rooms. If you don't have a reservation…"

She let the sentence dangle, allowing him to fill it in however he wanted.

"I'll take anything," he said, hoping she would pull a room out of a hat.

"I'm sorry, sir."

"What about later? Do you have anyone checking out? I won't need it until tonight anyway."

She glanced at the screen, but Evan could tell she was merely placating him. When she looked back, he saw the truth in her eyes. Even if she had a cache of rooms set aside, he wouldn't be getting one.

"Okay, then," he said before walking away.

"Have a great day, sir," she called after him.

"Yeah," he muttered. "Great day. Got it."

He fucking hated New York.

Luckily, he still had options. Not ideal, but he could share a room with Slade. He'd take the couch; he didn't care.

Dropping into one of the chairs in the lobby, he pulled out his phone. He shot Brantley a text to let him know he was there, then sent a quick one to Slade, letting him know he needed a place to crash.

The response from Brantley came almost immediately.

We're finishing up at Saoirse's apartment. She's not here. Put your stuff in your room and meet us at the Monolith in thirty.

Can't get a room. Hotel's booked. I'll take the couch in Slade's room.

Shit. Slade's sharing a room with Atticus. We'll head back there. Give us twenty.

With a sigh, Evan relaxed and waited for his team to show up. He hated sitting still. It felt like he was wasting time. He could always store his bag with the concierge and come back for it later. Maybe they'd find Decker, and he could return to Texas tonight. He wouldn't need a room. Or he could go down the street. There were half a dozen hotels in the vicinity. Surely, one of them had a room.

As he considered his options, his phone chimed with another text from Brantley.

Becs said you can share a room with her.

No.

No, no.

That wasn't happening. No way did he trust himself in a room with her. Especially after their argument last night. He would rather camp in this chair for the foreseeable future.

Before he could argue his point, another message came from Brantley.

Leave your stuff with the concierge and meet us at the Monolith.

10-4.

Resigned to his fate, Evan got to his feet and headed back to the check-in desk.

"They told us nothin', but they were nice enough," Slade mused as Brantley stood in the apartment building's lobby and processed the exchange they'd had with a very friendly yet ridiculously unhelpful concierge.

They'd come hoping to talk to Saoirse Kavanagh. According to the man with the radiant smile—it was fake, by the way—she wasn't home. He didn't buy that for a second, but Slade was right. The guy had seemed nice enough. He'd given them no information to help them, but he hadn't seemed opposed to talking. Provided they didn't ask anything personal about their esteemed resident. Whenever they mentioned Saoirse's name, some of the light faded from his eyes.

Brantley's phone buzzed. A text from Evan letting him know he had arrived.

He responded.

We're finishing up at Saoirse's apartment. She's not home. Put your stuff in your room and meet us at the Monolith in thirty.

Can't get a room. Hotel's booked. I'll take the couch in Slade's room.

"Shit," he muttered to himself.

All eyes turned to him.

"What's wrong, boss?" Slade asked a second before his own phone buzzed.

"Evan's here. They don't have any available rooms."

Brantley sent a follow-up message to Evan.

Shit. Slade's sharing a room with Atticus. We'll head back there. Give us twenty.

"What do you wanna do about it?" Reese asked from beside him.

"He can stay in my room," Becs offered.

Everyone's attention shifted to her.

She glanced at each of them. "What?"

"You wanna share a room with Evan?" Slade asked, chuckling.

"I didn't say I *wanted* to," she replied. "But there is a sofa bed that's not being used."

Brantley shot another message to Evan.

Becs said you can share a room with her.

"He can leave his stuff at the concierge," Reese stated. "That way, we don't have to make another stop. We can go right to the Monolith building."

Brantley sent the new instructions to Evan.

Leave your stuff with the concierge and meet us at the Monolith.

10-4.

With that problem solved, Brantley tucked his phone in his pocket and stepped outside. It was hot, more so because all the buildings blocked any hope for wind. The streets were crowded and growing more so as the day passed. If they weren't careful, they'd get swept up in the evening rush hour.

"You think we're wastin' our time goin' to see this Knox guy?" Slade asked, walking alongside Brantley as they headed down the sidewalk.

"Probably," he admitted.

Since they didn't have any other leads to go on, he figured it wouldn't hurt to try. You never knew what a conversation might turn up. But yes, since Kieran didn't know Decker's whereabouts and he was actually a family friend, he figured Knox Montgomery would be a bust.

Two hours later, as they were walking out of the Monolith, having no more information than when they'd gone in, Brantley was at a loss.

In a city with a population of eight and a half million covering over three hundred square miles, they didn't stand a chance of finding Decker. Certainly not if the guy didn't want to be found. And while Brantley didn't know that was the case, he was beginning to think it was. A seasoned operator like Decker would know to leave a few breadcrumbs for instances when he might find himself in hot water. From where Brantley stood, it looked as though the guy had purposely gone off the grid.

"Let's grab some food," Reese told him, clearly sensing his frustration. "We'll take a breather and regroup."

The entire day was a bust. They'd spent the morning working in the hotel's business center, communicating with Luca and Darius while Becs tried to work things from this end. When JJ'd gotten to the office, she'd summed up everything they had, which was pretty much nothing more than they already knew. Ronan Kavanagh, Kieran O'Rourke, and Knox Montgomery had netted them nothing.

Well, maybe that wasn't true. If they used deductive reasoning versus inductive, they were starting to see a pattern, and everything was pointing to Decker having gone rogue versus him having been taken. It was also leaving Z's participation in the whole thing questionable. From the outside, it appeared that Z was helping them find Decker, but Brantley was starting to suspect that they were being sent off course on purpose.

"Since you haven't spoken to Saoirse Kavanagh," Evan prompted. "Why don't Slade and I go to her apartment again? See if she's there."

It was almost three, which meant there was plenty of daylight left for them to search for their missing colleague. If only they had a destination to focus on. It wasn't like they could go door to door and ask people if they'd seen the man.

"She's got a penthouse apartment with more security than the Kavanagh building," Brantley told him.

"The reference is lost on him, boss," Slade said with a grin. "He didn't have the pleasure." Slade turned to Evan. "Seriously, man. If she's holed up at home, I doubt we'll get anywhere near her."

"He's right," Brantley agreed. "If she doesn't want us to know she's there, we aren't gonna know."

"We could watch it for a while. See who comes and goes," Evan offered.

"Have you ever *been* to New York?" Brantley retorted, gesturing toward the hordes of people that surrounded them. Picking one person out of this mob would be nearly impossible.

"It won't hurt to try," Slade added.

"Fine," Brantley told him, but he looked at Slade. "However, you won't be goin' with him. I want you to stay partnered with Atticus."

He could see Slade's confusion, but he didn't feel the need to elaborate. Brantley had watched Atticus at the club last night. He'd honestly been impressed. While Slade had practically glued his eyes to Becs's backside, Atticus had spoken to every person he came in contact with, flashing the photo of Decker that he had on his phone. For a guy who pretended not to give a shit about anything, Atticus could focus when he wanted to.

"I can go alone," Evan told him, glancing between him and Slade.

"Take Becs."

The man's eyebrows popped up so quickly that Brantley had to backtrack to what he'd said to ensure it hadn't been inappropriate.

"Somethin' wrong?" he asked, glancing between Evan and Becs.

"Not at all," Becs said at the same time Evan said, "No. Not a thing."

Weird.

While he sensed a potential storm brewing between them, Brantley didn't have the time or patience to delve into their problems.

"Good," he told them. "I'll check in with JJ, see if she has any suggestions on where to go next. Grab some food, and I'll let you know what I find."

"And I'll call Z," Reese announced. "See if he's heard anything."

The six of them stood there for a moment, and Brantley wondered what the problem was, but again, he didn't care to ask.

It wasn't until Evan, Becs, Slade, and Atticus headed in the opposite direction that Reese spoke up. "You realize what you just did there, right?"

"I split up the teams so we can cover more ground," he said, staring at his partner.

"No, you poked the bear."

Brantley glanced behind him in the direction the group had gone. "What bear?"

"Evan."

"What's wrong with Evan?"

Reese fell into step beside him, Tesha walking between them. "Nothin's wrong with him, per se. He's just got a thing for Becs."

Brantley frowned. "Really? I thought Slade had a thing for her based on the way he ogled her last night."

"There's a good chance that's true, too," Reese muttered.

"Are they fightin' over her?"

"Nope."

"You know that for a fact?"

Reese's eyebrows rose slowly. "Nope."

Brantley didn't get it. "It bother you?"

"What? That they're fraternizin'? No." Reese looked over as he pulled out his phone. "You call JJ. I'll call Z. Let's see what else we can do before we lose daylight."

With more questions than answers, Brantley grabbed his phone and dialed JJ's number. He hoped like hell she had an idea of where to go next. Otherwise, he saw no reason to stick around. And based on Reese's reaction yesterday, Brantley knew he was the only one.

CHAPTER FIFTEEN

"HONESTLY, Z, I DON'T KNOW WHAT MORE we can do."

Reese stared at Brantley while the man finished the conversation with Z. Reese had called his brother, but when Z told him he didn't have anything more for them to go on, Brantley had taken over the call. Evidently, JJ hadn't come up with anything else, either.

For the time being, they were standing still with no direction to go in. Now, as they sat at the table in the small hamburger joint they'd come across, Reese wondered if anyone had been doing the same thing when he was missing. He'd never gotten a full account of the search, and he figured that was because there hadn't been one. Not an official one. Reese had been one of many fallen soldiers who were left behind.

Had his teammates sat at a table like this one, trying to determine where, if anywhere, they should search next? Or had they hoped that he'd surface on his own?

"Give it a little more time," Z replied, his voice sounding through the speaker.

"Twenty-four hours, Z. That's all we've got," Brantley stated firmly.

"Fine. I'll file the flight plan for tomorrow afternoon. If you don't come up with anything by … let's say two your time, head to the airport."

"Will do."

Brantley disconnected and passed his phone back to Reese.

"Why're you lookin' at me like that?" Brantley prompted.

"Like what?" Reese hadn't realized he'd been looking at him like anything.

"Like I'm leavin' your fallen comrade behind to fend for himself. I would never do that, Reese. But Deck's not givin' us much to go on. I'm starting to think that was his plan."

Reese exhaled heavily, unwilling to admit he'd thought the same thing. More than once.

Instead, he glanced down at Tesha, who was snoozing by his feet, waiting for them to finish. "Mind if we head for the park? I'd like to give Tesha some downtime."

"Sure."

While Brantley paid the tab, Reese took Tesha out of the restaurant, waiting on the sidewalk. This street was lined with cars on both sides while more weaved down the center. People lingered at the corner while a few walked in one direction or another. At least they had a destination in mind.

Reese glanced around at all the concrete, his thoughts drifting to a much darker time.

The sun was setting, the cool air drifting in through the window. Reese wasn't looking forward to another night in this concrete box. It was difficult to look forward to much of anything anymore. Sometimes, he wished the freezing temperatures would put an end to everything. That he would go to sleep and not wake up. Not have to endure another day in this hole built for one.

However, the sun seemed to come up each day, bringing light to the hell he was living in.

No one was coming for him.

Was his country even bothering to look? Or had they already declared him dead? Was his family worried? Had they been told he was missing? Were they trying to find him?

The what-ifs were all he had to go on anymore.

At least his captors had stopped trying to torture information out of him. It wasn't like he'd had any information to give. He'd tried to convince them to demand a ransom. At the very least, someone would know he was still alive. He knew the US didn't negotiate with terrorists, so his life was as good as over, but it was the only ray of light he could see in his bleak existence.

But they weren't even doing that.

So what were they waiting for? Why were they bothering to keep him alive?

"Ready?" Brantley asked when he joined him a few minutes later.

Reese shook himself out of the memory, nodding and leading the way to Central Park. It was several blocks northeast of their current location, but he'd found that walking in New York beat sitting in their rented SUV or a cab going nowhere.

"What do you think happened to Deck?" Reese heard himself ask, although he hadn't meant to voice the question.

"Honestly? I think he's workin' on somethin'."

"For Sniper 1?"

"No."

They stopped at an intersection and waited for the *walk* light to change.

"He might act like an idiot, but Decker's not stupid."

No, he wasn't. Reese got the impression Decker liked to keep to himself, and he wasn't much of a team player, but his record with Sniper 1 Security was clean, save for a couple of hiccups when he'd gone off the grid. In those instances, no one had gotten hurt, and Deck had come back with one excuse or another. Personal shit, his file proclaimed. Other than that, he went on the jobs he was assigned, performed his duty, and returned. He'd been working for them for years.

Knowing that Decker had done this before made it difficult for Reese not to see Brantley's point. There was a good chance Decker was going to resurface in Dallas at any moment, and here they were, wasting precious man-hours looking for him.

"What do you know about him?" Brantley prompted as the walk sign flashed.

Reese moved forward, Tesha keeping pace at his side.

"Not much. Only what his employment file gave me. He grew up in Dallas. Didn't go to college. He was a bouncer at a few nightclubs before he went to work for Sniper 1."

"Why'd he want to work on the task force?" Brantley asked. "When I interviewed him, I thought maybe he was lookin' for a change of scenery, but I never saw him make an effort to fit in."

Brantley wasn't wrong. Decker had worked for the task force for such a short time, and he never engaged much while he'd been there. Reese never saw him in town, wasn't even sure where he'd been staying.

"I'm gonna have JJ dig into his personal life. Maybe this isn't about the Kavanaghs at all."

"Yeah," Reese said. "That's probably a good idea."

At this point, it was all they could really do.

BAZ'S FOOTSTEPS ON THE STAIRS PRECEDED HIS voice, alerting JJ to his presence before he appeared.

"You about ready to head home?"

She looked up from her computer screen, then to the clock on her desk, and finally over to Baz. "Yeah. I didn't realize it was almost five."

"You've been focused."

She had been. Ever since she got the text from Brantley asking her to dig into Decker's personal life, she'd been running searches to find every bit of information she could find. She was used to coming up empty when she did that but what she'd uncovered about Decker Bromwell had created far more questions than answers.

"You wanna swing by the diner for dinner?" Baz offered as she logged out of her computer and undocked her laptop. "It's Monday. I think it's clam chowder night."

The mention of her favorite soup caused her stomach to churn. It was crazy what pregnancy did to an appetite. She couldn't remember ever being repulsed by anything, but it was a frequent occurrence these days.

JJ shook her head. "Nope. No."

"Okay then. I can make somethin' at the house. We've got some chicken breasts. I could make stir-fry. Or—"

"Salad. I want a salad."

Baz took her laptop bag. "Salad it is."

"With sunflower seeds."

"Hmm. I'm not sure we have those."

"And mandarin oranges."

"I know for a fact we don't have those."

JJ headed down the stairs. “And a hard-boiled egg. And some of that chicken you mentioned. Actually, no. I want a Cobb salad.” She heard him chuckle. “With tomatoes and avocados and chicken and bacon.”

“They have that at the diner,” he said as he flipped off the lights.

JJ stepped outside. “I told you the diner sounded fine.”

This time, his laughter was more robust, and it put a smile on her face.

Their conversation lulled until they were in the truck.

While Baz stored her bag in the backseat, JJ got in and put on her seat belt. “I heard you on the phone earlier. Were you talkin’ to Charlie?”

“Yeah.”

“How’re they doin’?”

“Good. They’ve talked to almost every person in the neighborhood where the attempted abduction was.”

“They get anything that’ll lead the cops to an arrest?”

“Not yet. But it’s more than we had.”

“I bet Charlie’s ready to come home. She probably misses Autumn.”

“She does,” Baz agreed, starting the truck.

“How’s her mom? Do we need to do anything for her while she’s out of town?”

“Autumn’s taking care of that. She visits her every day in the assisted living center,” Baz explained. “Charlie says her mom’s really happy there. She’s making friends.”

That was good news. JJ recalled Charlie’s mom having disappeared not too long ago. She suffered from Alzheimer’s and had managed to wander off. They’d found her quickly, but she knew Charlie had been beside herself with worry. Rightfully so.

“I told them to finish up and come on back,” Baz continued. “She said she needed one more day, but they’d book a flight out tomorrow night.”

“Good.” JJ understood the need for the team to go off on their assignments, but she preferred when they were around.

“What did Brantley have you workin’ on?”

She peered over at him. “Findin’ information on Deck.”

“Like what?”

"I think he thinks this might be personal. That it doesn't have anything to do with Saoirse Kavanagh."

"So we believe Ronan? That he didn't hire Deck to keep an eye on her."

"Yeah. I think so." JJ wasn't sure about much of anything anymore. Every time she started down one path, it twisted and turned and dumped her into Nowheresville.

"What did you find?"

She leaned back in the seat and relaxed, placing her hand on her belly and rubbing lightly. "Nothin' yet. I'm doin' a full background on him." She looked at Baz. "When he was workin' with us, did you ever really talk to him?"

He flipped on the turn signal as they pulled out of Brantley's driveway. It made her laugh since it was a rural neighborhood—not much more than farmland, really—and there was never any traffic, yet Baz did it every time.

"I never got a chance. He's not really a forthcoming guy."

No, he wasn't. JJ had tried to engage him in conversation a few times, but Decker always managed to shut her down. Politely, of course. He wasn't rude or anything, but he never divulged much information about himself.

"I did ask him once why he wanted to make a change," Baz mentioned. "He went from bein' a personal bodyguard to lookin' for missing people."

It had been quite a leap, but JJ had never really thought about it. It was true, though. Baz had been a detective with the Austin Police Department. They'd encountered him when they were looking for Corinne Greenwood. As for Evan, he'd been a homicide detective, but he had experience looking for missing people since he'd been part of the search when his wife had gone missing years ago. And Slade and Atticus had both been bounty hunters. They were used to looking for people. Deck was like Trey in the sense that they ventured down an entirely different path.

Then again, JJ couldn't really talk. She'd been hopping from one company to the next, attempting to find something that fit her skill set. Not too many people were interested in hiring a hacker. When Brantley returned, she'd been working for her ex-boyfriend, Dante. A fact her best friend hadn't been at all thrilled about.

After what Dante did, she understood.

"What did Deck say when you asked?"

"He was kinda cryptic, actually. Said you never knew when your past would come back to haunt you."

JJ frowned. "He said that?"

Baz nodded.

She turned her attention out the window. His past had come back to haunt him? If that were the case, why would he have left the city he grew up in to come to Coyote Ridge? It made absolutely no sense at all.

NEVER IN HER LIFE HAD BECS EVER seen anyone as beautiful as Saoirse Kavanagh. She was almost too pretty to be real as she opened her apartment door and allowed them to come in.

When Evan suggested coming back here, Becs had expected to get booted by the concierge again. She'd been surprised when the man recognized her and told them that Saoirse had told him to let her know if they returned.

Surprise. We're here!

"Sorry it took me a minute," she said with an Irish lilt that turned her from stunningly beautiful to beguilingly intriguing.

Becs figured it was weird that she was practically drooling over this woman, but she couldn't help it. It wasn't an attraction thing. She didn't find women attractive in that way. It was simply awe. There was no other way to explain it.

"I had to call my brother," Saoirse explained. "He mentioned meeting some people from Texas."

"Yes, ma'am," Evan said as he scanned the interior of Saoirse's apartment. "We're here looking for a colleague, and we were hoping you might be able to help us."

"This is about Decker?" Saoirse led the way into a spacious living area lined with windows overlooking Central Park.

Becs feared she would start drooling. This time, it had nothing to do with Saoirse's beauty. It was the view that did her in. She couldn't imagine living in a place like this, having the opportunity to see such wonder every day. Beyond the glass was a field of green that went on forever, and in the distance was the blue water that hugged the island.

"Yes," Evan told her. "We were under the impression Decker was here on assignment."

"Keeping an eye on me," she said with a smile, gesturing for them to sit on one of the white leather sofas.

Becs eased down, sitting on the edge of the cushion, not wanting to get too comfortable. It took effort, but she kept her attention on Saoirse and not on the view of Manhattan.

"It wasn't so much a job," she explained. "He wasn't getting paid. He said he was in town for business and he had some free time. It was more like a personal favor. I had a few … issues that he was helping me with."

"Issues?"

"My ex."

"Lawson Nova?" Becs asked.

She waved a hand in dismissal. "It's all taken care of now. I'm no longer seeing … him."

Becs wanted to ask her what happened, why they broke up, but she didn't want to be nosy. Plus, Evan was the seasoned investigator. She was merely here because Brantley had paired them up.

"Do you have a history with Decker?" Evan asked.

A soft smile pulled at her mouth. "If you're asking whether we were intimate…"

"No," Evan said quickly. "I'm merely trying to find out what got him from Texas to New York. We were under the impression your brother called him and asked him to come here."

That seemed to surprise Saoirse. "Not that I know of. He did come to my rescue one night." Her gaze swung to the windows. "I was being hassled, and he stepped in. Took care of it. We got to talking."

"So he wasn't here specifically as your personal protection?"

"Not at first, no. When he realized I was upset about … what was happening, he offered to hang around." Saoirse frowned. "Is there something wrong? I thought Decker went back to Texas."

"We haven't heard from him in five days. He's missed his check-ins."

Saoirse sat up straight. "The last time I talked to him, he said he was heading to the airport."

"If he was, he didn't make it," Evan told her, his tone smooth and even.

Becs could see her concern. Saoirse clearly hadn't been aware of Decker's MIA status.

"Do you have a way to get a hold of him?" Becs asked.

"Just a phone number." Saoirse nodded to her cell phone sitting on the glass coffee table. "I texted him yesterday to thank him, but I haven't heard from him."

"Do you know if he was meeting with anyone else while he was here?" Evan asked. "Did he mention anyone?"

Saoirse seemed to consider the question. Becs held her breath as though that would help the woman come up with information that might help them find Decker.

When she finally spoke, Becs's hope faded.

"He seemed preoccupied, and he was on his phone a lot. But no, he never mentioned anyone specifically. I honestly thought he was eager to go back home. As I said, he wasn't being paid to watch me, so now that you mention it, I can see that it seems suspicious."

If this could get any stranger, Becs would be surprised.

"Thank you for your time, Ms. Kavanagh," Evan said, his tone polite, not a hint of the disappointment Becs was feeling.

"Here," Saoirse said as she got to her feet. "Let me give you my phone number. If you have any questions, feel free to call me anytime. And if I hear from Deck, I'll let you know."

Saoirse and Evan exchanged phone numbers while Becs stood quietly closer to the door.

"Thank you," Becs said when the other woman neared.

"My pleasure."

Becs's shoulders relaxed once they were in the elevator, but it lasted only a second. As soon as Evan looked her way, the scrutiny of his gaze had her tensing all over again.

"What?" Becs asked, feeling like a bug under a microscope.

"Nothing," he grumbled before turning to face the doors as the elevator descended.

When they were finally out on the street, Becs drew in a deep breath. Her smile was involuntary. It was the city. There was something about this place that felt magical. She figured it had more to do with growing up in a small, rural town than anything. It wasn't that she wanted to live in a big city, but visiting was certainly worthwhile.

"What's the smile for?"

"This place," she told him before thinking about it. "I've never been here before. I'm trying to enjoy what little I can. Have you ever been here?"

"A few times," he answered, less frustration in his tone.

"I got to see Central Park," she admitted. "A little of it, anyway."

Evan looked at his phone. "Have you heard from Brantley?"

Well, apparently, they were done with small talk.

Becs pulled her phone from the pocket in her backpack and tapped the screen. "Not yet."

"We should head back to the hotel. Regroup."

"Sure."

They walked in silence, and it didn't take long for Becs to realize their conversation last night had taken them back to the place they were in before they shared that kiss. Evan was once again ignoring her, as though by pretending to see right through her, she wasn't even there.

Becs considered apologizing, but she wasn't sure what she would be apologizing for. No, she hadn't always been a pessimist, but years of being let down by her ex-husband had put a sour taste in her mouth when it came to her expectations of other people. By not letting them in, Becs could usually avoid those moments when she would get her hopes up, only to have them crushed again.

She briefly wondered how Evan had breached those carefully constructed walls in the first place. It wasn't like he was a particularly friendly guy. He avoided her like the plague and had since pretty much they first started working together. Becs had mistakenly believed they'd been building a friendship forged over their love of their kids. She'd been wrong there, too.

"When we get back to the hotel," Evan said casually from beside her, "I'll talk to Slade and Atticus. See if I can bunk with them tonight. I'm sure we can figure something out."

"You don't have to do that. There's plenty of room. The couch folds out to a bed. I can—"

"It's necessary," he barked, cutting her off.

Becs felt her frustration; it began seeping into her bloodstream, heating her skin. There was a good chance her face was red because that was what happened when she got upset. She was a redhead, and her fair skin reflected every ounce of her emotions, whether she liked it or not.

"Whatever you need to do, Evan," she said through gritted teeth. "Whatever you need to do."

CHAPTER SIXTEEN

SLADE FELT LIKE A CAGED LION AT the zoo.

He hated hotel rooms. He'd once spent almost four whole days locked up in one with Jennifer, the two of them unable to keep their hands off each other. It had been early in their relationship. Back when he was just a kid, really. The good ol' days, he liked to refer to it. Back when he'd been stupid enough to believe the woman loved him.

Speaking of Jennifer…

His phone was blowing up again, but he'd silenced it earlier in the day when they'd been with Brantley and Reese. No matter what he told her, Jennifer wouldn't stop texting. At first, when she'd started messaging him months ago, Slade had been blindly hoping that she'd realized the error of her ways. It had taken him about thirty seconds of talking to her to realize she was up to her old games. His ex-wife was no longer happy, and she was looking for a way out.

Slade hadn't given her the opportunity to use him as an escape route. Not this time. Despite their near knock-down drag-out, Jennifer wasn't taking no for an answer. She mistakenly believed Slade would eventually take her back.

As if.

Ten years ago. Most definitely.

Five years ago. Maybe.

Now. No fucking way.

He would be a fool to believe Jennifer was anything more than a self-centered bitch looking out for only one person—herself—and using everyone around her as a source of entertainment.

That was what Slade had been for her. A puppet she could maneuver however she wanted. Someone she could get to do things for her that no one else would do. Hell, he'd done things *with* her that he'd never fathomed doing, period.

In some ways, Jennifer had changed him. He'd opened his eyes to other possibilities because of her. He seriously doubted she knew that.

"You gonna answer that?" Atticus asked from his spot on the couch. He had his foot propped on the cheap wooden coffee table, the remote in his hand, and aimed at the television.

"No."

"You ever considered blocking the number?"

He had. In fact, Slade had blocked Jennifer's number on more than one occasion. But he'd always removed it, fearful Jennifer might one day need him for something. As much as he hated her, he cared about her well-being, and well, the truth was, Jennifer wasn't exactly mentally stable. He worried that one day she might ask for the help she truly needed.

It was another lie he was telling himself in his effort to pretend his marriage hadn't been one giant waste of time. Although he liked to blame Spencer for his marriage failing, his brother wasn't the only one at fault. Jennifer was the one who was always seeking comfort from someone. She claimed she'd never gotten it from Slade, hence her reasons for running into the arms (and beds) of numerous other men. For the longest time, Slade had thought he'd done wrong by her, that he hadn't given her what she needed.

But the truth was, he'd tried. He'd really tried to make Jennifer happy. The problem was she would never be satisfied. Didn't matter who she was with; Jennifer was not going to be content with her life because she was searching for something that wasn't out there.

Atticus's phone chimed.

On Slade's return pace toward the window, he glanced at the man, watching as Atticus looked at his phone, smiling as he did.

"Please tell me that's not my brother," Slade grumbled.

"It's not."

"Yeah, right," he muttered.

Atticus's head snapped up, his eyes narrowed. "Why would I lie to you about that?"

"I don't know. Why do you lie about anything?"

"I don't."

"Right."

"What's your problem, man?"

That was a damn good question. One Slade didn't have an answer for. He knew the kid didn't deserve his wrath. The other night at Moonshiners, after Slade had confronted his brother, he'd thought Atticus had left with him. He hadn't been surprised. What little he knew about Atticus James made Slade believe him to be a liar and a cheat. He would do whatever was necessary to get his way.

He'd learned he was wrong a few minutes later when Atticus came back inside, alone and angry. Wrong about Atticus leaving and wrong about his initial assessment of his character. Atticus wasn't a bad guy, but Slade had been expecting the worst from him since the beginning.

Of course, there could be an entirely different reason Slade was trying to paint Atticus with an unflattering brush, but he wasn't about to go there.

Slade should've been relieved that Atticus had seen Spencer for who he was and didn't make the mistake of learning firsthand, but instead, Slade merely felt guilty for getting in the way of someone else's happiness. Who was he to determine whether Atticus could find what he was looking for with Spencer? But he hadn't seen past his blind rage.

Or jealousy?

No. Definitely not that.

"Look," Slade said, stopping near the door to the bedroom. He put his hands on his hips. "I'm sorry for gettin' in your business the other night. If you wanna hook up with Spencer, that's your decision."

"It is," Atticus countered. "But I'm not talkin' to Spencer. I haven't seen him since that night. I don't intend to."

Slade nodded, not sure he believed him but sane enough to realize that wasn't Atticus's problem.

It was his.

"Holy shit," JJ muttered as she stared at her computer screen. "Holy *holy* shit."

"Is everything okay in there?" Baz called from their home office.

"Yes," she said, her eyes glued to the information on the screen.

"Find something?"

More than something. JJ had found … well, she wasn't really sure what she'd found, but it was definitely something.

Toggling between screens, she went to her notes app and clicked the search icon. She typed in the name of the high school Decker went to.

"Oh, my God," she muttered when she realized she was right.

"Okay." Baz's voice was moving toward her. "I think it's time to share with the class."

She grinned and looked up at him. "Did you know Decker Bromwell attended the same high school as Kylie Walker?"

He frowned. "And that means what to me?"

"Well, for starters, they're the same age." As soon as the words were out of her mouth, she amended with, "Or they would be if … you know."

If Kylie hadn't died.

"And that means what?" Baz asked.

"They went to the same high school. They were the same age. They would've been in the same grade."

"Probably. But that still doesn't mean they knew each other."

"I knew everyone in my high school," JJ countered. "In every grade."

"True. But you went to school in a small town. One with only one high school."

"So?"

"Is it a public school they went to?"

JJ glanced down at the screen. "Yeah."

"Some of those schools have close to two thousand students."

JJ flipped screens and typed the school's name into the Google search bar. She chewed her lip as she skimmed the results, then clicked on one that showed the number of students per school for all Dallas schools.

Baz was right. The school had a little over nineteen hundred students with a student/teacher ratio of 17:1. So maybe they hadn't known each other. But it was still strange, right? Definitely not a coincidence because, according to Brantley, coincidences didn't exist.

"What exactly does that connection do for us?" Baz asked.

JJ looked up at him, processing the question. She didn't have an answer because … well, because it didn't really do *anything*, did it? A connection between Decker and Kylie didn't mean a thing. Not at this point, anyway. Maybe it would have a couple of years ago when they'd been searching for Kylie's killer. But now … now it was merely one of those things that caught your attention.

With a sigh, JJ relaxed. "You're right."

"I'm not trying to be right," he said, perching on the arm of the couch. "If you think that's a lead, by all means, follow it."

"No. It's not. I mean, it's not like I can call Kylie and ask her where Decker is."

Even as she said it aloud, the information still felt important. Was Kylie the reason Decker had joined the task force? He'd come on about the time they were looking for Juliet Prince. Maybe they had been friends back then. Perhaps he'd been looking to avenge her death like a lot of other people.

"I'm gonna take a shower," Baz told her as he stood tall. "Care to join me?"

Smiling, JJ set her laptop aside.

No way could she say no to that.

"I DON'T KNOW HOW THIS COULD GET any fuckin' weirder," Brantley grumbled from his chair in their hotel room.

After spending an hour in the park, allowing Tesha to play off-leash for a little while, they'd come back to their hotel room for a breather. Atticus and Slade had done the same, checking in via text message a short time ago. Brantley had informed them they didn't have any additional information from JJ or Z, but they would let them know when/if they did.

"You're talkin' about Decker, right?"

His gaze shifted to Reese. "Yeah. What did you think I was referrin' to?"

Reese grinned. "With you, there's no tellin' sometimes."

Brantley smiled, forcing some of the tension from his shoulders.

Evan and Becs were apparently on their way back after an interesting, although not enlightening, conversation with Saoirse Kavanagh. It was looking more and more like Decker had played them. He was out there somewhere, likely doing something he shouldn't be doing while they were wasting time and money hunting for him.

At least, that was what Brantley was hoping. He honestly didn't want Decker to be in trouble, but he intended to give the guy a piece of his mind the next time he saw him.

"What're you workin' on?" Brantley asked, glancing in Reese's direction. He was sitting at the small desk with his laptop open in front of him.

"Just checkin' in with the team. I messaged Darius and Luca earlier to see how they were doin' with the hotel search."

"Lemme guess? Nothin'."

"Nope. He said they've got a search runnin' on all hotels and motels in Manhattan, but so far, nothing's come up. He could be usin' an alias."

True. Or he could be somewhere else entirely.

"They could spend a year researchin' hotels in this city," Brantley muttered. "If Deck's off the books on this one, I doubt he used his real name."

"Luca said he asked Z if he knew of any aliases that Deck used, but he said no."

Brantley frowned. "For someone so worried when he called us, Z doesn't seem to be providin' much intel."

Reese shifted, twisting his upper body in the chair and peering over. "You're right. He's not."

"What's that look for?" Brantley asked, noticing the shift in Reese's countenance.

"I've just got this feelin'."

"About Deck?"

Reese nodded. "I went into this fearin' he was bein' held captive somewhere and that it was our duty to find him."

Brantley knew Reese's reaction was based on personal experience. He'd been held captive years ago, missing for eighteen months after he'd been captured in a failed training mission. A training mission of all fucking things.

It was understandable that Reese would resort to that way of thinking after that. It was also understandable that Z would expect his brother to react that way. Had that been Z's intention? To send them off course? Here they were, seventeen hundred miles from home, searching a city with too damn many people for one person without a whisper of a trail to follow. It was like finding a specific needle in a stack of needles. There was no chance of them finding Decker without some sort of lead. All the ones they'd had—the Kavanaghs—had netted them nothing.

"What's on your mind?" Reese prompted.

Brantley shook his head. "Nothin'."

"Don't lie to me. What were you thinkin' just then?"

Brantley didn't want to tell him he was starting to question Z's motives. He had nothing to base it on, and making an accusation like that could cause problems.

"Brantley."

Because he couldn't outright lie to Reese, he said, "I'm just wonderin' why Z sent us out here with nothin' to go on."

"You think he had an ulterior motive?"

Brantley shrugged. "It might've crossed my mind."

"He doesn't seem all that concerned," Reese mused. "He did when he called us Sunday mornin'. But not so much anymore."

Perhaps Z was merely good at hiding his concern. Could be he was exhausting every avenue, and they were meant to focus solely on their mission.

"The part I'm havin' a hard time with is what's his goal?" Reese said. "What does sendin' us out here do if we're not meant to find Decker?"

Brantley was wondering the same thing. And he had the same number of answers as Reese. A big, fat none.

CHAPTER SEVENTEEN

When Becs returned to her hotel room, she texted Brantley to let him know she was available if something came up. She didn't bother telling him that Evan had gone to Slade's room to see if he could find a place to sleep. That was Evan's problem, not hers. And at the moment, she wanted to do anything that would get her mind off Evan and the argument they seemed to be in the middle of.

So until Brantley had something for them to do, Becs wanted to run a few things, see if she could find something in New York that would've drawn Decker here. And she wasn't referring to the tourist sights.

She took a seat at the small desk in the room, pulled her laptop out of her bag, and plugged it in to charge. She logged in and found one of the message threads the team used to suss out ideas. Everyone was on it. Luca, JJ, Holly, Darius, and Elana. Jay had been on it before, but he'd left when he was promoted—his terminology, not hers—to investigator.

Promoted.

The word made her roll her eyes.

Based on what she'd seen today, she wasn't sure the job was a promotion. It was simply *different*. More boots on the ground versus fingers on the keyboard. They were all doing the same thing; they merely had a different method of doing it.

She typed up her message and hit send.

Becs: *Has anyone checked Decker's credit cards? When was the last time he used one?*

There was a good chance no one would answer her for a while, so she went to Google Maps and pulled up Manhattan. She skimmed the main attractions that showed up first. The Empire State Building, the Metropolitan Museum of Art. Those were the first things she noticed. Times Square. The Plaza, Union Square, Hell's Kitchen. They were all familiar names, which was likely why she honed in on them first. Anyone who watched television knew those names.

Didn't mean Decker had come here for that.

Her messenger app dinged, and a banner came across the top of the screen.

Luca: *I haven't checked his accounts. Don't have the info. I can get it if needed.*

Becs didn't respond since he hadn't asked a question, and she'd learned that he wasn't much for small talk. One time, she'd messaged back with a thank you after he answered her question, and she saw him shake his head. She'd done it to be polite and to ensure JJ knew she'd gotten his message since JJ was technically her boss. If Becs had known Luca would think she was an idiot, she would've kept silent.

Needless to say, she'd learned her lesson.

She continued to scan the map, clicking *transit* to see the subway lines. She started at the southernmost tip and began moving north. The financial district, Tribeca…

"If I ever go, I'd want to see the memorial site."

Holly was the one who mentioned the 9/11 Memorial when they'd been talking about places they wanted to visit. Becs wasn't sure what had gotten them on the subject, but she recalled it had been her, Holly, Decker, and Darius. Holly said she wanted to go to Las Vegas, and Becs had mentioned always wanting to visit New York City. Holly brought up the memorial. Luca had firmly stated he had no desire to visit a big city, and Darius had said that Hawaii was more his thing.

"It's definitely worth seeing," Decker said.

Holly's eyes widened. "You've been?"

"Yeah. I've got a…" He glanced down and away before finishing with, "A friend who lives in Chelsea."

"Do you visit them much?" Becs asked.

"No. Only once." He wouldn't meet her gaze as he shifted the topic and looked at Holly. "I took the subway to the memorial. It'll take your breath away, that's for sure."

Becs grabbed her phone and pulled up Brantley's number to send him a text.

I doubt it means anything, but I recalled a convo with Decker. He mentioned having a friend who lives in Chelsea.

His response came quickly.

Any chance he gave you a name?

Unfortunately, no. Like I said, I'm sure it's nothing, but he seemed kinda … off when he mentioned them.

Guy? Girl?

He didn't say.

Feel free to research and see if you can find something. Let us know if you do.

OK.

Becs set her phone on the desk and looked at the computer at the same time it dinged with a notification from the messenger app.

JJ: *Good question on the accounts, Becs. I'll follow up with Z. I asked him for the information yesterday. If he doesn't have it, I'll bypass him.*

Becs: *Let me know if you need me to run with it. I'm happy to.*

She leaned back and stared at the computer. Most of her job entailed a lot of back and forth, digging deeper into each layer they uncovered until something made sense. Unfortunately, in this particular case, whenever something started to, it went in an entirely different direction.

With a sigh, she looked at the clock. It was a little after five, so she should probably call Kaye and check in to see how Carly was doing. Before she picked up her phone, she remembered New York was an hour ahead, meaning it was only a little after four in Texas. She would give it some time before she called so she could talk to Carly when she was ready for bed.

Until then, she would do a little research on what was in Chelsea.

"You're welcome to sleep here," Slade offered as Evan stood near the door.

Evan had come to Slade's hotel room, hoping he could convince them to let him sleep on the sofa. Turned out Atticus was sleeping there since the room didn't have two beds. For a brief moment, he considered sleeping on the floor but changed his mind as soon as the thought formed. If he did, he would likely be in a world of hurt tomorrow. He couldn't remember the last time he'd crashed on anyone's floor. College, maybe.

"I'd offer to trade," Atticus said, looking up from his phone. "But I don't wanna weird Becs out. She's cool and all, but I don't really know her." Atticus's gaze swung to Slade, and he grinned. "Then again, you're the one who's got the hots for her. Maybe you wanna give it a shot."

Evan looked at Slade. "What's he talking about?"

"Nothin'," Slade said quickly.

Was Evan crazy, or was Slade blushing?

"He couldn't take his eyes off her last night." Atticus laughed. "Then again, half the guys in that club were starin' at her in that dress."

What dress?

Slade shook his head. "Trust me when I say it ain't like that."

Atticus laughed. "Are you scared of her or what?"

Evan waited for Slade to answer until he realized Atticus had directed the question at him.

"What?"

"You obviously don't want to sleep in her room. Did she do somethin' to freak you out?"

"Of course not."

Atticus sat up, looking between Evan and Slade. "Seriously. I'm happy to talk to her. I can be polite when I need to be."

"No," Evan said quickly, getting to his feet. "It's cool."

He picked up his bag and headed for the door. He was being an idiot. The last thing he wanted was for the team to think he had a problem with Becs. It was bad enough Luca was openly treating her like a leper. If they thought Evan was bothered by her, someone might start to get the wrong impression.

Truth was, Evan didn't have a problem with Becs. His problem was that he liked her, and at the moment, he wasn't sure where things stood between them.

"Well, if you change your mind, you can grab a patch of carpet," Slade offered. "We can get extra blankets and pillows."

Evan nodded as he opened the door and stepped into the hall.

He knew Becs was on the sixth floor because that was the button she'd pressed in the elevator earlier. As he started down the hallway toward the stairs at the end, he shot her a text, asking for the number. Her response was immediate and contained only the room number, which he figured didn't bode well for him. She was obviously upset after their argument on the street earlier. In all fairness, he could've handled it better, but he'd panicked when she'd gotten defensive.

Or maybe he was the one being defensive. Evan was a rational man. If he were wrong, he could admit it. And in this case, he honestly couldn't say. He hadn't liked a woman in so damn long…

He walked slowly, trying to come up with a way to smooth the waters. They had to work together, and as close as the team was, they would pick up on the tension immediately if he didn't fix this.

Perhaps he should consider pushing Becs in Slade's direction. Although his partner had rejected the idea, Evan knew him well enough to see the interest on his face when Atticus mentioned her name. They were certainly a far better pair than he would make with Becs. For one, they were the same age. Evan was eight years older than her. He had no business wanting a woman that much younger.

He arrived at Becs's room. Evan lifted his hand to knock, then dropped it, pacing away from the door.

If he hinted that Slade was interested, he could see her reaction. If she was keen on the idea, Evan could nudge her in that direction.

So what if the idea of her with Slade made him want to put his fist through the wall? Becs deserved someone who wasn't battered and broken, and Evan had been that way for so long that he'd gotten used to it. She deserved someone who would worship at her feet, and Slade was the kind of guy who would put his woman before all else. There were things in Evan's life that took precedence over everything else. And he wasn't talking about Sophia, although she was at the top of his priority list. No, there were other things. Things that would certainly interfere if he ever let himself be in another relationship.

Taking a deep breath, he moved to the door. This time, he let his knuckles meet the wood.

"Yes, hello," Becs said as she opened the door.

At first, Evan thought she was talking to him, but then he saw she was holding her phone to her ear.

"My name's Gladys Overwith, Decker Bromwell's assistant. I'm looking at his credit card statement, and it looks like he stayed at your hotel the last time he was in Chelsea. I think there might be a problem. It looks like he was charged for two rooms. Can you confirm that for me?"

She walked away, so Evan stepped into the room and closed the door behind him.

"No, I'm sorry. I don't have that information. Mr. Bromwell…" She laughed softly. "Well, to be honest, Mr. Bromwell's not very good at keeping track of his receipts. I know he likes to stay there, so there's a good chance he's stayed more than once."

Evan watched as Becs paced the room, her phone to her ear.

"July eighteenth?" She stopped walking, a frown marring her forehead before it cleared, and she continued. "Now that you mention it, that does sound about right. Can you tell me how many nights he stayed? I only expected him briefly, so the charge seems high. That's why I thought he got charged for two rooms."

Evan watched as Becs listened to the person on the other end of the phone. She walked over to the desk and began jotting something on the notepad.

"Yes. Uh-huh. Can you tell me this? Did he check out through the in-room system or at the desk?" She laughed, and while he could tell it was fake, he doubted the caller could. "He's always telling me they didn't give him a receipt. That's his excuse for not giving it to me."

She laughed again, smiling as she stared at the wall and listened to the caller.

"At the checkout desk. I knew it. I'm gonna have to water down his coffee for a week as payback. I knew he lost the receipt." Becs laughed again. "That's perfect. Thank you." She stood tall. "Actually, yes. If you'd send me a copy of that receipt, that would be great." She rattled off the email address. "Yes, thank you. You, too."

She disconnected the call and grinned.

"Gladys Overwith?" Evan prompted.

Her grin widened. "Yeah. You know. Glad it's over with," she enunciated slowly. "Gladys Overwith. It's a name we use when calling for information that we probably shouldn't be privy to."

"And the email address? Is it real?"

"Yep. We can thank JJ for that. It comes in handy at times like this. He would've been suspicious if I didn't want a receipt since I'm reconciling Mr. Bromwell's credit card statement and all."

Evan set his bag on the floor by the door.

"It only took four calls for me to find the right hotel." She leaned over and jotted more notes on the notepad.

"Right hotel for what?"

"Where Decker was staying. In Chelsea."

Evan frowned. He got the feeling there were details he was missing.

"Oh, sorry." She took a breath and sat in the desk chair. "I recalled a conversation we had at HQ. Me, Holly, Luca, Darius, and Decker. We were talking about places we wanted to…" She waved a hand. "Never mind. That's not important. Decker mentioned he had a friend in Chelsea. I only remembered it because he seemed off when he said it. Like, he didn't mean to mention it at all. But he did, so I thought I'd see if that friend was what brought him to New York this time. I still don't know if they were, but I did find out he checked into the Holiday Inn on July 18th and checked out on August 1st. He stayed for two weeks and checked out himself. At the front desk. Which means he likely wasn't under duress at the time."

Evan had to admit that was quite a bit of information she'd managed to obtain with a very simple question.

"I need to let Brantley know. I think we should go over there and check it out."

"Let's go," Evan said.

"What?"

"You and me. Let's go check it out. If we find something, we can call Brantley and tell him."

Becs stood slowly, her grin growing wider by the second. "Seriously?"

"Sure."

Her eyes danced with excitement. She morphed from being pretty to being downright gorgeous right before his eyes.

Evan felt that strange churning in his stomach. Suddenly, pushing her in Slade's direction seemed like the worst idea in the history of ideas.

CHAPTER EIGHTEEN

IF ATTICUS DIDN'T KNOW BETTER, HE'D SAY Slade was acting weird. Like the kind of weird that made it awkward to be around him.

"Hey, are you pissed that I told Evan you like Becs?"

Slade shot him a sideways glare.

"Look. I didn't mean to blurt it out. Sometimes shit comes outta my mouth before I can think it through."

"I don't like Becs," Slade said, his jaw set and his eyes narrowed.

Atticus backed up a step, holding his hands up in a sign of surrender. "Got it. You don't like her. I'll never mention it again."

He exhaled and dropped his hands, considering taking the stairs rather than waiting for the elevator while the air chilled to negative temperatures. It was safe to say Slade was definitely acting weird. Or if maybe not weird, he was acting very … unSladelike.

But then the doors to the elevator opened, revealing, *guess who*? Becs, who Slade doesn't *like*, and Evan. Woohoo.

"Fancy meetin' you here," Slade said. "Where're y'all headed?"

Atticus stepped in and to the side, leaving space in front of the doors as he waited for one of them to answer Slade.

Becs looked at Evan.

"To Chelsea," Evan said flatly.

"Chelsea?" Slade glanced between the pair. "To do somethin' fun?"

"To chase down a lead."

"No shit?" Atticus stood up straight.

Chasing down a lead beat going to the hotel bar with Slade, whose attitude was snippy because he didn't *like* Becs.

Sure, Atticus could've gotten past that part, but that wasn't his only issue with the man. A small part of him was still a little pissed at Slade for his reaction at Moonshiners the other night.

Atticus smiled at Becs and Evan. "Want company?"

"Sure," Evan stated, his eyes straight ahead as though looking at them would cause physical pain.

"Are you sure we didn't interrupt somethin'? Slade asked.

Becs's smile was forced at first, but then her expression softened. "Not at all."

"Who came up with the lead?" Atticus asked, simply because he thought they all might suffocate from the awkward tension if he didn't.

"Becs did." Evan nudged her arm. "Tell them."

Atticus listened as Becs told a story about a conversation she remembered having with Decker and about how she'd called several hotels pretending to be Decker's assistant, attempting to reconcile his credit card charges.

He remembered plenty of times he called someone, pretending to be someone he wasn't, to chase down a criminal who'd skipped out on their bail.

While Becs talked, they headed through the hotel lobby and out to the street.

"Cab or subway?" Becs asked.

"How far is it?" Atticus inquired.

"About two miles."

"I'm game for the subway," Slade answered.

"Me, too," Atticus chimed. He'd never been on the subway before. He figured now would be a good time to check it out just to say he did.

They walked two blocks to the 7th Avenue station, then underground.

It was exactly as it was shown to be on television. A little dim and a lot dirty. Atticus couldn't help but think about all those fictional crime shows when someone would get shoved to their deaths off the subway platform in front of a train.

Perhaps he should apologize to Slade one more time before they get to the platform.

The E train was the one they wanted, and since they didn't have passes, they had to pay. It took only a few minutes before they were waiting on the platform for the mass transit train to arrive. When Slade stood behind him, Atticus imagined himself flying through the air after Slade shoved him from behind. Flying, flying … then *splat.*

Okay. Maybe he would step *this* way. Just a little.

Slade glared at him briefly before turning his attention to the tracks.

The awkwardness from the elevator had followed them, hovering like a dark cloud over the city, threatening to burst at any moment. Rather than attempt to lighten the mood, Atticus checked out the people hanging out down there. There were more people than he'd expected. Then again, he was in a city of millions, and being that it was Monday night, they were most likely on their way home for the evening.

The train finally arrived, bringing with it a wave of hot air that passed through in a rush. Atticus grinned. *No, Death, you can't have me today.*

"What're you smilin' about?"

"You didn't shove me in front of the train."

Slade's eyebrows slammed down. "What?"

Atticus smiled again, then whispered, "Win."

They joined their fellow passengers inside. Atticus and Slade remained standing, leaving the seats for those needing them. Evan sat, but he suspected that was because Becs looked uncomfortable. As soon as his butt hit the seat, Becs was next to him.

If something wasn't going on between those two, the four of them were going to emerge at their stop to find pigs flying through the city. And whatever it was, they weren't on good terms at the moment.

Then again, Atticus had noticed the tension at HQ for a while now. At first, he thought it was Luca who'd caused it. Now he wasn't so sure.

Drama seemed to be a theme for the task force.

The Penn Station stop took eighteen minutes to get to, with a couple of stops along the way. He wondered how long it would've taken by taxi, considering all the other cars on the streets were attempting to go in the same direction and often weren't going anywhere at all.

"So what's the plan?" Slade asked as they emerged from the underground tunnel and back into the daylight. Thanks to all the shadows thrown by the buildings, it wasn't very bright.

"We've got four blocks to go," Becs informed him.

"I meant once we get there," he clarified.

"Oh."

Evan looked at Becs. "It's your lead. You make the call."

She chewed on her lip for a moment, then looked at Slade. "Why don't you and Atticus check out the restaurants and bars nearby? Decker checked out of the hotel, but that doesn't mean he left the city."

"And you think he's in Chelsea?"

Becs shrugged. "He said he had a friend here."

"At least we've narrowed it down some," Slade mused.

Atticus didn't bother to tell Slade that Chelsea was a neighborhood that spanned something like five hundred acres. Or so he'd read on one of the brochures he'd grabbed in the hotel lobby.

So, yeah, they'd narrowed it down, but it was still too big for the four of them to cover. Not without checking into more long-term accommodations first.

Becs was looking at them as though she wasn't sure she'd made the right choice. "I figured it wouldn't hurt to check."

"You're right," Atticus said when it was clear Evan and Slade were going to keep the constipated looks on their faces. "We'll split up and keep our search to a two-block radius of the hotel. I'll go south. You can go north," he told Slade. "We can meet up back where we start from in what? An hour?"

"Hour and a half," Slade said.

Atticus nodded. "Hour and a half. Got it."

They walked the next few blocks in silence. It was unfortunate he'd left his earbuds in the hotel room. He could've had music to accompany him on this evening stroll. Since he'd thought they were going to get their drink on, he'd left them.

He wondered if Brantley would've brought them anyway. Tucked them into one of the many pockets on his cargo pants. The thought made him smile.

He didn't know why, but he was having a lot of those WWBD moments. What would Brantley do when… Ever since he met the guy, he'd been fascinated. Not in a romantic way, although it was amusing to tease Reese by flirting with his man. He meant no harm, and he always watched for signs of when he was about to cross the line. He wouldn't do that. Not to either of them. But he did find it amusing to get a rise out of Reese and he was pretty sure Brantley enjoyed the fact that his soon-to-be husband was jealous.

It was all in fun, of course, but no, Atticus wasn't interested in either of them. Not like that.

No, his fascination was with the man himself—a real-life Navy SEAL who likely had more stories from his experiences than the entire task force combined.

He figured it partially stemmed from having wanted to join the military himself. Atticus had attempted to sign up when he turned eighteen, only to be rejected when they learned he'd spent a year in a mental facility when he was fifteen. He'd been in the foster system, and evidently, acting out at school to a certain degree was grounds for hospitalization. Atticus had sucked it up, but shortly after they released him, he ran away from the foster home he'd been placed in. He'd lived on the streets for a year before he turned eighteen.

Because of his troubled youth, Uncle Sam hadn't been interested in taking him. He'd been wandering since then, but now … he didn't want to get too excited, but he was starting to think he might've finally found a soft place to land.

"THANKS, JJ. LET ME KNOW IF YOU *do* find somethin'."

As Brantley ended the call with JJ—the second in the past hour—Reese could feel Brantley's tension rising. And it was steadily increasing with every passing minute. While Reese continued to review what little information Z had sent him on Decker and the bits and pieces JJ was unearthing, Brantley had started pacing.

"Goddammit," Brantley growled, throwing his phone on the bed.

Reese closed his laptop and stood. "I think you need a distraction."

"No, what I fucking need is to find Decker. This is bullshit. It's—"

Reese cut him off by shoving him onto the bed.

Brantley's eyes were saucer-wide as he stared back at him.

No, Reese didn't make a habit of manhandling Brantley, but he knew, in this instance, it was necessary. Brantley was getting himself worked up enough that a migraine was inevitable.

"Relax," Reese told him. "Lie back and relax."

"I don't—"

Reese covered Brantley's mouth with his hand and pushed him down so he was lying on the bed. Reese straddled his hips, staring down at him.

"I'll remove my hand, but I want you to be quiet. Understood?"

Brantley's blue-gray eyes glittered with a promise of retribution, but he finally nodded.

"Good."

Removing his hand, Reese inched backward and got off the bed.

"Take off your shirt, then turn over."

Brantley's eyes narrowed, and his lips parted.

"Quiet," Reese repeated.

While Brantley removed his shirt—dramatically jerking and tossing—and flopped over onto his stomach, Reese removed both of their shoes. He went to his bag and retrieved the bottle of lubricant.

"I'm not in the mood," Brantley grumbled, glaring at him as Reese approached.

Reese barked a laugh. "Is that the biggest lie you've ever told?"

Brantley grunted.

"I hate to disappoint you," Reese told him. "But I have no intention of fuckin' you."

Another grunt.

Reese laughed. "I promise you'll enjoy this just as much."

"Doubtful."

"Fine." Reese joined him on the bed, straddling his thighs. "Maybe not *just* as much. But I won't disappoint. Now close your eyes."

Reese squeezed a generous amount of the liquid into his hands and began massaging Brantley's back. He remained silent—they both did—for a good ten minutes while he worked some of the tension out of Brantley's shoulders. It took effort. The man was as taut as a bowstring.

When he felt Brantley go limp beneath him, he knew he'd fallen asleep. How he did that, Reese would never know. The man could go to sleep in seconds. It was a skill he'd acquired during his time in the Navy. Reese hadn't been in special forces, so he'd never experienced the sporadic chaos that special operators did, but evidently, they were trained to recoup their strength by catching sleep whenever they could. And they did that by shutting themselves down in an instant. It was quite interesting to witness.

While Brantley snoozed, Reese got off the bed slowly. He went to the bathroom and washed his hands, then looked at the shower in the mirror's reflection. His mind drifted to the time when a shower hadn't been a luxury for him. He'd been allowed to wash with a bucket of water and a sponge once every couple of weeks. He hadn't understood why his captors had bothered. For the longest time, they hadn't given him a reason for why they were keeping him alive at all. One day, he'd asked.

"Why?" Reese asked, shivering from the chill in the air and the fever that racked his body. "Why don't you just kill me?"

White teeth flashed behind the dark beard. "You're worth nothing to us dead."

"I'm worth nothing to you alive, either."

"We'll decide that. Don't discount yourself yet."

When he'd finally been rescued, Reese had spent far too much time sitting on the shower floor. For days after, he would seek solace there, letting the water rain down on him until it ran cold. It was an attempt to get clean, both physically and mentally. While it had removed the grime from his skin, it hadn't done anything to wash away the memories.

Shaking off the past, he turned to find Brantley standing in the bathroom doorway. He was naked, his eyes gleaming with the promise of retribution he'd seen earlier.

"Strip," Brantley grumbled as he moved toward the shower to turn on the water.

Reese didn't bother to tell him they'd showered that morning. It was moot. They weren't getting in because they were dirty. They were getting in because that was what Brantley wanted.

"I'm not in the mood," Reese mocked even as he stripped off his shirt.

"You're always in the mood." Brantley's hands were on his chest before the T-shirt hit the floor.

It was true. He was.

Sex had never been quite as thrilling as it was with Brantley. Not necessarily because Reese had never been with another man before. It was simply more intimate. Not merely physical. And Reese looked forward to those intimate moments he shared with this man.

"Fuck, I could touch you all day," Brantley rumbled near his ear as he kissed Reese's neck.

Maintaining his indifferent attitude, Reese grunted. "I can't strip if you keep doin' that."

"Then let me help."

Reese had to grip the edge of the counter when Brantley jerked his jeans down his legs, dragging the denim to the floor.

And then he was staring down at Brantley, sucking air into his lungs as desire flooded his bloodstream.

"Perfect," Brantley rasped, leaning in to kiss the head of Reese's dick. "I could do *this* all day, too."

"Oh, fuck." Reese hissed, his head falling back as Brantley took him to the root.

"Forty days, then this…" Brantley stroked him firmly. "This is gonna belong to me."

Reese sighed. "Already does."

"Yeah, but I'll have a piece of paper that makes it official."

Admittedly, it thrilled Reese that Brantley was so excited to marry him. He knew the wedding wasn't exactly Brantley's cup of tea, but he was making concessions because he knew Reese was looking forward to it. Reese couldn't exactly say why that was but being involved made it more real. Since there were days when he wondered how the fuck he'd gotten this lucky, Reese needed those preparations because they grounded him.

Brantley got to his feet, pressing his chest to Reese's before sealing their mouths. Within seconds, the kiss turned omnipotent, and the next thing Reese knew, they were in the shower, the warm water raining down on them. He held on to Brantley, letting his new memories overwhelm the nightmares that still attempted to invade from time to time. It was getting easier, but he still had his moments.

"Turn around. Put your hands on the wall."

Reese did as instructed, moaning and groaning as Brantley's hands moved over him, causing goosebumps on his skin. His cock was hard as steel and ached for Brantley's touch. He knew it would come, but not until Brantley was ready. Luckily, Reese had been honing his patience over the past two years since he met this man. He hadn't mastered the skill, but he was learning to be in the moment.

"Put your foot on the bench."

Shifting a step to the right, Reese did as Brantley wanted, lifting his leg and placing his foot on the bench. As soon as his skin touched the tile, Brantley's fingers delved between his ass cheeks, fondling his hole and making him moan.

"In forty days, this is gonna be mine, too."

"Already is," Reese chimed.

Brantley chuckled. "You're right. It is. I'm the only one who's ever had the pleasure. Which means you're all mine, Reese."

He loved when Brantley said shit like that. The man was an alpha male with a soft spot, and that made Reese want him even more.

Brantley moved in closer, his thighs pressed against Reese's legs, his cock sliding along the crack of his ass. Moments later, Reese was groaning as Brantley pushed inside him.

He held himself still as his skin prickled. Pleasure, unlike anything he'd ever known before this man, consumed him. It was always that way. Every inch of him felt Brantley like they were one person when they were like this.

"You feel so good," Brantley rasped against his shoulder, his arm banding around Reese's stomach. "I could certainly do *this* all day."

Reese inhaled and exhaled, riding the waves of pleasure as Brantley fucked him. Slow and deep, filling him completely. He maintained a brutally slow pace until Reese thought his head would come off his body. And just when he was reaching the point of frustration, Brantley fisted his cock, stroking in time with the languid pace. Reese gasped for air, welcoming the rush that preceded the release. He held on as long as he could.

"Come for me, baby," Brantley groaned. "Let go for me."

He did.

And a second later, Brantley was right there with him.

NEARLY THREE HOURS AFTER THEY LEFT FOR Chelsea, Becs was walking out of the subway near their hotel.

The trip had been a bust.

At least, she'd thought it had been. The guys weren't saying as much, but she was sure they would agree. According to Atticus, it had been necessary. He'd done his best to reassure her that they hadn't wasted their time looking for something that wasn't there.

Maybe he was right. If they hadn't gone, she would've wondered.

Then again, if she had told Brantley and Reese, there was a good chance they would've found Decker and would be preparing to go back to Texas.

Granted, they weren't miracle workers, but still. Becs couldn't help but be disappointed. She'd secretly hoped to be the one who found Decker. She'd even imagined the approval she would've seen in the eyes of her co-workers if they had.

But no. She'd led the team on a wild goose chase.

As they walked through the hotel lobby, their phones all chimed almost simultaneously. Becs pulled hers from her backpack.

"Brantley wants us to meet for breakfast at six o'clock," Slade announced.

"Oh six hundred," Atticus said with a chuckle, which made Becs smile. Yeah, she could practically hear Brantley and Reese saying it in the military speak they were used to.

"I guess that means drinkin' at the bar's outta the question," Slade added.

"You can," Becs told them. "But I'm gonna call it a night." It was later than she'd intended, and she wanted to call Carly before she went to sleep.

"Me, too," Evan said before following her toward the elevator.

They were silent on the way up.

"I'm going to call Kaye," Evan said. "Check in with Sophia. You want to talk to Carly?"

"Absolutely."

While Evan talked to his daughter, Becs slipped into the bathroom and changed into her pajamas. She washed her face and pulled her hair up in a ponytail to keep it out of her face while she slept.

By the time she was finished, Evan was saying good night. He passed her the phone.

Becs put the phone to her ear at the same time Carly said, "Hey, Mommy."

"Hey, honey." She slid into the desk chair, smiling simply because she could hear her daughter's voice. "Did you have fun today?"

She listened as Carly rattled off everything they'd done during the day. Every single thing, including what they'd eaten—the pancakes they had for breakfast, the peanut butter and jelly sandwiches they had for lunch, and the macaroni and cheese they had for dinner.

"Sounds like you had a good day," Becs surmised.

"I did. When are you coming home?"

"Tomorrow, I think," she said.

"Really?" Carly squealed. "Yay."

Becs grinned. "I want you to be good for Kaye until then, all right?"

"Yes, Mommy. Sleep tight. Don't let the bed bugs bite."

Becs laughed. "Good night, honey."

The call disconnected, and she sat there for a moment, clutching Evan's phone.

"You okay?"

Realizing he'd come out of the bathroom, her gaze shot to him. He was wearing shorts, but unlike the other morning when she'd woken him to tell him she was leaving, Evan had on a T-shirt. A shame, really. The guy looked really good without a shirt.

Pushing to her feet, she passed him his phone. "Yeah. Good night."

Before she reached the doorway to the bedroom, Evan called her name.

She turned slowly, holding her head up, hoping he wouldn't bring up the conversation they'd had last night. She didn't need him to tell her that now wasn't the right time for him to be in a relationship.

"Are *we* okay?" Evan asked, stepping toward her.

With her jaw set, she nodded.

His gaze shifted to her mouth, and Becs's heart slammed hard in her chest. She swallowed, then took a deep breath, trying to get air into her constricted lungs. When he looked at her like that, she could easily forget that she wanted to be friends. Or rather, that she didn't want to lose their friendship by starting something that would only end badly. And it would. Pessimism or not, Evan didn't want anything more from her, and Becs wasn't willing to risk their friendship for anything less than everything.

"I'm sorry if I did something to upset you," he said softly.

"You didn't," she whispered, staring into his eyes as he seemed to move even closer.

"I don't want to complicate things, Becs."

Evidently, he didn't realize he was sending some serious mixed signals. If he moved any closer, she was going to fall into him, and that complication was going to be inevitable.

His fingers swept along her jaw, and she gasped, hating that tears were forming.

"I can't stop thinking about you," he said, his voice soft and gravelly.

She swallowed again, her heart drumming in her ears. Becs wanted him to kiss her. She wanted to get lost in this man. For a brief moment, she even considered taking advantage of this one night they had. One night of passion would be more than enough. They could go back to being friends tomorrow.

Only Becs wasn't wired that way. She would fall in love with Evan even more than she already had, and if they made love, seeing him every day would be a heartache she didn't think she'd survive.

"Goodnight, Evan," she said, forcing the words from her mouth as she stepped back, reaching for the door to shut out the temptation once and for all.

Or at least it gave her the illusion that it did.

CHAPTER NINETEEN

Tuesday, August 9, 2022

IT WAS INTERESTING THAT HE USED TO sleep on hard cots in foreign countries more often than not, and now Brantley was uncomfortable in a plush, 4-star-hotel bed.

Sure, he'd napped for a few minutes earlier this evening when Reese had massaged his back, but that had never stopped him before. However, tonight, his brain wouldn't shut off. It was going ninety miles a minute, ticking off endless things he wanted to do/needed to do/should have done. None of it was important at this very moment. There was nothing he could accomplish from here in New York City, yet his brain didn't seem to give a shit.

So, when he didn't force his eyes closed, he would stare up at the ceiling, trying to figure out where the fuck Decker had disappeared to. More importantly, why?

Another twenty minutes passed, and Brantley glanced at the clock. It was 0147, which meant it was far too early to get up. If he'd been at home, perhaps he would, but not here. Not with Reese sleeping soundly beside him and Tesha snoozing on the blanket pallet Reese had created on the floor.

Brantley grinned. He loved how much Reese loved that dog. Just another side of the man Brantley had fallen hopelessly in love with. And they were getting married in thirty-nine days. He didn't even have to calculate anymore. He was tracking each day like a kid the week before Christmas.

That made him smile even more.

Only thirty-nine more days before—

His phone buzzed on the nightstand. He reached for it, not wanting the sound to wake Reese.

Brantley squinted at the brightly lit screen to see JJ's name and number.

She wouldn't be calling unless it was important. Only if she had a lead or if she were going into labor. Since she still had weeks to go before her due date, he had to hope this was about the case.

"Yeah," he answered softly.

"I hate to wake you, B, but Decker's phone just came online," she said urgently.

Brantley sat up, dropping his feet over the edge of the bed. "Where is he?"

"Believe it or not, he's only about ten minutes from you. Two miles from the hotel. A house in Chelsea. I just texted you the address. I'll see if I can get more information while you head that way."

"Thanks, JJ."

Brantley disconnected the call and tapped Reese's hip.

"Hmm?"

"Decker's phone's online. He's at a house in Chelsea. Come on. Get dressed."

"You want me to text the others?"

"No." Brantley wasn't about to wake them. Decker would either be there or he wouldn't. He didn't need the team with him to determine that.

Within minutes, they were dressed and in the SUV, Tesha panting happily from the backseat. While Reese pulled up the address on the navigation screen, Brantley exited the parking garage.

"Southwest on Seventh Avenue," Reese instructed.

Brantley turned right onto 7th, heading toward 55th Street.

"You're gonna turn right on twenty-first," Reese informed him. "Just past the Five Guys."

Brantley smirked. "Should I stop for food on the way back?"

"Maybe."

Brantley turned at the light.

"You're gonna turn left on 9th. It'll be the second cross street."

They passed 8th Street and down another block to 9th. Brantley had to wait at the light, and he felt his impatience gnawing at him. If they missed Decker, he was going to lose his fucking mind.

"Turn left on Twentieth," Reese instructed. "Should be the first street you come to."

At the light, Brantley turned left onto a narrow, one-way street. It was lined with parked cars and three- and four-story brick buildings—referred to as walk-ups—that were pressed together like pancakes. A couple of the buildings had scaffolding in front of them, signifying work was being done. There was a dumpster in the street in front of what looked to be a church. Most houses had steps leading to the front door, along with wrought iron fences blocking access to the basement and first-floor windows.

"It'll be on the left," Reese said as he skimmed the addresses.

They passed the church and then a small off-Broadway theater.

"Stop," Reese barked. "This is three-thirty-four, so only a few down is where Decker is. There was a spot a few houses back."

Thankfully, no one was behind him, so he backed up and parallel-parked in a small space between two Teslas. He turned off the headlights, and they sat for a moment.

"Let me scope the house first," Brantley told him.

"I'm comin' with you." Reese turned to look at Tesha in the backseat. "Lay."

She eased down into the lay position.

"Stay."

Brantley knew she wouldn't move from that spot until told otherwise.

Attempting to look like he was supposed to be walking down a residential street in the middle of the night, Brantley headed for the address JJ had given them. He stopped when he heard voices, keeping himself concealed behind a large tree.

Brantley glanced at Reese.

Reese nodded.

That was the house they were seeking. And those voices appeared to be coming from one of the lower floors. Maybe a basement apartment?

"Eddie, I told you, you can't keep doin' this."

That was definitely Decker.

The response was muffled, but it sounded like a female voice.

"I promise it'll be fine," Decker insisted.

"You can't make that promise. No one can," the woman hissed. "And you can't keep coming here. This is where I work. They depend on me to take care of their kids. If they see you…"

"I know," Decker said, his tone less aggressive. "I'm sorry."

"Please go," the woman insisted. "And don't come back."

"Seriously? That's how you're gonna play this? After everything I told you?"

Brantley listened, hoping to hear Eddie's voice. The only pieces he could catch were Decker's and the woman's.

"There's no other choice," she said harshly.

"Yes, there is. Come *on*, Eddie. You—"

"Stop, Deck. Please. Just stop."

When the voices went silent, Brantley backed up. Reese kept pace with him, moving until they reached the SUV. They slipped inside and waited.

"Good girl," Reese crooned to Tesha. "Relax."

Instantly, she sat up, her head between the seats as they waited for Decker.

"Are you gonna confront him?"

"Damn straight." Brantley saw no other way to handle this. Sniper 1 Security had sent a team looking for him. Someone had to set Decker straight because this was bullshit. You didn't go off the grid and leave everyone wondering where the fuck you were. Not when your job was sometimes dangerous, and the risk of being taken or killed was real.

Nine minutes passed before they saw Decker come out onto the sidewalk. He started in their direction, so Brantley waited until he was only feet from the SUV before he opened the door.

Instantly, Decker had his gun out and pointed directly at Brantley's chest.

"Relax, Deck. It's me."

"Brantley?"

"Yeah. Surprise."

"Jesus Christ. Don't do that shit," Decker growled.

"Do what shit? *Find* you?"

Decker slowly lowered the weapon, tucking it into the holster at his back. "What the fuck are you doing here?"

"I'll give you three guesses," Brantley snapped. "What the fuck are *you* doing here?"

Decker glanced down the sidewalk in the direction he'd come from. "Not here."

"Oh, hell no," Brantley told him when he started walking. "You get in the car, or I'm gonna knock on that door and wake up the whole fuckin' house until I get the answers I'm lookin' for."

Decker's dark eyes narrowed, but he finally huffed and got in the backseat.

"Hey, girl," Decker greeted Tesha.

Brantley looked at them in the rearview mirror. "If he tries to get out, attack him, Tesha."

She wasn't an attack dog, but Brantley didn't care. If Decker tried to bolt, he was going to attack the mother fucker.

Brantley pulled out of the parking spot and headed down the street toward the light.

"Who's Eddie?" Reese asked, forgoing pleasantries.

"What?"

Brantley glanced in the rearview to see Decker's eyebrows slammed down over his eyes.

"We heard you talkin' to a woman," Reese explained. "But who's Eddie? Her husband? Her brother?"

Brantley was still looking back, so he noticed the relief that smoothed out Decker's features.

"Brother," Decker said.

It was a lie.

Brantley had interrogated enough people to know when a man was lying. And Decker had gone from sheer panic to instant relief, his answer coming far too quickly. He was lying.

"No," Decker said when Brantley flipped on his turn signal. "Go down to Sixth. There's construction on Eighth."

Brantley turned off the signal and waited for the light to turn green.

"Who's Eddie?" Brantley asked.

"A friend."

"What's this friend running from?"

Decker huffed. "Running? What makes you think … he's running?"

"Why else would you go off the grid?"

"I wasn't *off the grid*," Decker countered. "I told Z I had some shit to take care of."

"So why'd he call us in a panic?"

"You'll have to ask him."

Brantley fully intended to because, based on Decker's reaction, Z knew exactly where Decker was and possibly what he'd been doing.

Which meant they'd been played.

"DID YOU FIND HIM?" JJ ASKED WHEN she answered her phone two hours after she'd given Brantley directions to Decker's phone.

"Yeah."

"Why don't you sound happy?"

"I'll explain it all when we get back to Texas."

"So that means you're comin' back? Today?"

"Yep. If Z did his part."

"I'll check with him," JJ told him.

"Wake his fuckin' ass up if you have to."

JJ didn't need to see Brantley's face to know he was seething.

"Is Decker comin' with you?"

"I told him to meet us at the airport at fourteen hundred. If his ass doesn't show up, he's no longer my problem."

JJ could hear the frustration in Brantley's tone, but considering it was the middle of the night, she didn't figure it was a good time to ask him for details.

"Okay. I'll call Z, make sure your transpo is arranged. Let me know when y'all are on the way back."

"Will do. Oh, and JJ."

"Yeah?"

"Thanks. We couldn't've done this without you."

She knew that wasn't true, but she liked that Brantley said it. More specifically, she liked that he believed it.

Decker Bromwell sat in his rental car, which was still parked on Eddie's street. He was trying to determine whether he needed to go back and warn Eddie that his team had been too damn close for comfort. He knew if he did, Eddie would panic, and rightfully so.

Brantley and Reese showing up hadn't been in the plan. Nor had Z's betrayal. He had no idea why his boss/friend would've betrayed him like that but sending the Off the Books team to New York could've cost him everything. Hell, it could've cost Eddie everything.

He felt his face flame from his anger, and he grabbed his phone and dialed. He didn't give a fuck what time it was.

"Tavoularis."

"What is your fuckin' problem? How could you do that?"

"Good to hear from you, too, Deck," Z said softly.

There was a rustling sound, then a squeak. Possibly from a door being closed. If he had to guess, Z was getting out of his warm, comfortable bed so he didn't wake his husband.

"Fuck you, Z. I told you, I've got this handled."

Z's voice was louder than before. "Yeah? It looks to me like you've got no fuckin' clue what you're doin'."

"Why? Because I don't jump when you snap your fingers? Jesus, Z. I told you I needed some time to figure it out."

"Did you?"

"Yeah. I told—"

"No. Did you figure it out?" Z barked.

"No. Not yet. But I will."

"No."

"No? What do you mean, no?"

"I want you on that plane tomorrow and back here."

"Here as in headquarters? Or here, as in Coyote Ridge?"

"Honestly, I don't give a shit."

Decker figured Z didn't care, but he knew the same couldn't be said for Brantley. No way was the man letting him back on the task force after this. Sad thing was, he understood.

"It's bad enough I can't keep Brantley and his team in line. I'm not lettin' you go rogue, too. You're off this for the time being, Deck."

"You can't do that."

"I just did."

"Goddammit, Z!"

Decker didn't get a chance to tell Z to shove his commands up his ass because the man hung up on him.

"Fuck," he snarled, gripping the steering wheel until his knuckles were white.

CHAPTER TWENTY

ATTICUS WAS PRETTY SURE BRANTLEY WAS A sadist.

What other reason was there for why their boss wanted them up at six o'clock in the morning for breakfast? Seriously.

Granted, Atticus had passed out early last night, but still. The day wasn't meant to be started until after sunrise, and from what he could tell, the sun wasn't up yet. Not for another half hour or so, anyway.

But Atticus was up. He wasn't sure Slade was, though. The man hadn't emerged from the bedroom yet, and Atticus needed to take a piss. He considered heading downstairs to the lobby and using the restroom down there, but he wasn't sure his bladder wouldn't burst before then, and he didn't look forward to explaining why he was standing in a puddle in the elevator.

Slade would just have to suck it up.

Atticus turned the knob to the door as slowly and as quietly as he could. The room beyond was dark, which meant Slade was still asleep. Atticus would give him until he finished in the bathroom, then he would stumble through like a bull in a china shop just to wake his ass up. It would serve him right.

He moved slowly to the bathroom and paused when he heard a soft grunt from the direction of the bed.

"Oh, God," Slade moaned. "Fuck. Suck me, Atticus."

Atticus's eyebrows shot up to his hairline. Was the guy dreaming? Or was he inviting Atticus to join him?

"Yeah. Like that." Slade gasped and sighed. "Just like that."

His eyes adjusted to the near pitch-blackness, and he made out Slade's outline in the bed. He certainly wasn't asleep. The blankets were shoved down to his knees, his hand was curled around his cock, and he was moving it up and down, his hips pumping upward on every third stroke.

"Suck harder … oh, yeah … I'm gonna come in your mouth."

Feeling flushed, Atticus hurried to the bathroom and closed the door, praying Slade didn't hear the door close. He leaned against it, dragging deep gulps of air into his lungs. He fumbled for the switch on the wall and flipped it. The room brightened instantly.

This had to be a dream. One of those inspired by the body's needs. He had to pee, so his brain worked that into the dream. No way had Slade said his name. No fucking way.

And if, by some strange chance, he was awake, Slade was fucking with him. Had to be. Hell, the other night, Slade's eyes had been glued to Becs's willowy body all damn night. No way was he jacking off, pretending Atticus was the one giving him pleasure.

He recalled the conversation he'd had with Carson. He could practically hear Carson's gruff baritone in his ears.

Sharin' a hotel room with another man. Should I be worried?

I don't know. You think Slade swings that way?

Rumor is he might've dipped his wick a time or two when he was with the missus. Kinky sex games or some shit. His wife was all about mixin' it up.

No way. Atticus hadn't believed it then, and he didn't believe it now. Slade wasn't gay. Atticus was asleep. That's what it was.

He moved to the sink and turned on the water.

Instantly, the urge to pee intensified. He went to the toilet and stared down, praying this wasn't a dream and he wasn't about to wet the fucking bed.

He relieved himself with a sigh, then flushed the toilet. No doubt that got Slade's attention because Atticus heard a thud on the other side of the door.

So if Atticus wasn't dreaming and Slade wasn't asleep … what the fuck was going on?

He turned back to the sink and washed his hands. He grabbed his toothbrush from the toiletry bag he'd stashed in here. He brushed his teeth while he stared at his reflection, frowning as his brain tried to process what he'd heard.

By the time he was finished, he had again convinced himself that Slade was fucking with him. Which meant Atticus had to pretend he hadn't heard. And why would he let Slade know anyway? It wasn't like he was interested. No, Atticus's interest was back in Coyote Ridge. A tall, handsome electrician who, according to the texts Atticus had received yesterday, was waiting patiently for Atticus's return.

Exhaling heavily, he put the travel cover on his toothbrush and tucked it into the bag. He stood at the door for another minute before he scrounged up the nerve to open it.

"You ready?" Slade prompted when Atticus emerged from the bathroom.

Atticus glanced at him, watching as Slade rummaged through his bag, not looking at Atticus.

"We've got fifteen minutes to get down there," Slade noted. "And you know Brantley's motto."

Oh, yeah. He knew it. "If you're early, you're on time. If you're on time, you're late," Atticus said, reciting the motto JJ drilled into everyone to protect them from Brantley's wrath.

"Exactly."

As he went to grab his clothes from his bag, Atticus had to wonder whether he'd imagined the whole damn thing.

THERE WAS A REASON EVAN DIDN'T SLEEP on the sofa. Every time he did, he woke up with knots in his back.

This morning was no different. It took ten minutes to get to his feet after stretching as much as possible to contort his body back into something resembling normal.

Not that the sofa bed hadn't been comfortable. Truth was, Evan had slept pretty well. He'd passed out to thoughts of Becs in the next room. It had been his only option when his brain drifted wildly out of control. When he started thinking about slipping into that big bed with Becs, he'd shut the thoughts down and started counting backward from five hundred. He couldn't remember what number he'd stopped on, but it worked.

The door to Becs's room opened, and she stepped out. "The bathroom's free if you need it."

"Thanks," he grumbled, scratching his chin.

"I'm gonna head down."

She didn't even look at him when she spoke.

"Becs?"

She didn't turn around, her hand already on the door handle. "You want me to order you coffee?"

"That'd be great."

With that, she slipped out, leaving Evan to stare after her.

He knew he'd fucked up last night when he'd nearly kissed her. It hadn't been intentional. He simply couldn't help himself. Ever since their kiss in his kitchen, he'd been thinking about her non-stop—more than he had before, which had been all the damn time, too.

But now his thoughts involved kissing her, and clearly, they weren't on the same page anymore.

"Shit," he grumbled as he headed for the bathroom.

Fifteen minutes later, Evan emerged, showered, shaved, and ready for the day. He grabbed his phone and the room key Becs had given him, then ventured down to the hotel's restaurant to meet the rest of the team.

He was the last to arrive, which caused all eyes to shift to him. He didn't bother looking at his watch. He wasn't late, but he was cutting it close.

"Mornin'," Reese greeted as Evan pulled out a chair.

"Good morning," he replied, dropping into the seat beside Slade, skimming all the faces at the table to see if he could determine what he'd missed. If Atticus's bored expression was anything to go by, he hadn't missed anything yet.

"I ordered for you," Slade told him.

Evan had been partnered with Slade long enough that the guy knew what he ate for breakfast. Most of the time, it was toast and coffee, but when he went all out, he preferred his eggs over easy and his hash browns extra crispy.

"We're heading back today," Brantley announced as Evan took his first sip of coffee. "We found Deck last night."

All heads snapped in the boss's direction, which told Evan that news hadn't been shared before his arrival.

"Where was he?" Atticus asked.

"Is he all right?" Becs asked.

Brantley nodded at Becs and answered Atticus with, "A house in Chelsea."

Becs looked at Evan.

He smiled at her. "You were on the right track."

"Right track?" Reese asked.

Becs recapped their eventful evening.

"You were even closer than you thought," Brantley noted. "We found him on Twentieth Street."

And they'd been on 23rd. Definitely close.

"Was he okay?" Becs's tone was rife with worry.

"Perfectly fine," Brantley grumbled. "He was on his own. Willingly."

A complete waste of time, then.

Not that it would do him any good to let it bother him. During his career in law enforcement, he'd chased down many leads that had gotten him nowhere. That was part of it. When searching for someone, you did what was necessary to get the result you wanted. And since finding Decker had been the ultimate objective, they could count this as a win. Even if he hadn't been missing as Z had thought.

"He's meetin' us at the airport," Reese relayed, probably to keep Brantley from getting angrier than he already was.

Evan understood. They'd wasted so much time looking for a man who wasn't missing but rather hiding that they'd neglected other cases that could benefit from the time they dedicated to them.

"Is he comin' back to the task force?" Atticus asked.

Evan watched Brantley and Reese, waiting for an answer.

"Fuck no," Brantley said firmly. "He can go back to Dallas."

For some reason, that made Evan feel a little better.

Based on Reese's expression, he hadn't been expecting Brantley's harsh response.

And his partner must've sensed the silent question because Brantley elaborated, looking at each of them as he spoke. "I know we've all got personal shit that takes us away from the job. That's expected. You prioritize the way you need to. But you don't do it like this. You don't run off and tell no one where you're goin'. I don't have a problem with you needin' time off. Take it. But tell me where you're goin', and by God, be there when I'm lookin' for you. Understood?"

No one spoke, but heads nodded all around.

Evan respected Brantley for his straightforwardness. He would tell it like it was, making it simpler for those around him to follow. Evan understood why Brantley didn't want Decker working for him. Considering he couldn't bother to call to say he was all right, Evan figured that was for the best. A team was only as good as its weakest member. And the last thing they needed was someone who might disappear when they needed him most.

"You've got the next few hours free," Reese said. "Check-out's at nine, so be sure to do that, then we'll meet at the airport at fourteen hundred. We'll leave an hour before in case you want to ride with us."

Evan noticed Becs checking her watch. A second later, her eyes were practically glowing as she looked at Atticus. "You wanna go check out the sights with me?"

"Love to."

And that told Evan all he needed to know about where he stood with her.

AS SOON AS JJ WALKED INTO THE barn, she looked around, eager for the team to arrive so she could tell them it was time to move on from this case. They had done what they'd set out to do—find Decker Bromwell—and while he hadn't actually been missing, they had succeeded. Brantley and Reese had confirmed his whereabouts and instructed him to come home. That was the most they could hope for.

Unfortunately, no one was there. Not even Darius, who was known to sneak in early to see if he could beat her.

Her gaze shifted to the electronic board mounted to the wall. Someone had left it on last night, and the screen showed a photo of Decker and a few bits of personal information. It was the official file they'd created for him to track the various pieces of information they gathered. It was stored on a shared drive and backed up in the cloud so everyone had access.

With coffee cup in hand—the only caffeine she was allowed for the day—she walked over to it and tapped the screen to bring up the full details of the file.

JJ stepped back and stared at it, impressed by how much information they'd ascertained in such a short time. Far more than she would've wanted someone to find out about her if she hadn't truly been missing, that was for sure.

A moment later, the door opened behind her.

"All good?" Baz asked.

"Yep. Just lookin' at the fruits of our labor."

"You want your bag upstairs?"

She glanced at him over her shoulder and smiled. "Yes, please."

While he carried her laptop bag upstairs to her office, JJ skimmed the information on the screen, then clicked on the icon for the timeline of events. It started with a phone call from Z on Sunday, August 7th. That call played in her head as she looked at the screen. Z had sounded worried. Not quite frantic. More like frustrated. And definitely determined to find one of his missing agents.

The team then went to New York, also noted on the timeline. They'd met with Ronan Kavanagh, who also hadn't sounded worried, JJ recalled. Considering the information they'd received had said his sister was missing, that was when it had started to go off course. At least for her. Had Z attempted to determine Saoirse's whereabouts, or had he assumed she was missing since he hadn't heard from Decker? And why would he assume anything?

There'd been a definite change in Z's attitude once the team landed in New York. As time went by, he hadn't sounded quite as concerned for Decker's well-being. Because Brantley was on the case? Or for another reason altogether?

What had changed for him because, based on this timeline, nothing had changed for them until the very last second. It was as though Z had known something all along. Something he hadn't told them about.

Had Z found out where Decker was and didn't want to own up to sending them for no reason? Or had Z known more than he was letting on in the beginning? Something about the whole setup felt off to her. Like they'd been used. But why would Z do that? Maybe he thought they would come up empty, and he could check off the box saying he'd done his due diligence. But they'd never failed him before, so why them? And why now?

JJ clicked out of the timeline and glanced at the dark line that connected Decker's photo to an image of his high school. She clicked on the image to bring up the notes she'd added. Like Baz, no one else thought the connection Decker might have with Kylie Walker was significant. Luca had chalked it up to coincidence. JJ knew better. There was nothing coincidental about Decker joining the task force. For one, they'd had numerous applicants, yet Z had insisted they add Decker to the team. Why? What value had he added while he was there? He'd helped on a few cases, but he hadn't done anything extraordinary.

Footsteps sounded on the stairs. JJ quickly closed the screen, taking it back to the image of Decker and the lines that connected all the notes they'd added.

"You need me to do anything for you before I call Charlie?" Baz asked.

"No," JJ said, skimming the screen. "I'm gonna—why do they do this? I bet it was Luca. Probably an acronym for something stupid."

She stepped forward and tapped the image of a Post-it note with the initials A B. When a file didn't have a photo, there was a Post-it icon to note there was information in it. She tapped on it.

As soon as the screen changed, she stepped back and gasped. "What the fuck?"

"Is that a picture of Allison Bogart?" Baz asked, coming to stand beside her.

"Yeah," JJ muttered as she read the notes, which provided her nothing. Nothing of importance anyway. Basic information they'd already had when she applied to join the task force.

"JJ..."

She looked at Baz. "What?"

"Let it go."

She frowned. "Let it go? Seriously? You want to say that to me after you find out that somehow, some way, there's a connection between Decker Bromwell and Allison Bogart?"

"Maybe it was misfiled," he said, but she heard the skepticism in his tone. He didn't believe that for a second.

"It wasn't," she assured him.

"It's done, JJ. They found Decker. That was the job. Right now, we've got other things to focus on."

"Like what? What could possibly be more important than figuring—"

"Brantley and Reese's wedding," he said, cutting her off.

Oh. Right. The wedding that was taking place in thirty-nine days. She had countdown blocks on her desk to remind her that time was running out to plan her best friend's big day.

"Not to mention, a peanut to be born shortly after that."

JJ took a deep breath and looked back at the screen.

"If you start digging into that"—Baz's tone was smooth and even—"you and I both know you won't stop. At the cost of all else. And right now, I think the last thing we need is to deviate from the path."

He was right. They'd already gone off course simply finding Decker. They'd been pulled away from almost every case they worked on to focus their efforts elsewhere. Now that Decker was found, they had more important things to focus on.

"And if Brantley or Reese get wind of it..." JJ said softly.

She knew they would want to know how they connected. Allison Bogart had been with the task force for too brief a time to even resonate in their memory, so the fact her name was in the notes meant that someone had come across it while researching Decker. That meant there was a thread to pull, so it didn't matter if it was now or a month or two from now, she would be able to pick up where someone else left off.

Baz put his hand on her shoulder and gently squeezed.

"You're right." JJ stepped forward and closed the file. She went one step further and added a password lock so it couldn't be accessed or deleted. If someone wanted to see it, they would have to find her.

In the meantime, she would do her best not to think about it.

Based on the expression on Baz's face, she knew he realized the same way she did that that was impossible.

CHAPTER TWENTY-ONE

"DID YOU NOTICE THE CHILL AT BREAKFAST?"

Brantley looked around, confused. They hadn't even gone outside, so how would he have noticed it was cooler? "What?"

"The tension? Between Evan and Becs?"

Brantley smiled. "You know, one day, you're gonna realize I don't pick up on that shit like you do."

"Sure you don't." Reese rolled his eyes.

"Fine. Maybe I noticed. But if you haven't noticed, I'm doing my best to keep my nose out of their personal lives. I've got more important things to focus on. Like you."

Reese's chin tucked downward, and Brantley knew he was blushing.

"You enjoy that, don't you? Makin' me blush?"

Brantley responded with a grin. Damn right, he enjoyed it. Why wouldn't he?

Reese shook his head and rolled his eyes playfully. "I'm gonna take Tesha to Central Park again. Figure I'll give her a couple of hours to sniff around. You wanna come with us?"

"Of course I do."

"If we go now, we'll have plenty of time to check out before they come in and kick us out."

Brantley fell into step with Reese, heading for the door leading to the street. "Do you think there's a problem between Evan and Becs?"

"I don't have a clue. I figure I'll check in with her when she gets back from sightseein' with Atticus. I told them to store their things with the concierge or in the SUV."

"That's why Atticus wanted the keys," Brantley mused.

The walk to Central Park took twenty minutes. It was rush hour for a lot of people, so the streets were crowded with vehicles, and the sidewalks were crammed with bodies hurrying toward their destination. Thankfully, it wasn't quite so bad when they reached the park. At least not once they'd made it into the park, past those looking to make a quick buck off unsuspecting tourists. They deviated from the main road and onto one of the secondary paths.

"Are you good with how this ended with Decker?"

Brantley was surprised that Reese asked but not surprised by the question. It was the same one he'd asked himself this morning after he explained what had happened to the team. The whole thing felt anti-climactic. It should've been a good feeling since Decker was alive and well, but Brantley still had reservations about how it all went down.

"No," he admitted. "I think there's somethin' goin' on that Z's not telling us. I don't appreciate being used to further whatever agenda they've got."

"You think that's what this is?"

"Yeah."

"You've got JJ lookin' into it, don't you?"

Brantley had expected Reese to ask him that, so he'd stopped himself before calling JJ and asking her to stick with it. They had too many things going on right now to worry about Z's motivations. Brantley was sure he had his reasons. As for whether they were altruistic or not wasn't his business. The guy was technically their boss. He could send them wherever he wanted.

"No, I don't," he said honestly. "I wanted to. I even thought about it, but there's too much goin' on right now for her to go down that path. Hell, she's still stuck on findin' the woman she suspects to be Harrison Rivers's first victim. Last thing I need is for her to get swept up in something else."

"So you won't be lookin' into findin' out who this Eddie person is?"

Brantley smirked. Reese knew him all too well. "I didn't say that. But I intend to keep it from JJ for as long as possible."

"Are you gonna ask Luca to help?"

Brantley cocked an eyebrow and looked at Reese. "Seriously? And risk JJ's wrath when she finds out I went behind her back?"

Reese laughed. "Fair point."

"No. I think I'll keep this one between us for now." He linked his fingers together and pressed his hands out in front of him. "I might surprise you, Tavoularis. Maybe I'll become a hacker extraordinaire."

Another laugh bellowed out of Reese. "Sure you will."

Reese released Tesha from her leash while Brantley dug a tennis ball from one of his cargo pockets and handed it to Reese.

When Tesha took off after it, Brantley turned to Reese. "Do you know something I don't? About Z or Decker and whatever this is?"

Reese met his gaze. "I wish I did. I don't have a clue what Z's up to, but I'm with you. I think somethin's goin' on."

"Does it bother you that he sent us on a wild goose chase?"

Reese's expression darkened. "It's not the chase that bothered me so much."

"It was the circumstance," Brantley supplied.

"Yeah." Reese exhaled heavily. "I can't say I've minded the trip. But I don't like spinnin' my wheels any more than you do."

Brantley was more worried that this particular case had stirred up bad memories for Reese. He knew Reese had been worried that Decker had been taken, and then the worst-case scenarios began to run through his head. Now that they'd seen that Decker was fine, he would be able to move past it. Or pretend he had, anyway.

Brantley figured Reese would never truly move forward until he dealt with what happened to him during his captivity. He didn't know the details, but he knew enough to worry.

"When you're ready to talk about it," Brantley told him. "I'm here to listen."

Reese's gaze snapped to his face. Surprise registered.

"What? You didn't think I'd put two and two together? Come on, Reese. I'm not as obtuse as you think I am."

"I don't think that," Reese countered adamantly.

"No, but you think I don't notice the small things." Brantley met his stare. "When it comes to you, I notice *everything*."

Reese's Adam's apple bobbed in his throat as he looked away. "I've dealt with it."

It was a lie. They both knew it, but Brantley nodded. "Okay."

And just like anytime the emotions started churning too deep, they both locked it up inside and pretended they were fine. It was how you made it through the day when you'd been through a traumatic ordeal. As long as you didn't think about it or talk about it, you could pretend it never happened.

Until you couldn't.

SLADE WAS PACKING UP THE REST OF his things when there was a knock on his hotel room door. He glanced at the clock, ensuring he hadn't passed checkout time. He hadn't, which meant the knock was likely his partner's.

He opened the door to find Evan standing in the hallway, head hung down, bag slung over one shoulder.

"Give me a minute. I need to finish packin'."

"How much shit did you bring with you?" Evan chuckled as he stepped into the room.

"Hardly anything. My problem's not the amount of stuff. It's procrastination."

"You're good at that."

Yes, he was. And today, he was proving it. Ever since he'd woken up this morning, he'd been off. He knew exactly the reason, but he was doing his best to pretend that it hadn't happened. Because if it had … if Atticus had come into the room while Slade was … doing what he'd been doing…

Had he heard him? Did Atticus know that Slade was fantasizing about…?

Shit. He didn't want to think about that.

"What's up?" Evan asked. "You're acting weird."

"You're one to talk. You go first."

Evan glanced around. "Atticus isn't here, is he?"

"Nope. Packed up, then took his stuff and left with Becs."

Evan huffed and dropped onto the couch, which was no longer pulled out into a bed.

Slade wasn't surprised by the silence that followed. He could tell Evan wanted to talk, but he had to prepare himself for that. Slade never had that problem. He tended to vomit up his emotional baggage whenever he felt like it. Often at the expense of those around him.

Finally, Evan exclaimed, "I kissed Becs."

Slade stopped moving and turned to look at his partner/friend. "Last night?"

Evan shook his head. "No. The other night. Before she left for New York."

"At your house?"

Evan nodded.

"Did anything else happen?"

"No."

"So why exactly do you look like your nuts are in a vise?"

Sure, Slade understood the concept of blue balls, but from a single kiss? Or maybe Evan was suffering since he'd been pining for this woman for so long. One kiss could've sent him right over the edge.

Evan's forehead pinched. "You know, you could use some less disturbing comparisons."

"Touché. Now answer the question. Was it terrible or what?"

Evan stared at his hands in his lap. "It was incredible."

"One kiss?"

"Yeah."

"Then my question still stands? Why do you look like—"

"Because she thinks I'm having second thoughts."

Knowing Evan, he was. Hell. He was probably having third and fourth thoughts. The guy spent far too much time thinking.

But Slade asked anyway. "Are you?"

"No."

"Really?"

"You sound skeptical," Evan grumbled.

"Because I know you."

"Fine. I was."

"Past tense?"

"Am," Evan corrected.

"So she was right to think that."

"No," Evan stated firmly. "She didn't know that at the time."

"Maybe she picked up on it."

Evan looked up. "She couldn't have. She left for New York, and I hadn't talked to her. Then, when I did, she said she wasn't expecting anything from me."

"Are you expectin' somethin' from *her*?"

Based on the single-shoulder shrug Evan gave, it was apparent he had been.

"I screwed it up," Evan muttered. "I screwed it up before I even had a chance with her."

Yeah, well, Slade knew a little bit about that. He was pretty sure he'd done the same thing just a few hours ago.

"There's always time to make it right," he told his friend, even though he didn't think that was the case for himself. "At least as long as she's talkin' to you."

And as long as she didn't walk in on you masturbating while calling out her name.

Slade felt his face grow warmer. For the past few months, he'd hidden his secret infatuation with Atticus. Mostly because he didn't understand it himself. He barely liked the guy. How the fuck could he want to…to… To do whatever his dirty mind could conjure up. And Jesus. Some of those fantasies he'd been having were downright raunchy.

Evan was looking at him, and Slade prayed he hadn't said any of that aloud.

"I probably shouldn't be talking to you about this."

Slade frowned. "What? Why? We're friends. That's what friends do."

Evan's eyes raked over his face as though he were looking for the truth. The man's next words explained why.

"Atticus mentioned you couldn't take your eyes off her at the club."

Shit.

He'd honestly hoped Evan wouldn't bring it up. It hadn't been like that. Yes, he had stared at Becs. Partly because he'd never seen her dress like that, and she was hot when she dressed up. But mostly, he'd stared at her so he wouldn't risk staring at Atticus. It was one thing to do it in the office because he could claim to be lost in thought about a case. It was something else entirely when they were out in public.

"Do you…?" Evan lifted a shoulder and dropped it. "Do you have a thing for her?"

"No."

"Something tells me that's a lie."

Slade chuffed a mirthless laugh, then walked over to the upholstered armchair and flopped down into it. "Can I tell you somethin'?"

"If it's about you and Becs, no."

"It's not." Slade could feel Evan's eyes boring into him. "It's about someone else."

"I didn't realize there was someone else."

"There's not."

"So it *is* about Becs?"

Slade groaned. He didn't want to tell Evan this, but he knew if he didn't, the guy would continue to hound him about Becs. Knowing Evan, he would use Slade as an excuse for not seeing where things went with her. Slade had known for a while now that Evan was attracted to her. That was the only explanation for the way he tried to keep ten feet between them at all times.

"I don't have the hots for your girl."

"She's not—"

"I've got the hots for … for … Atticus," he blurted.

That shut Evan up quickly.

Slade could feel those all-seeing eyes drilling through him, and he couldn't bear to meet the man's gaze.

"I didn't realize…"

"What? That I'm gay?"

"Well … yeah."

"I'm not." He took a deep breath in through his nose and exhaled before looking at Evan. "Well, I am, but I'm not. I like women, too. Just not always as much as I—Jesus fuck. I can't believe I'm tellin' you this."

"You're bisexual?"

"Yes. No. Maybe. It's more of a…" Slade wasn't even sure how to describe it. "A situational attraction."

Evan chuckled. "So you're confused?"

"More than you know, man. More than you know."

Evan nodded his head as he stared at Slade.

"Don't act like it makes sense because it doesn't," Slade told him. "It wasn't until the other night at Moonshiners when I saw Atticus talkin' to Spencer that I realized this thing … it's become an obsession." Slade met Evan's gaze. "Shit. You don't want to hear about this."

"Of course I do. That's what friends do, right? They spill their guts."

"Don't mock me," he said without heat.

"I'm not." Evan sat up straight. "Honest to God. I want to know."

"Please don't say anything. It'll pass. I know it will."

"Do you want it to?"

Slade answered honestly. "Yeah."

"Why?"

"Because the last thing I want is to find myself in over my head the way I was with my ex-wife. Once in my lifetime is more than enough for me."

"So when you were with Jennifer…"

"Did I like men?" Slade said for him.

"Yeah."

Slade considered his answer for all of a second, then blurted out the truth. "Jennifer's the one who made me realize I liked men in the first place."

Evan's forehead creased. "How'd she do that?"

"She introduced me to my first bisexual encounter."

"Oh."

Yeah. That was a good word for it. Jennifer had enlightened him about sex in many, *many* ways.

"I think once we're back home and I've got shit to keep me busy, I'll move past it," Slade told Evan, although if that were true, he would've moved on already. He'd been telling himself the same damn thing for the past two months.

Slade had a history of getting attached and latching on for long periods. It had happened with Jennifer and almost happened with one other person after that, and now Atticus. It was a trend. A sickness, if you will. Slade knew it wasn't healthy to form that sort of obsessive attachment to anyone.

Evan obviously picked up on the fact Slade was done with this conversation because he said, "We've got a couple of hours before we leave. You want to do anything before then?"

Drink himself stupid. That was what he wanted to do, but Slade said, "Find a souvenir shop. I wanna get my momma somethin'."

Evan stood. "Cool. Let's do that then."

AS THE PLANE PREPARED TO TOUCH DOWN in Texas, Evan bolstered the courage to talk to Becs. For the past four hours, he'd sat within hearing distance of her, but she hadn't said a single word to him. When she wasn't flipping through pictures she'd taken during her brief sight-seeing tour with Atticus, she was talking to the man. From what he gathered, they'd had fun, and it looked like they'd forged a friendship from the adventure.

Could've been you.

That voice in his head had been mocking him with shit like that for the past several hours. Yeah, yeah, yeah. He could've offered to take her to see the sights. He probably should've. He didn't. His loss, he knew.

One of the pilots came over the speaker to announce they would be landing soon and to buckle their seat belts. Since it was a private jet, no attendants would be marching up and down the aisle to ensure they were doing as they were told. Even so, everyone clipped their belts. Everyone except Atticus who decided he needed to use the restroom first.

Or at least that was what he appeared to do, but based on the glance he shot Evan, the one that said, *Now's your chance, idiot,* his move was intentional.

Taking the cue, Evan got up and switched seats.

Becs was once again looking at pictures, but her head snapped up when she realized he wasn't Atticus.

"Are you coming to the house to pick up Carly?"

Her eyebrows furled. "Of course."

Great. And now she thought he was hounding her about her parenting skills.

"You want to grab some food first?"

She chewed on her bottom lip for a moment, then shook her head. "No. I'll have dinner with Carly. I've missed her."

"Understood."

Evan sat quietly for a minute. Then another. And another until the silence was so thick not even the deafening sound of the plane's engines could drown it out.

There were a thousand things he wanted to say to her, but he blew it by what came out of his mouth next.

"Would you mind if I got a ride with you to my house?"

Her pretty blue eyes skimmed his face briefly before she plastered on a smile. It was a fake one. Like you give the delivery guy when he brings your order earlier than expected.

"Sure."

"Thanks."

As he sat there waiting for the plane to deposit them safely on the ground, Evan felt eyes on him. He looked at Decker, but the guy had his head back, eyes closed. He hadn't said a word the entire flight. Not him.

He glanced over to see Slade staring at him, a worried expression on his face.

Or perhaps that was discomfort that was creasing his brow.

Maybe it had something to do with the fact that Atticus was sitting beside him now, and Slade wanted to rip Evan a new one for putting him in that position.

As much as he wanted to worry about his partner's unrequited obsession with the new guy, Evan was more concerned about the state of his friendship with Becs. It was hard to believe that a few ill-timed sentences could take them from that incredible kiss to the blizzard of the century. She was freezing him out, and he couldn't deny that he deserved it.

He wanted to make it up to her. But how? He had no idea what would make this situation better.

He didn't even know why it mattered to him. His interest in this woman went against every promise he'd made to himself since Gayle was murdered. He swore he wouldn't allow himself to be truly happy until he found the bastard who killed his wife and at least seven other women that they knew of. At the very least, Evan owed her that.

It was the very reason he had joined the task force. He'd hoped to utilize their skills to hunt down the man responsible for the brutal rape and murder of young, unsuspecting women. The police and FBI had been at it for years, but based on the information he received from the friends he'd left behind in Florida, they'd gotten nowhere. The consensus was the serial murderer had gone into hiding. Or maybe he was dead.

That should've been good news. But for Evan, it simply meant he would never get any closure.

"Hey." Becs's cool fingers brushed over his wrist. "Are you okay?"

Realizing he was clutching the armrest like his life depended on it, he forced his hands to relax.

"Are you a nervous flyer?"

"What?" Evan shook his head, realizing she thought his tension had something to do with the plane landing. "No."

"Sorry," she whispered, pulling her hand back.

He realized he'd snapped his response. "No." He reached over and touched her hand. "I'm sorry. I was thinking about something. I—"

Evan had no idea what he'd intended to say. But he knew one thing. If he wanted a life, any life at all, he was going to have to renew his efforts to finding that sick bastard who killed Gayle. Perhaps then he'd be capable of giving a woman like Becs everything she deserved.

CHAPTER TWENTY-TWO

Wednesday, August 10, 2022

Reese had been expecting it, so he wasn't surprised when he woke up on Wednesday to find Brantley's head covered with a pillow. His breathing was shallow, which signified he was in tremendous pain.

There was very little light in the room; only the glow from the front porch light breached the slats of the blinds, but he knew it was more than enough to increase the pain if Brantley were to open his eyes.

Being as quiet as he could, he got out of bed and went to the bathroom. He grabbed the bottle of pills from the medicine cabinet and shook one out into his hand. He filled the glass he kept by the sink with enough water for Brantley to down one of the pills. Last but not least, he soaked a washcloth with cold water, wrung it out, and then took everything into the bedroom.

He put his hand gently on Brantley's shoulder, not wanting to surprise him.

"Keep your eyes closed," he instructed as he moved the pillow.

Brantley grunted.

"Here," he whispered. "Take this."

Reese covered Brantley's eyes with the washcloth and put the pill in Brantley's mouth. He held the glass to Brantley's lips, helping as much as possible.

Once that was done, Reese set out to take care of everything else. He closed the heavy curtains he'd hung a couple of months ago. The very curtains Brantley had made fun of him for adding. Reese had taken the good-natured ribbing just like had with all the upgrades he'd done to the house, not telling Brantley that he'd added the curtains for this reason alone.

It pained him to see Brantley in agony. Especially since there wasn't anything anyone could do. There wasn't a magical potion that would make a migraine go away, but being in a dark, quiet room would help some, and hopefully, the medication would do the rest.

On his way out of the bedroom, he tapped the thermostat in the hallway down a couple of degrees, wanting to keep the room cool before going to the kitchen to grab a can from the refrigerator.

Tesha lifted her head to watch him move across the room.

"He'll be all right, girl. He just needs to sleep."

Reese returned to the bedroom with the can, easing it beneath Brantley's neck, knowing the cold pressure would alleviate some of the pain.

When he returned, Tesha was sitting on the couch, focusing on the hallway. She had slept soundly last night, curled up on the couch, glad to be back home. He got the feeling she knew Brantley wasn't feeling well because she didn't jump up with excitement, instead watching the hallway as though that might make Brantley emerge sooner.

"It's just you and me, girl," Reese told Tesha as he grabbed his shoes from the closet in the hallway.

Reese had learned to stash clothing around the house so he didn't have to bother Brantley when he was like this. If they were lucky, Brantley would get up in a few hours. If not, it would be dinnertime before the headache subsided. Reese intended to ensure no one interrupted Brantley in the interim.

"Come on, girl. Let's go for a run."

An hour and a half later, after their run and after Reese took a shower in the guest bathroom, he was dressed and ready for the day. He didn't cook breakfast because the scents could make Brantley nauseous. Instead, he grabbed a plastic tub of cantaloupe and grapes for himself, as well as Tesha's food, and took both to the barn. He settled Tesha in with her breakfast before starting the coffee.

The team hadn't arrived yet, but he knew JJ and Baz would be coming shortly. He'd closed the curtain on the back door to signal that they shouldn't come in. It was something JJ had suggested to ensure they didn't walk in on something that would make her want to bleach her eyes out. Her words. Brantley had teased her relentlessly since JJ was prone to joking about *wanting* to watch them.

The thought made Reese smile as he realized Brantley never did close that curtain. If Reese didn't know better, Brantley figured the simple fact someone could walk in at any time made their mid-day encounters hotter. He wasn't wrong.

Reese had just poured his first cup of coffee when the door opened.

"When did it start?" JJ asked, her forehead creased with worry.

"He didn't wake me up, so I don't know."

"Poor Brantley." Her attention shifted to Tesha, and she grinned from ear to ear. "Hey, girl. You miss me?"

Reese watched as JJ knelt to give Tesha hugs and kisses and sneak her a treat, as though Reese couldn't see her.

When she stood up, she noticed he had been watching.

"What?" she said with a smile. "Ramona has been experimenting with dog-friendly treats. I picked it up on my way here."

He knew that if Ramona Weber, the owner of Batter & Bliss, was cooking treats for dogs, it was because JJ had asked her to.

"So what did you do with Deck?" JJ asked as the door opened and Baz strolled in carrying her bag and a box filled with what could only be donuts.

"He took the jet to Dallas," Reese told her, then looked at Baz. "I made coffee."

"Thanks."

JJ pulled out a chair beside the box of donuts and sat. "Did he say anything on the flight home?"

"He did not."

"Did B interrogate him?"

"No."

"Is he mad? Brantley, I mean."

"He's not thrilled." Reese understood Brantley's frustration with Decker. Not because of whatever he'd been doing but of how he'd gone about it. Going off the grid was stupid and reckless. At the very least, he could've maintained his check-ins, and no one would've been the wiser.

Reese watched as JJ took a donut from the box. Her gaze bounced from Baz to Reese to Tesha, then to the donut in her hand. She was stalling, but he couldn't imagine why.

"Did I forget to do something?" he asked when Baz disappeared into the small kitchenette for coffee.

"What?"

"You're actin' like you need to tell me somethin'. Did I forget to do somethin' on the checklist?"

"Oh." She flashed a smile. "Nope. The wedding's right on track."

That was a relief.

"For now," she amended. "You've got the tux fitting comin' up, and y'all need to get the marriage license. It's good for eighty-nine days, and we're well past that now, so whenever y'all can work it into the schedule."

Reese realized she wouldn't meet his eyes when she talked. He knew JJ well enough to know when she did that, she was hiding something.

"What else?" he prompted.

She took a bite, then looked up at him, her eyebrows lifting slowly. "Hmm?"

"What aren't you tellin' me?" Reese glanced back as Baz returned. "What's goin' on?"

JJ sighed.

"JJ." Baz exhaled. "We talked about this."

"I didn't say nothin'," she said around a mouthful of donut. "He's *Professor Xing* me."

"Professor X?" Reese guessed, not sure he was deciphering her words correctly. "What the hell does that mean?"

"You're reading her mind," Baz explained. "You know. *X-Men*."

Reese huffed, turning his attention back to JJ. She wouldn't meet his gaze.

"Tell me," he insisted.

"It can wait," Baz told him. "There's too much goin' on right now."

Reese narrowed his eyes and glanced between them. "What's it have to do with?"

"Decker," JJ blurted.

"What about him?"

Baz glared at JJ.

JJ glared at Baz.

A second later, she hopped up from her chair and waddled over to the electronic board they used when they were reviewing case files as a team. She quickly pulled up an image of Decker. She tapped on it, and several more pictures appeared, as well as file folder and Post-it note icons.

Reese watched as she clicked the Post-it that had the letters "A B" on it. A login prompt popped up, and she typed in a password.

As soon as the image appeared, Reese frowned, moving closer. "Is that…?"

"Allison Bogart," JJ filled in. "Yeah."

"Why do we have a picture of her?"

"That's a damn good question," JJ retorted, looking at Baz.

Reese skimmed the notes. "Who found this?"

"I assume Luca, but I don't know for sure."

Reese looked at both of them again. "Deck knows Allison?"

"Looks that way."

"Reese," Baz said, coming to stand between him and the board. "I really think this is somethin' we should hold off on lookin' into right now."

"Why?"

"Because there's a lot going on. Your wedding." He glanced at JJ. "The baby. If we start lookin'—"

"We might go down a rabbit hole," Reese said. "I agree."

"You do?" JJ exclaimed.

He definitely did. With the wedding roughly a month away and JJ's baby due in two and a half months, they couldn't afford to get sidetracked by something that could mean absolutely nothing.

"What if it has something to do with Kylie?" JJ asked.

Reese frowned. "Kylie's dead, JJ."

She swallowed, and her eyes rounded. "I know that."

"Then what would it matter?"

She shrugged.

It wouldn't. And that was the problem. Regardless of what the connection was, it didn't matter. It couldn't. Nothing was going to bring Kylie back. Certainly not Decker Bromwell or Allison Bogart.

"I told her to keep it but to put it aside for the time being," Baz explained.

"I agree." Reese looked at the screen again.

Even though he knew putting it aside for now was the right thing to do, Reese couldn't help wondering how that information came about. How the fuck was Decker connected to Allison? Obviously, it wasn't a coincidence that she'd applied to join the task force at the same time Z had assigned Decker to be on it. Reese had always wondered about her disappearing act. She hadn't done well on the only case she assisted with, and the next thing he knew, she was gone. Was this why? Had her interest in joining the team merely been a ruse?

And how the hell was it tied in with Decker?

"Close it," Baz told JJ.

She did.

Reese looked at her and waited until she met his gaze. He doubted for one second that JJ was going to let this go. It wasn't in her nature. And Baz had already admitted that he'd told her to keep it quiet, yet it was the first thing she told him when she saw him.

"Do not let Brantley get wind of this. Understood?"

JJ nodded, and Baz said, "We won't."

"I'm serious," he reiterated. "No matter what. He doesn't need to know. Not until after the wedding."

"Agree," JJ said softly.

Reese shook his head as he turned away. The last thing he wanted was for Brantley to get wind of this. There would be no stopping him from seeking the truth. But Baz was right. They had too much going on, and there was a good chance it was all a weird coincidence.

Sure it is. And the sky is green, grass is blue, pigs fly, and cats swim.

ATTICUS PULLED DOWN THE DRIVEWAY, BYPASSING THE two trucks parked by the house. The gate was open, which meant he wasn't the first to arrive, but that was always the case. He'd tried at least twice to get there before anyone else but failed both times. The error in his logic wasn't only because Reese and Brantley lived a few yards from their office, which meant they were technically always there.

No, he hadn't expected to beat them. But he had hoped to show up the rest of the team. Then he realized Baz and JJ were always there. Or it seemed they were, anyway. Atticus was dedicated and all, but he was not coming in at the ass-crack of dawn to try to get there before them. Sometimes, he was sure they'd stayed the night, maybe camped out on the couch in JJ's office.

He parked his truck inside the gate, ensuring he didn't get blocked in when everyone else arrived. As he made his way to the barn, he looked at the back of Brantley and Reese's house, noticing the curtain that covered the sliding glass door was covered. Based on deductive reasoning, that meant Brantley had one of his debilitating migraines. Evidently, Reese closed the curtain to ensure no one stopped by to chat.

Atticus kept walking, trying not to smile so much his cheeks hurt. It wasn't easy since he'd received a text message from Carson a short time ago telling him he wished he was waking up with him this morning. Atticus wished the same thing, but he was playing it safe. That was the only reason he hadn't gone to Carson's as soon as they touched down yesterday evening. Instead, he'd returned to his motel room and crashed, sleeping until his alarm went off at five.

And here he was.

He typed in his passcode, waited until the lock disengaged, and pulled open the door to the barn. As soon as he walked inside, he realized there was a reason people didn't come in that early. Baz, JJ, and Reese were standing at the electronic board, an animated conversation taking place. He couldn't make out *what* they were saying, but there was an edge to Reese's tone.

To announce his presence, he cleared his throat and greeted Tesha, pretending he hadn't noticed anything else.

When Reese turned around, he looked worried but quickly masked it with indifference before forcing a smile. "Mornin'."

"Good morning," Atticus replied. "Looks like I'm early."

"Never too early to get here," Reese said, his shoulders relaxing. "Plus, I wanted to talk to you, anyway."

Aw, shit. Nothing good came after those words. Anytime someone wanted to *talk* to him, they usually wanted to criticize or threaten.

"Should I pack my shit now?" he asked, already feeling defensive.

Reese frowned. "No." He exhaled sharply. "It's not bad, Atticus. Not at all. Come on. Let's go in here."

"Can I get some coffee first?"

Reese's eyebrow quirked. "You don't drink coffee."

"I know."

Reese shook his head and chuckled. "Seriously." He pointed to the conference room. "Get in there."

Atticus led the way, stopping just inside the room.

"Close the door," Reese said as he marched past.

And he said it wasn't bad. Right.

Atticus closed the door but refrained from sitting even though Reese did.

"I told you, it's not bad."

"Forgive me if I don't believe you."

"Sit, Atticus," Reese demanded, his tone sharper than Atticus had ever heard it.

He sat.

He looked around the room.

He fidgeted.

He did everything but look at Reese because he knew what was coming. Reese said it wasn't bad, but that was because he likely believed he could deliver the news with style. The man had a way with words. He could probably give Atticus his walking papers and make it look like it had been Atticus's idea.

"We were watchin' you in New York."

His gaze snapped to Reese. That didn't surprise him. Atticus knew he was still within his probationary period. Back when Brantley had offered him a job, he'd told him he needed time to assess him. His ninety days were officially up this week, so it looked like it was time to get that assessment.

"And?"

"I think it's time…" Reese sat up and put an elbow on the table. "To get you a partner."

Atticus's mouth opened, but he closed it just as quickly. He'd been gearing up for an explanation or excuse. Now he was stunned speechless.

Reese grinned. "What did you think I was gonna say?"

"Pretty much anything but that."

"Brantley and I talked last night. Your probationary period is up. Provided you're still interested, we'd like to welcome you permanently to the team. Are you?"

"What? Interested?" Atticus did his best to hide his excitement. "Yeah. Damn straight I am."

Reese smiled, and Atticus was sure it was the first time the man had ever really smiled at him.

"Good." Reese relaxed again. "I know you've been workin' one-offs with Baz for the past couple of months, but once you've completed the training course, we'll set you up with your own cases and add you to the rotation for assignments. Once you have a partner, that is."

Atticus's brain replayed the words, and he backed up. "Training course?"

"In Dallas. It's an all-inclusive, six-week-long course. It's mostly interactive, combat training, firearms … that sort of thing. So I think you'll do fine."

Evidently, Atticus's inability to sit still for long periods hadn't gone unnoticed by his bosses.

"And yes, before you ask, everyone here's been through it. Investigators, anyway."

Atticus had figured as much.

"While you're gone, Brantley and I are gonna put out some feelers to get you a permanent place to live. You can't go week to week in a motel anymore."

Well. Looked as though his inability to sit wasn't all they'd noticed.

"Okay. And a partner? Will I come back to one?"

"Probably not. But we'll start lookin'. I'll ensure you've got a say in who we hire."

That surprised him.

Atticus couldn't remember the last time anyone asked his advice on anything. He was a loner. Had been for most of his life. It was the reason he'd taken up bounty hunting as a career. It allowed him to work on his own and not worry about checking in with anyone. But a partner … having watched Slade and Evan, Brantley and Reese, plus Charlie and Jay, he could see how it might be beneficial. Not to mention, watching Brantley's reaction to Decker going off on his own the way he had, Atticus was starting to see the logic of having someone watching his back.

"When do I leave?"

"Monday. If you have anything you need to store, bring it here. We'll figure out a place for it."

Atticus didn't have anything. He'd sold or given away all the possessions he'd owned before he took the job. He had his clothes, and that was about it.

Reese pushed to his feet and held out his hand. "Welcome to the team, Atticus."

He swallowed a lump that formed in his throat but managed to shake Reese's hand without busting into tears. "Thanks. I appreciate it."

"No," Reese said with a grin. "*We* appreciate it. Seriously."

Atticus remained in the conference room, staring after Reese when he walked out. He wasn't sure what he'd done to deserve this, but he knew, no matter what, he was not going to let Reese or Brantley down.

After all, they were the only people who'd ever given him anything worth living for.

Brantley woke up to the emptiness in his head caused by the migraine medicine. Like he had cotton between his ears. He disliked the feeling but would take it over the headache any day.

His body was stiff, which told him he'd spent far too long in bed. He knew before looking that it was later in the day, but he glanced at the clock anyway.

He groaned.

The headache had better be gone. It was damn near dinnertime.

"Shit," he muttered, sitting up slowly.

For the next few hours, he would be moving slowly, his body's defense mechanisms firing on all cylinders, attempting to avoid anything that might cause another headache. He hated those damn things.

He took a shower and felt better for it despite his stomach rumbling like a freight train. Since the thought of food didn't make him nauseous, he figured he'd see if Reese wanted to order something. Or maybe they could go to the diner. Reese deserved to have someone else cook after he'd spent the day taking care of him. Brantley would offer to do it, but he knew better. Reese would shoulder him out of the way and take over. Brantley didn't blame him. He was good at many things, but cooking wasn't one of them.

When he emerged from the bedroom, he was greeted by Tesha, who was waiting at the door. She did that when she heard someone moving around in the room.

"What's up, girl?"

Her tail thumped happily against the hardwood as she sat up.

Brantley bent to scratch her head. "Where's Reese?"

She stood and trotted down the hall, clearly expecting him to follow.

He found Reese on the couch, eyes closed, arm out, hand holding the remote.

Brantley smiled, his heart swelling in his chest as he took in the sight. Never had he loved anyone the way he loved this man.

Tesha let out an excited yip, which woke Reese instantly.

"Shh. You'll wake—" Reese's gaze slammed into him. "You're awake."

"And you're not," Brantley teased.

"Just dozin'."

"You hungry?"

Reese nodded. "You want me to cook somethin'?"

"I was thinkin' we could go to the diner so you don't have to."

"You sure you're up for it?"

"Yeah." Brantley had accepted that he would suffer through the migraines, but he wasn't willing to allow them to stop him from living his life.

"How'd the day go?" Brantley asked when they were seated at the diner.

"Good."

"Anything new?"

"Cases?" Reese shook his head. "No. I talked to Z."

"How'd that go?"

"I tried askin' him about Decker, but he blew me off. Said he was just glad we found him safe and sound and that he was back. I asked where he would be assigned now. Z said he wasn't sure. It was obvious he didn't want to talk about it."

"Probably worried you'd ask too many questions." Brantley was convinced Z had purposely sent them after Decker. He just couldn't understand why.

Was it to get them out of Coyote Ridge? From what he could tell, nothing had happened while they were gone. Or so they could investigate the Kavanaghs? That seemed unlikely since Z hadn't asked anything about their conversation with Ronan or Saoirse.

Or was it because Z wanted them to actually find Decker and see what he was doing? Brantley had no idea who Eddie was or how he played into this, but he got the feeling he was a big piece of the puzzle.

"What can I get you boys?"

Brantley didn't bother with the menu. "I'll take a double cheeseburger. Well done. With fries and a piece of peach cobbler."

The waitress smiled and jotted it down.

"I'll have the chicken pot pie," Reese added.

"Any sides?"

"No," Reese told her. "And we'll take two sweet teas."

"Bread before your meal?"

"No thanks," Brantley told her, knowing Reese wouldn't eat it and Brantley didn't need it.

"I went out to Camp K-9 today," Reese informed him when they were alone again.

"How'd that go?"

"Weird."

Brantley chuckled, waiting for the punchline.

"Today's Ava's birthday."

"And that made it weird?"

"No. It was the whole encounter. Trey was…" Reese shrugged. "I can't explain it, but somethin's goin' on with those three."

"Those three? Or Trey and Magnus?"

"All of 'em."

That was interesting. Brantley knew that Trey and Magnus had gotten close when they'd been looking for Ava. He also knew that Ava and Magnus were close when they were younger. But how that translated to all three of them, he wasn't sure. Maybe he should reach out to Trey and ask.

The next hour passed while they ate their meals. Small talk was minimal, but it wasn't uncomfortable. Brantley enjoyed spending time with Reese. Even if it was simply sharing a meal in silence.

"Oh, I meant to tell you, I talked to Atticus today," Reese said, pushing his plate away.

"Yeah? How'd he take the news?"

Reese's grin was wicked. "I'm pretty sure I almost made him cry."

"He's a good kid."

"Yeah. He is. And I think he's a good addition to the team."

"You tell everyone else?"

"I did. Charlie and Jay got back mid-day, so I made the announcement with everyone there."

"How'd *they* take it?"

"JJ sent Baz out to get cupcakes, so I'd say it went well." Reese wiped his mouth with his napkin and set it on his plate. "Slade asked who he'd be partnered with. I told him we'd be hirin' someone soon."

Brantley knew how tight knit the team had become. He doubted that had gone over well.

"I told 'em to let you or me know if they had someone in mind who might be a good addition. Luca mentioned he had a cousin—"

"No," Brantley snapped.

Reese laughed. "That's what I said. I told him we had our fill of Switzers and didn't need anymore. Holly thanked me for sayin' it."

"Sounds like it's gonna—"

"Excuse me. I hate to interrupt," a man said as he approached their table.

Brantley glanced up at the guy and reassessed his initial estimate. He wasn't sure the guy was a man. Not from a chronological aspect, at least. He looked more like a kid. Probably seventeen, maybe eighteen. His jaw was lined with acne, and he had braces on his teeth.

"Yeah?" Brantley prompted, wanting the kid to get on with it. As it was, Tesha was sitting up, her full attention on the interrupter.

"Do you know Molly?"

"Molly who?"

"Just Molly."

Brantley frowned and looked at Reese. He turned back to the kid. "No. Can't say I know a Molly. Sorry."

The kid grinned like an idiot. Almost like that was the answer he'd been hoping for. "Cool. Thanks."

Brantley watched as he walked past the other tables toward the front door. It didn't appear he had anyone with him, nor could Brantley see anyone in the parking lot waiting. But as he reached the door, the guy glanced back over his shoulder and grinned. It was the eerie kind of smile. The kind someone flashed when they thought they knew something you didn't.

"What the hell was that about?" Brantley asked, looking at Reese.

Reese was peering back over his shoulder, tracking the kid until he left the restaurant. "No idea."

"Well, with that weirdness behind us, what d'ya say we call it a night?"

Clearly as eager to get out of there as Brantley, Reese motioned for the waitress.

CHAPTER TWENTY-THREE

Friday, August 12, 2022

"Hey, congrats, man. I hear you're headin' to Dallas next week."

Slade's gaze snapped up, his eyes locked on Atticus and Luca talking a few feet away.

"Yeah. Six weeks, I hear."

"It's fun," Jay said, joining the conversation. "Really fun. I dreaded the idea of six weeks away, but it was worth it."

Feeling eyes on him, Slade looked to his right. Evan was watching him closely. His partner had been doing that for the past few days as they settled in after the trip. Thankfully, Evan hadn't brought up what Slade had told him, but he figured it was only a matter of time. Especially if Slade didn't get his act together and stop getting distracted by Atticus.

"You doin' anything to celebrate this weekend?" Luca prompted. "Before you head out, I mean."

"I've got plans," Atticus told him. "I'm hanging out with a friend."

"Anyone I know?"

Since Luca knew practically everyone in Coyote Ridge the same way Slade did, he figured it was a stupid question.

"Carson Briggs," Atticus told him.

Slade's chest got instantly tight, and he turned his attention to his computer screen.

"I know Carson," Luca said. "I was best friends with his brother, Jaxson, in high school. You two seein' each other or what?"

"I wouldn't go that far." Atticus chuckled. "We're friends."

Yeah. Sure they were. Slade knew exactly the kind of friendship Carson offered. The guy had an eerie way of finding a guy when he was down and worming his way into their life. Slade knew firsthand. He'd spent nearly a year with Carson dragging him around by his dick.

It damn sure didn't surprise him that Carson would be interested in Atticus. He was just his type. Young, hot. And likely open for some heart-stopping sex. That seemed all that Carson needed—a spark. From there, he was capable of amping up the intensity to the nth degree. Slade knew from experience.

Not that he spent time dwelling over what might've been with Carson. He'd gotten over him a long time ago. Not quite as long ago as he would've preferred, but he wasn't heartbroken anymore. He'd stopped thinking about their time together in the negative sense and reflected on the good times. Slade wouldn't deny he'd enjoyed the hell out of himself. Carson had taught him things he'd never imagined possible. At least not when it came to sex. To say the guy liked kink was an understatement.

But what Slade had thought was something real had turned out to be one of Carson's many games. Carson was like Spencer in that regard. Minus the traitorous affair. Carson didn't sleep with other people's wives. And not because Carson was gay. He was a good guy. A standup guy. He merely had an issue with settling down.

Or he had. Back when Slade had been his entertainment.

"Well, you watch out for that one," Luca told Atticus. "He's squirrelly."

"I don't even know what that means."

"Trust me, you'll figure it out."

Slade fought the urge to look up. He sensed Atticus's confusion, but no way was he going to weigh in this time. He'd done that already by getting in between Atticus and Spencer. Atticus could figure this one out on his own.

"Why do you look like you've got your … what was it? Nuts in a vise?" Evan asked, his voice too low for anyone else to hear.

Slade rolled his eyes. "It doesn't sound the same comin' from you."

Evan laughed. "Yeah. I realized that as soon as it came out. You want to grab a beer after work?"

"Yeah." Anything to keep him from thinking about Atticus and Carson together.

If the mental image of the two of them together wasn't so fucking hot, he was certain the idea would've repulsed him.

Damn certain.

AS BAZ DROVE HOME FROM HQ, HE considered stopping at the grocery store before going to the house. It would save time. Usually, he would've picked JJ up, whether at the house or the office, so she didn't have to be alone. She preferred it that way.

These days, though, she was exerting her independence to convince him that she was okay. To prove her point, she had slipped out of the office early after closing out the last of the details on Decker's case. When they didn't have a case keeping them busy, she preferred slipping out early on Fridays. As soon as she mentioned leaving, Baz had immediately offered to go with her, but she had reminded him that she had driven herself that morning.

Those reminders were coming a bit more frequently these days. JJ's routine was changing, and she was becoming more independent. He knew she was doing it because she wanted him to believe she was no longer scared to be by herself. Whether that was true, he didn't know for sure, but Baz knew bringing it up would only cause an argument, so he didn't make a fuss about it. He trusted her to know what was best for her.

Baz would've preferred to chauffeur her everywhere she needed to go, but JJ had told him it was weird. Again, her way of making them both believe she was moving forward, one step at a time. It had taken her a long time to get over what had happened the night before her house exploded, and Baz understood. She'd been drugged that night, and while nothing had been done to her physically—thank fucking God—it had been traumatic to wake up in a pool of blood. Turned out to be animal blood, but the damage had been done, regardless.

To help her move forward, Baz suggested they replace her car with a new one. He'd been driving her everywhere she needed to go for a solid year at that point. At first, she'd blown him off, using the excuse that it was more cost-effective to ride together. Then, once a month, he would bring it up. By the sixth time he made the suggestion, she pretended to be excited about the idea. For his sake, he knew. So back in June, they bought her a Toyota RAV4, newer and nicer than her previous one, which had also been decimated in the house explosion.

These days, she made an effort to drive herself at least once a week, giving him time to work with the rest of the team on open cases once they returned from the field. Today, she'd left him at the office when he was set up in the conference room with Charlie and Jay, going over what they'd learned during their time in Chicago. Her timing had been intentional. Had he not been in the middle of something, he would've left with her.

If he had to guess, she'd gone straight home, unlocked the front door, disarmed the alarm, then locked herself in, resetting the alarm.

She was taking baby steps, and he was proud of her. She still wasn't comfortable being alone for long periods, but she was learning to do it. Baz assured her she would one day be back to normal, urging him to leave so she could have some time to herself.

Baz decided he *would* go to the grocery store before he went home. If nothing else, to show her he trusted her judgment and wasn't hovering, although he was prone to do just that.

He told Siri to call JJ and waited until her voice sounded through the truck's speaker.

She answered on the first ring. "Are you on the way home?"

"Yeah," he told her. "I thought I'd stop at the grocery store first."

"Ooh. Yay. What're you makin' for dinner?"

"I guess it depends on what you'd like."

He could tell she'd stopped typing, but she didn't respond immediately.

As was the case when he asked her that question, JJ gave her full attention to determining the answer. He never knew what she was going to come up with, but he always looked forward to hearing it.

"How about spaghetti?" she finally said.

"With meat sauce, meatballs, or chili?"

"Chili. Definitely chili."

"With beans or without?"

He could tell she pondered the answer before saying, "With."

"Anything else? Garlic bread? Chocolate mousse pie? Cookies? Nutella?"

"I'll send you a list."

"Perfect. It'll take me fifteen minutes to get there, so start making the list now."

JJ laughed. "Fine."

Baz disconnected the call and focused on the road.

With traffic, it took him twenty minutes before he was pulling into the parking lot. Although he loved the house and the small town, he wouldn't deny that it was inconvenient at times like this. Driving to the next town over for groceries or a restaurant that didn't serve comfort food was a chore. But he figured it was a fair trade. Their daughter was going to grow up in a town with roots, and he couldn't ask for more than that.

Forty-five minutes later, Baz was making his way toward the check-out registers. He was taking his time, ensuring JJ wasn't going to add anything at the last minute. She'd been sending him a steady stream of things she wanted, so he wouldn't put it past her.

He stopped on the seasonal aisle to waste a few minutes. It was there he noticed a guy watching him.

Maybe he wasn't necessarily watching him, but he was glancing in his direction again and again until he finally approached. The guy was younger than he first thought. Late teens, if he had to guess, with shaggy red hair and acne blotching his face. His green eyes were almost cold, but he flashed a smile, presumably to put Baz at ease.

It didn't work, but Baz took into account that the kid was carrying a bouquet in one hand and a greeting card in the other. Perhaps he wanted advice on what else to get his girlfriend.

"I hate to bother you, but I've got a question," he said with a metallic smile, the light glinting off his braces.

Baz expected him to ask about gift ideas, so the question that came out of his mouth shocked him.

"Do you know Molly?"

Baz frowned, looking around to see if someone else was nearby. They were alone on the aisle.

"I … uh…"

The guy's expression didn't change, nor did he move. He was regarding him with a smile, like they were two friends catching up.

"It's a simple question. Do you know Molly?"

"Molly who?" he countered.

The pleasant expression on his face slipped off, and what remained caused a chill to dance down Baz's spine.

"Wrong answer."

Before Baz could say anything, the guy spun on his heel and stomped off in the other direction. He glanced back once. His countenance was unreadable, but the way his eyebrow quirked was meant to say that wouldn't be the last Baz would hear from him.

"What the fuck?" Baz muttered before pushing his cart in pursuit. When he reached the end of the aisle, he looked both ways, but the guy was gone.

Feeling like someone was watching him, Baz checked out at the register and then headed for the parking lot. He looked around, hoping to find the guy so he could ask him who the fuck he was. Several people were loading groceries into their cars, and others were walking into the store. None of them were the guy with the flowers.

Clearly, he was losing his mind. Had he imagined the whole thing? Stress could do that to a person, and God knows Baz was dealing with stress. He was attempting to keep JJ from picking up on it, but he was anxious about the baby. More specifically, the health of JJ and the baby. Every time they went to the doctor, he feared the worst. He had no idea why, but sometimes fear wasn't logical. They were both healthy, the doctor had assured him.

Baz reached his truck and pushed the cart near the back wheel. He opened the back door and began transferring the things into the truck.

A car pulled up behind his truck, and he flinched, turning to see who it was. Turned out to be a man waiting for someone to back out of a space close to the door.

"You're losin' it, Buchanan," he muttered to himself.

After returning the cart to the rack that held them, he walked back to his truck and closed the back door. He opened the front to get in and noticed the flowers the guy had been holding were sitting in his seat. There was a card.

He snatched it up and opened it. A note was scrawled in neat little block letters: YOU SHOULD'VE SAID YES. MOLLY'S THE LOVE OF YOUR LIFE, REMEMBER?

Baz stepped back and searched the parking lot. He saw a woman getting into a car a couple of aisles over. She could've been Molly based on her height and build, but she was wearing a ball cap, so he couldn't see her hair. Before she got into the car, she turned toward him and smiled.

Fuck.

It was her.

An SUV pulled forward, blocking his view. When it finally moved past, the car and Molly were gone.

How the fuck had she found him?

CHAPTER TWENTY-FOUR

ATTICUS HAD NEVER BEEN ON A DATE before.

Although Carson hadn't come out and said that was what this was, it was obvious. Atticus had met Carson at the diner for dinner, then halfway through the meal, Carson suggested they go to the concert in the park. Evidently, it was an event that took place every Friday night in August. Atticus wouldn't say it was really his thing, but he had a good time, then accepted Carson's invitation to go to Moonshiners to grab a drink.

Now, here they were, nursing beers at a table near the wall while half of Coyote Ridge paraded through the place, greeting people they knew. It was too loud to hold a conversation, but that didn't stop Carson from making small talk. Atticus kept up, listening as Carson gave him the scoop on the people he knew. Most of which were family. Atticus didn't even attempt to memorize all the names this time. He'd forgotten the others already, so he figured it was pointless.

"That girl there … that's Honor. She's secretly datin' Luca. You know him."

"If it's a secret, how do you know?"

Carson chuckled. "*They* think it's a secret. But it's all over town. Evidently, someone saw 'em makin' out at the bookstore."

Interesting.

"That's Jaxson," Carson said, nodding toward a tall cowboy in the corner. "He's my oldest brother."

"Is he married?"

"Nope. But he's got a thing for one of the sisters who run Dead Heat Ranch. I don't know which one. Not sure I wanna know."

Atticus grinned, but as soon as it formed, it fell away as Slade approached their table.

Please, God, don't let him stick his nose where it doesn't fucking belong.

"Carson," Slade greeted with a terse edge to his tone.

"Slade. You know Atticus, don't you?"

Atticus glanced at Carson. Was he imagining that, or had it sounded like Carson was taunting Slade?

"We work together," Slade said, only glancing at Atticus briefly.

Carson leaned back in his chair, regarding Slade carefully. "I heard y'all shared a hotel room."

This time Slade did look his way, but Atticus couldn't tell what he was thinking.

"What brings you out tonight?" Carson asked when no one said anything.

"Just chillin' after a long week."

Atticus watched the two of them practically face-off, although there were at least three feet between them. Since they were the same age and had grown up in the same small town, he figured they had history.

Neither of them said anything for a moment. Long enough for Atticus to feel a bead of sweat trickle down the center of his back. He did not want a repeat of what went down the last time he was here, but there was a good chance he was about to witness round two.

Slade looked ready to rip Carson a new one, but a guy walked up. Atticus had never seen him before, and he'd seen most of the people who came to this bar at least once. He would've remembered him. Wild red hair and cold, dead eyes weren't something you would forget.

"Hey, man. I need to ask you a question."

The guy was directing it at Slade.

"What's up?"

"Do you know Molly?"

Slade frowned. "No. Can't say I do. Why?"

The guy ignored Slade's question and turned to Atticus. "What about you?"

"No. I don't know any Molly."

Dead Eyes nodded as though that was the answer he expected before turning to scan others in the place. Before he could walk away, Mack was walking toward him.

"I'll need to see ID," Mack said gruffly.

"No worries, Pops," the kid said with a laugh. "I was just leaving."

Atticus watched as Mack escorted him to the door.

"What the hell was that about?" Atticus wondered aloud.

"Probably lookin' for drugs," Carson said. "Maybe he thought y'all could hook him up. Isn't there a street drug called Molly?"

"Yeah," Slade said, still watching the door. "Ecstasy is referred to as Molly."

Great. Just what this little town needed: pill-popping teenagers wandering around.

Finally, Slade's gaze cut to him. He jerked his chin. "Watch out for this one, kid." Slade's eyes shifted back to Carson. "He's a squirrelly one."

Carson laughed as Slade walked away.

Yeah, there was definitely history there.

Atticus wasn't sure he wanted to know, but he asked anyway. "What was that about?"

"It was just a guess. I don't do drugs," Carson said.

"Not the drugs," Atticus clarified. "I meant with Slade. What's up with you two?"

Carson tipped his beer bottle to his lips and stared after Slade. "Nothin' that's worth repeatin'."

Why was it that Atticus found himself attracted to people Slade seemed to have a problem with?

Carson turned his full attention to Atticus, twisting to face him more fully. A warm hand pressed against Atticus's thigh as Carson leaned closer.

"What'd'ya say we go back to my place?"

Atticus met his stare, fascinated by the sparkle in Carson's blue-gray eyes. "Okay."

The drive to Carson's house took less time with Atticus following him. He wasn't sure that was necessarily a good thing. The closer they got to the little white house with the black shutters, the more nervous Atticus became. He wasn't sure what he had to feel anxious about. He knew what was going to happen, and he welcomed it.

Or he wanted to welcome it, but now he wasn't so sure. Twice now, someone had used the word squirrelly to describe Carson. What the fuck did that even mean? Was it some sort of twisted euphemism? Like Carson liked to play with nuts?

Although he didn't know what Luca's definition of squirrelly was, he got the feeling it had to do with his inability to stay in one place for long. Meaning Atticus would likely wake up tomorrow and find himself kicked to the curb.

But hell, if that was the case, he had nothing to worry about. He wasn't looking to settle down. He wanted to get laid. And right now, he was so damn horny he couldn't worry about the consequences.

He parked his truck behind Carson's big white van—obviously, something he drove for work—and got out, walking toward the door as though he was filled with purpose and not wild chaos. Anticipation, at least in this case, was not his friend.

Atticus tried to play it cool as he walked up to the house. He looked around, noticing that the neighborhood was quiet. No nosy neighbors watching him go inside. Didn't mean there weren't any peering out the windows, and he would almost bet money someone was because the back of his neck itched like he was being watched.

"You want somethin' to drink?" Carson offered as he closed the door behind Atticus.

"No, I'm—"

He didn't even get the word out before Carson had him pinned up against the wall. Carson kissed him like he was starving, and Atticus was the main course. And just like that, the events of the night faded away, and he wasn't worried about creepy neighbors or drug addicts looking for their fix. His entire world zeroed in on the man kissing him and the heat that exploded in his veins from the proximity.

"I don't know what it is about you," Carson mumbled against his lips. "I can't stop thinkin' about you."

Atticus knew how he felt. The same affliction plagued him. Keeping his distance these past few days had been hell, but he refused to let Carson know how eager he was. How desperate he felt when he thought about Carson kissing him like this.

Carson's hands slipped beneath Atticus's T-shirt, pushing the cotton higher and higher before finally pulling back to drag it off him.

"I want you naked," Carson said, his gaze hot as it raked over his chest.

Atticus knew he wasn't much to look at. He wasn't tall like Reese. He wasn't muscular like Brantley or Slade. And he wasn't lean and sculpted like Luca. He was skinny, more so than he probably should've been. The only difference between now and when he was a scrawny kid was the fact he was no longer pasty white. But that was about it.

"What's this from?" Carson asked, his thumb brushing along the four-inch scar on the lower right side of his abdomen.

"Appendectomy," he said, closing his eyes and letting the sensation take over. He didn't want to talk about how his appendix had ruptured when he was eleven or that he'd spent nearly a month in the hospital because of an infection that had nearly killed him.

When Carson's hands fell away, Atticus opened his eyes, watching as Carson reached behind his head and grabbed a fistful of his shirt before dragging it off.

Atticus's breath caught in his lungs when Carson revealed his ripped physique. He was all lean muscle, every inch defined. He was tanned from apparent time in the sun, his skin sleek and smooth. The muscles on his abdomen were distinctly sculpted, forming a perfect six-pack. The corded muscle along his hips angled downward, forming a V that disappeared beneath the waistband of his jeans. He was the kind of guy Atticus fantasized about fucking. The kind he wanted to spend hours exploring with his tongue.

Carson moved in again, pressing their chests together, sending sparks dancing under Atticus's skin.

"This…" Carson nipped his lower lip. "This is what I've wanted. To be skin to skin with you."

Their lips melded again, tongues gliding as Carson freed the button on Atticus's jeans. He gasped when Carson's knuckles rubbed against his dick as he dragged the zipper down.

"I'm gonna worship you, Atticus," Carson whispered, his lips brushing his chin before caressing his neck. "I'm gonna worship every fuckin' inch before I fuck you."

Carson pinned his hands to the wall above his head, then kissed his way down his arm, starting at his elbow. Lower, lower. He paused near his armpit, nipping the delicate skin before moving on, shifting over so he could bite Atticus's nipple.

"Oh, fuck." He pressed himself into the wall, letting the pleasure consume him.

It was evident Carson was taking cues from him because he pinched Atticus's other nipple as he lowered himself to his knees. He grunted, his cock kicking hard from the flare of pain.

Staring down at the man, Atticus gasped for breath as he watched everything play out. The way Carson pushed his jeans down his legs, the way his big fingers circled Atticus's cock.

"I was right," Carson said. "You do have a beautiful cock."

This man was going to kill him with his commentary. Atticus wasn't used to so much conversation. Hell, most of his encounters had been over at this point. Slam, bam, thank you, man. There was never much foreplay, certainly nothing like this.

Carson's gaze lifted as he licked the head of Atticus's dick. Atticus watched in fascination as the man took him to the root, swirling his tongue around the head before pulling back. He did it again and again until Atticus was lightheaded from pleasure. All the while, Carson stripped Atticus's clothes off, leaving them in a pile by the door.

"Carson… oh, fuck." He didn't want to come yet, but if the man kept doing that, he was going to.

But then he heard it. The distinct rumble of an exhaust.

"What's that?"

Carson continued to stroke him. "Slade's truck."

Oh, shit. "Is he *here*?"

"No." Carson licked the head of Atticus's cock again. "He lives across the street."

Great. They were neighbors.

"Does he … come over here?"

"Not anymore."

Atticus frowned. "What does that mean?"

Carson smiled as he got to his feet, taking Atticus's hand and leading him through the house toward his bedroom.

"I need more room to do what I really wanna do," Carson said, as though an explanation was necessary.

Atticus followed, but he couldn't stop thinking about Slade. In his head, he pictured the guy coming to the door, interrupting them so he could tell Atticus that Carson was squirrelly.

"Are you related to Slade or something?"

"Nope," Carson said, gently shoving Atticus onto the bed.

Atticus shifted back on the pillows and watched as Carson stripped. "Friends?"

Carson's eyes narrowed. "Not anymore."

"Falling out?"

Carson grinned, joining Atticus on the bed. "I used to fuck him."

The gasp that escaped was involuntary. That was the last thing he'd expected Carson to say.

"Slade's…?" He couldn't get the word out. It wasn't possible. The guy wasn't gay. He'd been married to a woman, for fuck's sake.

Oh, God. Fuck. Suck me, Atticus. Yeah. Like that. Just like that.

Slade's words filled his head; the memory of Slade lying on the bed, jacking off, made Atticus's dick swell even more. It was wrong on so many levels, but he couldn't help it.

"Mmm." Carson straddled Atticus's thighs and curled his fingers around his cock. "Are you thinkin' about me or Slade?"

"What?" Atticus knew his face was tomato-red.

Carson grinned. "You like the idea of me fuckin' Slade?"

Well, now that he mentioned it, he could see the appeal of watching two smoking hot guys like them going at it. He wondered who the alpha in that relationship was. Carson was definitely the alpha here, but Atticus couldn't imagine Slade letting Carson top him.

Not that he would ask. He didn't want to think about Slade. Certainly not right now, when the man Atticus had been fantasizing about for the past few days was about to make his dreams come true.

"Turn over," Carson said, lifting one of his legs to give Atticus room to move.

He rolled over onto his stomach.

"On your knees."

Atticus pulled his knees forward, lifting his ass in the air.

He sighed as Carson leaned over him, pressing a kiss between his shoulder blades. His hands began to roam, starting at his shoulders, working their way down his back. Atticus sighed, relaxing as Carson caressed him.

By the time he reached his hips, Atticus was back in the present, focusing only on the man behind him.

"That's what I want right there," Carson moaned, gripping Atticus's ass cheeks with both hands. He spread him wide, and a moment later, Atticus felt the warmth of his breath an instant before his tongue invaded.

The guy wasn't pulling his punches tonight, that was for damn sure.

"Oh, fuck yes." Atticus clutched the comforter, rocking back against the intrusion.

Carson reached around and fisted Atticus's cock. "You like havin' your ass rimmed."

"Yes," he hissed, unable to deny it.

"Enjoy it. Once I'm inside you, I'm gonna want to stay there forever."

Atticus's asshole clenched, eager for Carson to fill him with his cock.

He heard Carson chuckle, and a second later, a finger pressed against his hole.

"Is this what you need?"

Atticus relaxed as Carson pushed his thick finger inside him, slow and deep. It felt so good.

"What about when I do …. this?"

"Fuck!" Atticus's entire body tensed and jerked when Carson pressed against his prostate. The sensation was unreal, making his head spin as Carson massaged that delicate spot. The sensations overwhelmed him. His skin was tight, his scalp tingled. He was going to come with Carson fingering his asshole.

"Don't," Atticus rasped. "Not yet … oh, God, not yet."

Carson slowed, easing up on the prostate massage, but he continued to finger him. Atticus was aware of Carson moving, leaning toward the nightstand beside the bed. He heard the slide of a drawer opening and then closing. A moment later, something cold dripped on his hole, coating Carson's fingers and making the glide easier.

Atticus rocked back against two fingers scissoring inside him. "More," he pleaded.

Carson added a third finger, making Atticus moan.

"Take it," Carson grumbled. "Fuck yourself on my hand."

Atticus wasn't shy. He did exactly that, rocking backward, impaling himself on those thick digits. It wasn't enough. It would never be enough. He wanted Carson pounding into him.

"Fuck me, Carson," he whispered. "I want to feel you."

The fingers slipped out, followed by the distinct sound of foil ripping and a condom being rolled on. Atticus looked back at the beautiful man about to fuck him into oblivion. Their eyes met as Carson guided his cock to Atticus's hole.

Carson's blue-gray eyes blazed with passion. "You ready for me?"

"God, yes." He faced forward, pressing his chest to the mattress so he could press back against Carson's cock as it split him wide.

He hissed and moaned, letting the pleasure wash away the initial pain. He probably should've gotten a look at the man's dick so he would've known what to expect. It felt like he was being fucked by an eggplant.

"Fuck, you're big," Atticus groaned.

"I probably should've warned you," Carson said, the words hissed through gritted teeth. "You're so fuckin' tight … God, Atticus."

Finally, the pain diminished, and pleasure consumed him as Carson began fucking him. Deep and slow at first, gliding in, retreating. In. Out. Again and again, the waves of pleasure were crashing over him. Atticus reached between his legs and stroked his cock, keeping pace with the delicious thrust and retreat.

"More?" Carson asked.

"Yes."

Carson unleashed on him then, drilling into him hard and deep. He gripped Atticus's hips, holding him in place while he rammed inside. Faster and faster until their combined groans echoed off the walls.

"Atticus … fuck … I'm gonna come."

Atticus jerked his cock roughly, riding the waves one after the other until he couldn't hold on. Carson impaled him impossibly deep and held himself there, his cock pulsing inside him. Atticus let go, coming in his hand as he gasped for air.

"I could get addicted to you," Carson whispered as he fell to his side, pulling Atticus against him. Carson pressed a kiss to his shoulder. "In fact, I think I already am."

Atticus couldn't deny he liked hearing it, even though he wasn't sure it was something he was ready for at this point in his life.

"I'm leaving," he blurted.

Carson pulled back, propping up on an elbow and peering over Atticus's shoulder. "What?"

"Six weeks," he added. "I'm going to Dallas for six weeks."

"When?"

"Monday." Atticus twisted to look at him. "It's for training. I'll be back, though."

Carson rolled in the opposite direction, getting to his feet.

Atticus watched him as he disappeared into a connecting bathroom. He heard water running for several minutes.

When Carson didn't return after five, Atticus figured that was his cue to leave, but before he could get to his feet, Carson returned with a washcloth. Atticus frowned and then flinched when he realized Carson's intention. He cleaned him gently before slipping back into the bathroom.

Atticus's face was hot when Carson returned, crawling into the bed once again.

Carson pulled him closer, leaning down and smiling. "I guess we better not waste time then, huh?"

CHAPTER TWENTY-FIVE

Saturday, August 13, 2022

THE SUN WASN'T UP WHEN BRANTLEY OPENED his eyes.

He was in his bed, curled up beside the man he loved. The house was quiet, and his head wasn't pounding. It was going to be a good day. How could it not when this was how it started?

Rolling to his side, he put his hand on Reese's chest, listening to his deep, even breaths. After a minute, Reese's hand covered his, gently caressing.

"Thirty-five days," Brantley whispered, kissing Reese's shoulder.

He couldn't explain his need to countdown until they were married, but he'd been doing it day in and day out, getting more excited with each passing day. As he'd told Reese before, Brantley had never imagined his wedding or even what life with a partner would look like. Not before Reese. There was a point in his life when it hadn't been an option, and then when it was, he hadn't expected to find someone he would want to spend the rest of his life with.

"What're you thinkin' about?" Reese mumbled, his voice gravel rough.

"You." Brantley kissed his way to the center of Reese's chest, shifting over him as he did. "The day I met you."

"Mmm." Reese's hands moved to his sides, then his back, roaming softly.

Keeping the conversation to a minimum, Brantley homed in on his goal, kissing his way down Reese's stomach, pushing the blanket and sheet off in the process. When he settled his shoulders between Reese's thighs, Brantley smiled to himself, licking along the side of Reese's shaft, teasing him awake fully. It wasn't long before Reese was stiff and throbbing, his cock pulsing in Brantley's mouth.

Brantley took his time. This wasn't a sprint, it was a marathon, and he wasn't eager to do anything else. At least not until he'd had his fill of this man. It would never be enough, but it was a damn fine way to welcome the day.

Reese cupped his head, guiding Brantley as he bobbed up and down on his cock, licking, sucking, teasing. He could feel the heat of Reese's gaze as he watched him, his brain no longer struggling to come online. They were in the moment together.

"God, that feels good," Reese groaned. "Make me come, and I'll return the favor."

Oh, Brantley could certainly do that.

He continued his leisurely pace, ensuring Reese got the full experience. When Reese began thrusting his hips, fucking Brantley's mouth, he took him as high as he could without sending him over, then doubled his efforts until Reese was crying out his name, coming down his throat.

"My turn," Reese said, tugging Brantley's arm, urging him to come closer.

Brantley crawled up Reese's body, kissing along the path he'd taken earlier. When he reached Reese's mouth, he detoured for a few minutes, grinding his cock along Reese's thigh, working himself up with every passing second. And when he couldn't take anymore, Brantley straddled Reese's head, gripping the headboard and fucking Reese's face. He didn't rush, pumping his hips, letting Reese take him to the hilt again and again. When he came, satisfaction bloomed in his entire body, and his chest expanded.

No matter how they came together, no matter what it entailed, making love with Reese was unlike anything he'd ever experienced. And he was looking forward to years and years of explorations to come.

Thirty-five days and counting.

SLADE WOKE UP ON SATURDAY MORNING AND went right to his home gym. Originally, it had been two separate bedrooms, too small to do much in either. He'd removed the wall between, eliminated the closets, and converted it into one space that served a functional purpose.

Over the years, he'd spent a good chunk of both time and money getting the room to his liking. He'd painted the walls bright white, replaced the old fan with an LED light, and laid 7mm thick rubber flooring over the original hardwood. There was a television mounted high enough to see from almost every angle, and one wall consisted of mirrors that were taller than Slade and covered the width of the room. Fans were mounted in the corners for when he needed them.

As for the equipment, it was top-notch. He'd pinched pennies and saved for all of it, and now he had everything he needed. A treadmill sat in one corner, a rowing machine in another, and a heavy bag in another. There was a variety of free weights lining the walls. In the center was a cable machine that got the most usage.

He grabbed a water bottle from the small refrigerator he kept stocked. He twisted off the cap and took a sip as he headed for the windows to open the blinds. He tried to tell himself he wanted more light in the room, but the truth was he was looking to see if Atticus's truck was still parked in front of Carson's house.

It was.

Last night, when he'd come home, he'd noticed it, and it had been like a sucker punch. Sure, he'd seen the two of them at Moonshiners, but he'd fooled himself into thinking they would go home separately after that. It was a lie he told himself, yeah, but he'd believed it. He hadn't expected the feeling to be quite so intense, but it confirmed what he'd suspected. He wanted the man. Part of him had expected to feel a twinge of jealousy for Carson, but it never came. He'd moved on from that obsession a long time ago. Unfortunately, it appeared he was forming a new one. For a new man.

And just like every time he acknowledged it, his frustration ratcheted up a few notches.

Setting the water on the top of the refrigerator, Slade settled in to burn off some residual anger.

Two hours later, after a gruesome workout and a shower, Slade drove into town. He went to Batter & Bliss every Saturday morning for coffee and a cronut, a specialty item that Ramona Weber only made once a week. According to her, making croissants from scratch was a labor of love, and that labor was intensive. Hence, her reason for only making a limited supply one day a week.

"Good morning, Slade," Ramona greeted with a wide smile from behind the pastry case.

"Mornin'."

"I've got your usual ready and waiting," she told him, gesturing toward the register.

He grabbed a couple of napkins and made his way to the register, pulling his wallet out of his back pocket.

"Is this a working weekend?" she asked as she tallied his total. "Or do you actually get some downtime?"

"So far, it looks like I've got some downtime." He knew from experience that could change at any second, but he'd learned to enjoy the quiet whenever he could.

"That's good. I saw your mom and dad yesterday." Her gaze shifted to one of the tables as though she recalled Holden and Rose sitting there as they did every Friday morning.

"I'm supposed to have supper with 'em tonight," he said as he swiped his credit card.

"That should be fun."

No, it would be hell on earth, especially since his brothers generally stopped in. Slade wasn't looking forward to being in the same room as Spencer, much less having to sit at a table and actually converse with him.

"Thanks for this," he said with a grin, grabbing the bag and the coffee cup.

"Have a good day," she called after him as he headed for the door.

He reached it at the same time he saw Carson walking toward him. If he hadn't been pushing the door open, he would've turned around and avoided the confrontation. Instead, he held his chin up and walked outside.

"Mornin', Slade."

Slade didn't respond, choosing to assess the man instead. He looked happy. Exactly like a man who'd spent the night with Atticus should look.

"Don't be jealous, Slade. It's not a good look for you."

"Fuck you," he muttered, opting to walk away.

Before he could pass, Carson grabbed his arm and stopped him.

"You're still welcome in my bed anytime."

Slade glanced down at Carson's hand on his arm, then up to his face and frowned. "Would be kinda crowded, don't you think?"

Carson's eyes heated. "I'm not so sure. I brought you up last night. Atticus seemed quite thrilled by the topic."

Slade did his best not to react. The thought of them talking about him while they were… He shrugged off the erotic images that formed.

Carson's voice lowered. "His cock was extremely thrilled."

"He's a good kid," Slade hissed. "Don't fuck with him."

"That wasn't a kid in my bed last night," Carson stated firmly, his eyes hard. "He's a grown man."

Yeah, Slade knew that. Calling him one was a habit he couldn't break. Or perhaps it was merely his way of attempting to keep his distance.

"Enjoy it while you can, Carson," Slade seethed. "Once he realizes you wanna set him up so you can watch, he'll be on his way."

"I wouldn't be so sure. I think Atticus is kinkier than you know."

With a wink, Carson walked inside the bakery, leaving Slade to stare after him.

His thoughts drifted to the night Carson had convinced Slade to pick up another guy at a bar. The night had ended with Slade fucking someone else while Carson watched from the shadows. He'd known then that he wasn't capable of being with a man like Carson. He wasn't the sort who enjoyed hooking up with some random stranger. And since Carson had an extreme voyeur fetish, there was no way they could've worked.

Taking a deep breath, he turned and walked away, refusing to consider how that night would've been if it had been Atticus he'd fucked while Carson watched.

"Hey, you!"

Slade's head snapped up, and he shoved all those inappropriate thoughts aside as JJ came strolling toward him.

"You're out and about awfully early," he said in greeting.

"I know. I couldn't help it. I'm a sucker for cronuts. Maybe you could talk her into makin' 'em every day. That way, me and the peanut can get our fill."

"Don't think I haven't tried." He held up his bag to show her he had the same addiction.

"Tell me she's got more." There was a sincere hint of panic in JJ's tone.

"She's got plenty," he assured her with a laugh.

"Oh, thank God. It's weird. Once I get my mind set on somethin', I have to have it. If I don't, I obsess about it until I do. I don't get this whole pregnancy cravin' thing."

Slade laughed.

JJ rubbed her belly. "I won't keep you."

"Enjoy."

"Oh, trust me. I will."

Slade watched her waddle toward the door and slip inside.

For a brief second, he thought JJ's interruption was going to get his thoughts off Atticus and Carson. He was wrong. Now that Carson had planted the damn seed, it looked as though his thoughts were officially derailed.

CHAPTER TWENTY-SIX

"GOOD MORNIN', RAMONA," JJ CALLED OUT AS she walked into Batter & Bliss.

"JJ!" As usual, Ramona came out from behind the counter to give JJ a hug and lightly rub her belly.

The first time Ramona had done it, JJ had been shocked. Now that it was a weekly occurrence, she found she looked forward to the excitement in the woman's eyes when she walked in the door. JJ didn't have many people in her life who looked forward to seeing her. Baz, his parents, Brantley and Reese. Sometimes, the rest of the team. The list was short, that was for sure. Thankfully, only Ramona was into the belly-rubbing thing because it was a bit awkward, but she could endure simply to feel a sense of belonging.

"What can I get you today? I've got fresh—"

"Cronuts!" JJ exclaimed. "Lots and lots of cronuts."

Ramona laughed as she headed behind the counter. "How many is 'lots and lots'?"

"Three? No, make it four. That way, I can save some for this afternoon."

"Anything to drink?"

JJ looked at the glass-front refrigerator that was sitting on the counter. She opened the door and grabbed an orange juice. She set it on the counter, then went back and grabbed a chocolate milk for Baz. He'd been acting weird since last night, so she figured maybe that would get him out of his funk. When she'd asked what was bothering him, he'd shrugged it off. She figured he'd encountered a snippy cashier at the grocery store. They tended to sour his mood. That or he was fretting over a case, but she knew interrogating him wouldn't get him to open up. He truly believed he was protecting her if he didn't discuss the cases he was working on.

She wasn't sure why he would think that since she had no problem hashing out her case problems. She found it helped to talk them out with him.

"Can you add a long John to my order?" JJ asked. "They're Baz's favorite."

"Coming right up."

While Ramona grabbed one from the pastry case and slid it into a bag, JJ pulled her phone out of her pocket. Her wallet, which carried her license and one credit card, was magnetized to her phone. The only problem with it was if she bumped it just right, it would pop off. But it was too convenient for her to change it, and she hated carrying a purse.

Ramona took the orange juice and chocolate milk, placed them in a plastic bag, then tucked the two white bags of pastries inside.

"Here you go, hon." Ramona passed the bag to her. "Tell Baz I said hello."

"I will."

With treats in hand, JJ left the bakery and headed for her car. She'd parked around back because there were only a few spots in front of the stores that lined Main Street, and none had been available when she arrived.

As she was nearing the end of the building, a man appeared.

JJ smiled at him as she passed, keeping her attention on where she was walking. Pregnancy made her clumsy, and now that her belly was getting bigger, her center of balance was off.

"Hey, ma'am!"

JJ turned and noticed the guy was walking toward her rather than the way he'd been going. And they were now on the side of the building where no one could see them. Before getting pregnant, JJ wouldn't have thought twice about a stranger approaching. These days, she was extra cautious.

"Can I ask you a question?"

Feeling a tad unsettled, JJ stopped, hoping she could answer his question and he would be on his way.

As he approached, JJ cataloged his features just in case. His shaggy red hair looked like it hadn't seen a brush in a week. His face was dotted with acne and pockmarks from old scars. He had green eyes. Darker than hers but not quite emerald. There was a noticeable scar on his chin and another on his eyebrow. They weren't terribly old scars. Probably within the past year.

He was taller than she was, but not by much. Probably five eight. He had a slender build, and his clothes were dirty like he'd worn them for more than a few days.

"What's up?" she prompted, her unease intensifying as he got closer.

He invaded her personal space, stepping too close for comfort. JJ met his gaze and held it, pretending he didn't scare the shit out of her.

His eyes raked her face with definite scrutiny.

She wanted to tell him to get on with it but held her tongue. She didn't know this guy, and based on his expression, he wasn't too thrilled to be up this early on a Saturday.

Finally, he tilted his head slightly to one side. "Do you know Molly?"

And just like that, every ounce of warmth disappeared as a cold chill swept through her.

BAZ PACED THE LIVING ROOM.

At this rate, he was going to wear a hole in the new hardwood.

JJ had left for the bakery an hour ago. He knew from experience that getting there and back, plus the few minutes inside, took half an hour at most. He was giving her the benefit of the doubt, though. JJ was a talker, and she knew nearly everyone in this town, so it wouldn't surprise him if she had stopped to chat with someone.

He didn't want to call her because he didn't want her to know he was panicking. She deserved to have time to herself. He'd told her that a million times. Calling her would make him look like a hypocrite.

But with every passing minute, he got more and more agitated. Ever since last night, encountering the guy with the flowers at the grocery store, he'd been on edge. The more he thought about the woman he thought was Molly, the more freaked out he became. He'd thought that part of his life was behind him. That he'd left that crazy bitch at the hospital. She'd called him a few times after, but he had quickly blocked her number. The last thing he wanted was to lead her to believe he had any interest whatsoever.

Last night, when he'd come home, he'd opted not to share that information with JJ. He didn't want to worry her. Considering they'd both had more than their fair share of Molly Ryan during the time Molly pretended to be pregnant with Baz's baby, the last thing he wanted was to bring her up again.

She was in the past.

"Find my friends," he muttered as he came to a stop in the living room.

He recalled the app that would allow him to see where JJ's phone was. Since she always had it on her, it was as good as a GPS tracking device implanted in her skin.

Baz grabbed his phone and pulled up the app. He tapped her picture, and it brought up the locator map. He waited for the map to update and then exhaled his relief when he saw she was at the bakery.

"She'd tell you not to worry," he mumbled. "You're actin' crazy."

More so because he was talking to himself.

Plus, he didn't really know if that had been Molly.

Except for the card. That was pretty damning evidence.

But Molly was harmless. A little on the crazy side because of her obsessive compulsion, but harmless nonetheless.

Exhaling heavily, Baz set his phone down and went to the kitchen to empty the dishwasher.

An hour later, his attempt to remain calm had failed him completely.

He was a wreck as he got in his truck and headed for the bakery. JJ's phone still showed to be there, so he was hoping she simply lost track of time. He figured driving by would give him a chance to confirm she was all right. If she were talking to someone, he would keep right on going. No harm, no foul.

This is nothing, he told himself.

Nothing at all.

He spent the few minutes it took to drive into town with the radio up. He let Randy Houser attempt to drown out the anxiety. "Still that Cowboy" played through the speakers, and for a brief moment, it helped.

Baz pulled onto Main Street and drove by the bakery. The sun bounced off the glass, making it impossible to see inside, so he skimmed the cars parked on the street. He didn't see JJ's, so he kept going, circling behind the buildings where there was overflow parking.

Relief made him light-headed when he saw her car. He pulled up beside it, grabbed his phone, and dialed her number. He just needed to hear her voice. When she answered, he would play it off as a joke, telling her he was starving, and if she didn't hurry back, he would blow away in a breeze.

The call rang and rang, then ended with her voicemail prompt. "You've reached JJ. You should know better than to call. I do all my communicatin' via text. Try that."

Baz disconnected. He shot her a text.

You comin' home anytime soon?

He sat patiently, waiting for her to answer. Ten minutes later, when the text still didn't show to be read, his panic surged again.

"Fuck it." Baz got out of his truck.

He glanced in her car as he passed. Maybe she was hiding in the backseat. His current level of crazy would allow for that sort of outcome.

She wasn't.

Baz kept walking. He took the long way around, slipping between the real estate office and the bakery, coming out at the corner where the two met. He opened the door to the bakery and peered around, searching for JJ. She wasn't there.

"Good morn—Oh, hey, Baz." Ramona grinned. "Are you coming back for more cronuts for JJ?"

Baz tried to school his expression. "What do you mean more? Was JJ here?"

Ramona's smile fell. "Yeah." She glanced at the clock on the wall. "Probably an hour ago. She's not home?"

"No."

"That's odd. She got you some chocolate milk. I figured she was heading there after this."

She was supposed to. He didn't tell her that.

"Maybe she went to the bookstore," Ramona suggested.

Baz forced a smile. "Yeah. Probably. Thanks."

He made a beeline for the bookstore, which was just past the real estate office. It was closed.

Clutching his phone in his fist, Baz walked back to the parking lot, going the other way this time. As soon as he turned the corner, he came to a stop. A bag was on the ground, the contents scattered across the concrete—a bottle of chocolate milk, a bottle of orange juice, and two other small white bags.

And JJ's cell phone. The magnetic wallet that always fell off was a few inches away.

Baz fought the panic that strangled him. He dialed his phone, calling the only person he knew who could help him.

"What's up? It's supp—"

"Brantley."

"Yeah?"

"Oh, Jesus God."

The levity in Brantley's tone disappeared instantly. "Baz? What's wrong? Is JJ okay? The baby?"

"Fuck." Baz tried to get air into his lungs, but they were too tight.

"Baz," Brantley snapped. "What happened?'

"She's gone," he gasped.

"What do you mean gone?"

Baz took a deep, strangled breath. "She came to the bakery. Her car's here. She's not. I've looked everywhere. She's … oh, God. She's missing."

"Stay put. We'll be right there."

Stay Tuned

I hope you enjoyed this installment of the Off the Books Task Force. Relationships are forming, and new things are coming to light about the past. They'll continue to do so because it's not over for Brantley and Reese, JJ and Baz, and the rest of the task force. There's a new mission underway. Quite possibly, the most important mission of all.

Each book in this series is a full-length novel involving a new case and the continuation of the relationships between them all. And I promise not to keep you waiting long for each installment.

If you enjoyed *Off Course*, please consider leaving a review.

Acknowledgments

I know, I know. You don't like the ending. I don't either.

With that said, I don't want you to hate me. I promise there will be more very soon. I didn't do this lightly. There is a method to my madness, and if you read the dedication at the beginning of RAFE, you know that something is coming. Something big. I'm propelling the story forward for a reason. Things have to happen before that "something big" comes to be. You should notice the pattern if you're keeping up with the Walker universe. Be patient. It'll be worth it.

Now for my thanks…

My husband is always at the top of the list because he allows me to live my dream, and he has dinner with me every night, even if he thinks I might spend too much time talking to imaginary people. I'm okay with that as long as I don't have to cook.

Next is Chancy Powley. She motivates me to plug the holes before she can find them. I never catch them all, but I think she'll agree that I've improved immensely over the past decade.

I can't forget Jenna Underwood. Although she keeps moving, and always east—and farther from me each time—I still like her. She insists on proof of life when I don't answer the phone after too many weeks, which means she cares. For that, I'm grateful.

Nicole Nation 2.0, for the constant support and love and for those of you who have my back. You've been there for me from almost the beginning. This group of ladies has kept me going for so long that I'm not sure I'd know what to do without them.

And, of course, YOU, the reader. Your emails, messages, posts, comments, tweets… they mean more to me than you can imagine. I thrive on hearing from you; knowing that my characters and stories have touched you somehow keeps me going. I've been known to shed a tear or two when reading an email because your support brings so much joy to my life. I thank you for that.

About Nicole Edwards

New York Times and *USA TODAY* bestselling author Nicole Edwards lives in the suburbs of Austin, Texas, with her husband, their three fur babies, and the youngest of their three children, who has threatened never to leave home. When Nicole is not writing about sexy alpha males and sassy, independent women, she can often be found with a book in hand or attempting to keep the dogs happy. You can find her hanging out on social media and interacting with her readers - even when she's supposed to be writing.

Connect with Nicole

I hope you're as eager to get the information as I am to give it. Any of these things is worth signing up for, or feel free to sign up for all. I do my best to keep each one unique and interesting.

Nic News: If you haven't signed up for my newsletter and want notifications regarding preorders, new releases, giveaways, sales, etc., then you'll want to sign up. I promise not to spam your email, just get you the most important updates.

Ramblings of a Writer Blog: My blog is used for writer ramblings, which I am known to do from time to time.

Nicole Nation: Visit my website to get exclusive content you won't find anywhere else, including sneak peeks, A Day in the Life character stories, exclusive giveaways, cards from Nicole, or join Nicole's review team.

Nicole Nation on Facebook: Join my reader group to interact with other readers, ask me questions, play fun weekly games, celebrate during release week, and enter exclusive giveaways!

Instagram: Basically, Instagram is where I post pictures of my dogs, so if you want to see epic cuteness, you should follow me.

Naughty & Nice Shop: Not only does the shop have signed books, but there's fun merchandise, too—plenty of naughty and nice options to go around. Find the shop on my website.

Website:	www.NicoleEdwards.me
Facebook:	/Author.Nicole.Edwards
Instagram:	/NicoleEdwardsAuthor
TikTok:	/@nicoleedwardsauthor
BookBub:	/NicoleEdwardsAuthor
Goodreads:	/nicole_edwards

BY NICOLE EDWARDS

THE WALKERS

ALLURING INDULGENCE

Kaleb
Zane
Travis
Holidays with The Walker Brothers
Ethan
Braydon
Sawyer
Brendon

THE WALKERS OF COYOTE RIDGE

Curtis
Jared (a crossover novel)
Hard to Hold
Hard to Handle
Beau
Rex
A Coyote Ridge Christmas
Mack
Kaden & Keegan
Alibi (a crossover novel)
Trey
Rafe

THE JAMESONS OF COYOTE RIDGE

Hot Chocolate Wishes

BRANTLEY WALKER: OFF THE BOOKS

All In
Without A Trace
Hide & Seek
Deadly Coincidence
Alibi (a crossover novel)
Secrets
Confessions
Bounty
Off Course

Austin Arrows
Rush
Kaufman

Club Destiny
Conviction
Temptation
Addicted
Seduction
Infatuation
Captivated
Devotion
Perception
Entrusted
Adored
Distraction
Forevermore

Dead Heat Ranch
Boots Optional
Betting on Grace
Overnight Love
Jared (a crossover novel)

Devil's Bend
Chasing Dreams
Vanishing Dreams

Misplaced Halos
Protected in Darkness
Salvation in Darkness
Bound in Darkness

Office Intrigue
Office Intrigue
Intrigued Out of The Office
Their Rebellious Submissive
Their Famous Dominant
Their Ruthless Sadist
Their Naughty Student
Their Fairy Princess
Owned

Pier 70

Reckless
Fearless
Speechless
Harmless
Clueless

Primal Instincts

Chase (Volume 1-3)
Capture (Volume 4-6)
Claim (Volume 7-9)

Sniper 1 Security

Wait for Morning
Never Say Never
Tomorrow's Too Late

Southern Boy Mafia/Devil's Playground

Beautifully Brutal
Without Regret
Beautifully Loyal
Without Restraint

Standalone Novels

Unhinged Trilogy
A Million Tiny Pieces
Inked on Paper
Bad Reputation
Bad Business
Filthy Hot Billionaire
RULE

Naughty Holiday Editions

2015
2016
2021

BECAUSE NAUGHTY CAN BE OH SO NICE®

Printed in Dunstable, United Kingdom

80343826R10151